HIGH
WATER
HELLION

HIGH
WATER
HELLION

by
Glynn Marsh Alam

MEMENTO MORI MYSTERIES
New York

Memento Mori Mysteries
Published by
Avocet Press Inc
19 Paul Court, Pearl River, NY 10965
http://www.avocetpress.com
mysteries@avocetpress.com

AVOCET PRESS

Copyright ©2006 by Glynn Marsh Alam

Library of Congress Cataloging-in-Publication Data
Alam, Glynn Marsh, 1943-
  High water hellion : a Luanne Fogarty mystery / Glynn Marsh Alam.
     p. cm.
  ISBN-13: 978-0-9725078-6-8
  ISBN-10: 0-9725078-6-8
  1. Fogarty, Luanne (Fictitious character)--Fiction. 2. Women detectives--Florida--Tallahassee Region--Fiction. 3. Tallahassee Region (Fla.)--Fiction. 4. Women divers--Fiction 5. Hurricanes-Fiction. I. Title.
  PS3551.L213H54 2006
  813'.54—dc22

                            2006003192

Printed in the USA
First Edition

Thanks ever so to cousin Bobby Wilder, whose stories of mating alligators and central Florida flora and fauna helped inspire this book.

Southern storms and mating seasons bring together strange swampfellows. When all that spasmodic reptilian behavior spawns baby alligators who run down to the lake and rest on the still grass cover, the storm knows how to pick them up and fly them to the ditch across the road. No matter. If the storm keeps its pace, water will find a way to cover the entire distance between lake and ditch, hiding the road, and the baby gators will again sit atop their birth centers. The storm isn't finished yet. It gives the lake tentacles that stream into ancient tobacco barns, potting sheds, and ramshackle houses. People stand knee deep in the murkiness, dodging beavers, snakes, and the odd misshapen lump of material that rises in a particularly bad downpour, material that could be anything from a homeless person's kit to something of a more deadly nature.

CHAPTER ONE

"She insisted on an autopsy. Put it in her will. But she didn't take the chance on someone reading the will long after she was buried. She told people—the neighbors, her church circle, the coroner himself."

"And that's where she is right now?" I pulled the phone away from my ear and looked at it in disbelief. Tony Amado, self-centered sheriff's detective, was asking, almost pleading, for my help. It was on a personal matter.

"She even left some money to pay for it in case the county wouldn't."

"Is the body at the coroner's?" I asked Tony and took a deep breath of humid swamp air. The May morning cool had worn off, and I had been sitting too long on the porch. This was supposed to be the dry month when northern Florida needed rain, but my skin dripped with humidity, a sure sign of an afternoon monsoon.

"Yes! Luanne, I thought you understood that." Tony paused. I could imagine him swallowing those words along with the attitude. "Yes, she's in the morgue. The coroner knew she wanted that autopsy and decided not to raise the issue with her estate. He'll get around to it as long as I don't push for release of the body."

I sighed and brushed drops of perspiration from the back of

my neck. My fingers got caught in wet tendrils of hair, and I remembered I'd wanted to get a haircut—maybe even a color—today. Tony's call interrupted my rather mundane life of the moment. I'd taught my last linguistics class for the semester. Vernon—whose presence had felt almost interfering lately—joined forces with some divers in another county to look for a man's body off St. George Island. He wanted me to join him, and I could have, but I needed space to breathe and begged off.

My neighbor, Pasquin, haunted my front porch still, but I bit my tongue the last time he was here. He kept on and on about why didn't I marry old Vernon. I should quit chasing after things that had lives lower than a cottonmouth full of rat. I felt my skin flare and the roots of my hair rise along with my blood pressure. I kept quiet, and Pasquin knew he'd hit what he called my "touchy female temper." He bid his goodbye and headed home through the dark swamp. Now, it seemed to be Tony's turn. Detective Amado, macho supreme, needed someone who could swim—the way he referred to a professional diver—to help him locate something, just what he didn't seem to know, supposedly dumped by his recently deceased aunt.

"Tony, I've never been to Ocklawaha. It's a long drive, right?" I felt my solitude waning and dreaded having to work when my head said I needed to be alone. On the other hand, a nasty little giggle sounded off inside me. Tony would always go for a male to help him out, so that meant that I was the only one left. The help he needed wasn't police work. He was asking me to come and stay at his aunt's house as a personal favor.

"You'll find it outside Ocala, but there's a long way to go out from there. Just follow the signs that guide you to the place where Ma Barker and her son were killed."

"Oh, joy, a town with a past."

"Bring your scuba gear and outdoor clothes."

"Why outdoor? There's no camping involved with this, is there?"

"No. It's just the house is in the country, on a lake, and you'll find it a bit rugged."

I looked around me, at my refurbished swamp house that needed painting every few years, then gazed out the window at the encroaching growth. Tangled vines with spring flowers nearly blocked the small dirt road that led to a main highway. Among the tall trees and massive scrubs, every amphibian and reptile known to the northern Florida, crawled about looking for food and shelter. I knew rugged.

"Where will I sleep?" I asked, knowing Tony might make me pay for a motel somewhere.

"This is a two bedroom house. Has an extra bath." I heard the urgency in his voice now, an almost "pretty please" about to burst forth.

I sighed. The plea was too much. "All right, Tony, give me directions."

With my acquiescence, he conjured up some of his old defensiveness. "This isn't a job, now. You do understand it won't be a paid assignment?"

"Yes, Tony. I am assuming I'm doing you a personal favor for which you shall be grateful into eons of time and will, of course, call upon me for all future diving jobs before you go hunting for a male. And," I smiled to myself, "you'll let everyone know, as I will, that I helped you with this matter."

Silence greeted me, then a gruff, "You got a piece of paper to write down the directions?"

Getting an early start next morning meant contacting Pasquin about the house. This old man had been my swamp companion for too many years to ignore my call for help now. He picked up the phone and his voice perked up when he heard it was me.

"Thought you'd be ticked at me, ma'am." He used the affectionate address he'd called me as a child when he visited my father and me and told stories of the swamps.

"I was, and you'd best lay off the marriage stuff and let me be or you'll get no more biscuits and tea on my porch." I backed off then and explained I needed him to check the house daily. "And feed Plato if he comes around."

"If he doesn't find you at home, he sniffs around here."

Plato was my swamp dog. Not mine really, but I had rescued him from starvation as a puppy and he acted like he knew that. My place was safe territory for him, but the swamp in general was his habitat. He answered to no one.

"I got your key. Better give me the detective's phone number."

With scuba gear in the back of the Honda station wagon and my red canoe on the top, I traveled south, meaning I went from gentle hills in Tallahassee to flat land in central Florida. Just as many swamps and lakes here, but the trees were shorter and the road stretched out in front of me without a single dip. High reeds surrounded most of the ponds and lakes. I knew the snakes that would be hiding in the tall grasses, and there would be another one I wouldn't come across at my northern swamp house—the deadly coral snake. I shuddered. "First one I see, Tony, and I'm on the road going backwards."

According to his directions, I traveled three paved back roads after leaving Highway 27 to reach Tony's aunt's place. The final road was barely that, paved enough to make the tires run smoothly but trailing off in broken pieces into watery ditches. This was lake country. High grass, thick with recent rains and springtime, nearly blocked the lanes. The road wound around water holes, deep sink-holes leading to nowhere. At a point where two lakes nearly met—and probably did in heavy rains—I slammed on the brakes.

In the middle of the pavement, a reptile, the size of a petrified tree trunk and just as prehistoric, rose up on its four legs and lumbered toward the lure of water, or what was in it. As he left the pavement, he made a croaking sound, louder and more urgent than a frog, but just as primordial. "Lovely," I thought. "It's gator mating season which means hurricanes too." I slowed to gaze into the lake to my left. The bumps across the water were hard to read. Maybe they were humping gators just under the surface, and maybe just logs. A long wailing croak put the period on that sentence. "Gators," I said. "Tony has asked me to come down here to look for something in his aunt's lake, during alligator mating season." I realized I had stopped in the middle of the road when a truck behind me beeped.

I waved and pulled over to the side of the narrow pavement. The truck, looking as though it hadn't seen a downpour in several days, drove up beside me but made no move to continue. Through a missing passenger window, a man, young enough to be my son, missing a tooth off to one side, grinned.

"You lost, ma'am?" He didn't wait for me to answer but turned off his truck, slid out the driver's side and headed for my car.

With a quick glance, I noticed that the nose of his truck edged pretty close to the front of my car and a hurried exit could land me in a drainage ditch. I slipped my hand under my purse that lay in the passenger seat and gripped the small twenty-two semi-automatic.

"Any problems, ma'am?" The man leaned toward me; his dirty white tee had a faded logo partially obscured by grass and dirt spots. He brushed against the half-open window.

"Just looking for a Priss Lane," I said. "I was told it was down this road."

"Yeah?" The man chuckled and revealed the remnants of chewing tobacco, probably the reason for his rotting teeth. "You a relative of old lady Keen?"

"Friend of her nephew. He's at the house, waiting for me." I adjusted my hand on the gun, feeling for the safety.

"She was quite a character." He looked up and pointed toward a curve in the high reeds. "Go round that bend and pretty soon you'll see a painted sign that says PRISS LANE in bright blue paint. Just above it are three painted cats—yellow ones. Them's old Miz Keen's cats. Had more than three but that's about all the sign could hold. Named each one of them Miss Priss—Priss One, Priss Two—you get the picture." He grinned again, showing no inclination to move away.

"She sounds entertaining," I smiled back at him.

He shook his head and turned the smile into a frown. "Could be mean as hell, too. I did some work on and off for her, but she never was satisfied. Had to be perfect, just perfect."

"What kind of work?"

"Digging. That's what I do, dig holding ponds, drainage ditches. Fix it so's people's backyards don't fill up with water during a hard rain."

"Hurricane season must keep you busy."

"Don't dig during the 'canes. After one, I usually help with the cleanup." He gazed at me, and I noticed the eyes had changed. They had taken on the dreamy soft glow of a man looking at a woman. It was time to leave.

"I'd better get going. You want to move your truck a little?"

He nodded and backed away, straining to see the top of my

car. "You planning on using that canoe in Miz Keen's lake?"

"You never know." I shifted gears.

"Take care during the season. Some gator may take you for a mate." He grinned even wider as he headed toward his truck. He had one leg in the driver's side when he lifted his head and yelled, "Didn't get your name, ma'am."

I thought about doing the nasty routine and telling him I hadn't offered it, but I figured I might need allies during my stay with Tony. I shouted, "Luanne."

He nodded, yelled back, as he pointed to himself, "Stubbs," and started up his truck.

Less than half a mile of following Stubbs, he slowed at a break in the reeds and waved toward his left, pointing directly downward toward a brightly painted sign. As waved at him he drove off, throwing up dirt clods until the reeds engulfed him.

Miz Keen must have been a tidy soul, I thought, as I gazed at the sign. Not a bit of weather wear, like it had been painted in the last three months. I smiled at the thought of aloof cats called Miss Priss and drove down the two ruts that made up the driveway to a house built of cement blocks and sitting squarely on the ground.

"Now why did I expect to see a white cracker house?" I said as I moved from the car to the front door. Someone had painted the concrete drive a dark red color, setting it off like a scab in green grass that needed mowing.

"I see you found it all right," said Tony as he opened the front door. He stood with his hands on his hips, white ironed shirt, crisp jeans, combed hair. The hair, dark from his Cuban heritage, accented the large black eyes in a pale face. Most women found him handsome, kind of exotic, but it wore off once they got to know him.

"You don't look worse for the wear, but you never do." I looked past him into a room full of clutter on the floor. "This room looks about like your office."

"You got luggage?" He ignored me and headed for the car. I followed him to unlock the trunk.

"When are you going to get a new car, Luanne? You need something with a remote." He hoisted out my one bag, avoiding the slight overhang of the canoe. "Doubt you'll need this," he said, nodding at the canoe.

"Are you kidding? It's alligator mating season, Tony. This canoe may save my life." I slammed shut the back of the station wagon and followed him inside. "You know, if I have to dive for something, I need a buddy."

"I know that. I've hired a fellow in town to go with you if need be." He glanced my way, then turned his eyes upward as he pushed open the door.

I followed him through a tiny living room decorated with once-white wicker furniture, across linoleum tiled floors cluttered with what looked like hardcover notebooks. We went down a short hallway and into a master bedroom.

"This was my aunt's room." Tony put down the suitcase and turned to me. "Don't worry. She died outside on the grass. Not here. All clean linen and stuff." He waved his hand toward a master bath.

"I'll be fine, Tony. Ghosts don't bother me."

I joined him again in the living room and pushed aside a stack of notebooks to sit in a large peacock chair.

"This your usual clutter or did your aunt leave it this way?"

"I found these notebooks in stacks in her walk-in closet. The topmost one belongs to this year. They go back nearly fifteen years when she moved into this place. That was the year her husband died, and she couldn't live in her St. Pete house anymore. She bought this." Tony stopped and flipped through the pages he had been reading. "She was pretty eccentric, you know. I'm not sure if she was just looking for adventure and made up a lot of stuff." He shot me a glance. "But according to these books something sparked her interest, and then she got on that kick of telling everyone she wanted an autopsy when she died."

"Is that in the notebooks, too?" I slid one off the top of the stack next to me.

"All over the place. Look, you can go through all these. They make good stuff to read at night, but I want to bring you up speed. Why I needed you to come down here and dive."

I shot him my own glance. "During gator mating."

Tony shook his head. "I didn't decide when she was going to die."

"How did she die?" I eased back into the peacock chair and relaxed, satisfied to get Tony's version of things. I planned to read the journals later.

"Neighbors found her lying face down in the grass between here and the lake. Doctor thinks she had a massive heart attack while walking out there. She fell hard enough to get grass stains on her face."

"Any reason to doubt it?"

Tony shrugged. He gazed at the floor. "She had clogged arteries, but the doctors didn't advise a bypass because of her age. Had her on lots of drugs and a diet. Knowing my aunt, she took the medicine but ate what she pleased. Like her doctor said, no one gets suspicious when a ninety-year-old drops dead."

"Unless, of course, she's been insisting on an autopsy and she's written strange things in her journals." I opened a notebook that was dated four years back and read for a moment. "Listen to this."

Seems to me it ruins the ground. Ferguson lets them do it. All we can do is complain about the noise. Kids doing what they called muddin' this Saturday morning. Making all sorts of noise in the open area behind Ferguson's house. What's the fun in sliding your car around in all that mud?

"There's more about the muddin' in several of the journals," said Tony. "It's a way of letting off steam, I guess. Happens after a rain, when the ground is good and soaked. Kids just race their cars around in a circle, slinging mud and sliding the wheels."

"Who is Ferguson?"

"Man who owns lots of land just south of the lake. It's got a big field where the muddin' takes place. He's in his eighties and mean as the devil, so I hear. Haven't met him yet."

I gazed around the walls. Except for paintings and photographs of orange cats, there was no indication of a family.

"She had a husband?"

"Three of them. She was my mother's oldest sister and the only one with a streak of adventure. My grandpa said it was more like a streak of mischief. She said she wanted to see the world, but the only way to do that for a woman who grew up in the Depression was through marriage. First husband abandoned her down in Miami. She outlived the next two. Never had any kids." Tony leaned back in his chair, the wicker creaking with the movement. In spite of his neat appearance, he looked tired. Emotion was not something he wore well. It was one thing to investigate the brutal murders of strangers, but to nose into the death of one's own relative—well, it must hurt.

I stood up. "Let's take a walk."

Outside, the summer sky showed no signs of dimming even though it was nearly six. The chorus of mating gators kept up its roar across the lake. Occasionally, we'd hear the splash of something near the shore and two long black streaks would head toward the depths. The green grass around the yard area needed mowing, and, beyond it, tall reeds blocked the view of the neighbor's yard.

"She was found here." Tony pointed to a grassy area to the side of a worn path. "It looked as though she had been down on the dock and was returning home. The markers are mine, by the way."

Tony had used small red triangles to mark his aunt's position on the ground.

"She was off the path completely," I said. The markers showed her body to be almost perpendicular to the path. "Could she have been thrown this way by a heart attack?"

"Doctor says so," Tony shrugged. "When the local police called me, I told them to take a photograph before moving the body. Fortunately, someone had the sense to do that."

"And they're sure it was a heart attack?" I touched the ground at the spot where Miz Keen's face hit the grass. It looked bent and brown in one spot. "Is there something in the grass?"

"Vomit remnants. The doctor says it's not uncommon for that to happen."

"So a scene investigation was done?" I lifted my eyes to see a brown lizard scoot into the reeds.

"Sort of. The doctor examined her here. No sign of foul play, he said."

I heard something rustle in the reeds. Another lizard darted into hiding. The reason for the hasty retreat caught my eye. At the edge of the stalks, an orange tabby cat the size of a wild boar stalked with one foot raised. It waited until something caught its eye and it pounced. Like the head majorette in a parade, he trotted around the house, a lizard tail wiggling out the side of his mouth.

"One of the Miss Priss cats?"

"You know about them? If it's a Miss Priss, it's not coming around the house to be fed." Tony's eyes followed the cat until it disappeared between some hedges. "The neighbor said the cats came from a bunch of kittens dropped off around here. They kept having kittens, and my aunt would take in the friendly ones."

"And since cats don't hang around water much, the gators are too lazy to move away from the lake's edge to have them for lunch." I knew this from my own neck of the woods where only clever dogs, like Plato, avoided the urge to bark and harrass gators. Cats considered that kind of thing beneath them.

"Yeah, cats thrive around here."

"Your aunt died two days ago. When will this autopsy take place?"

"I'm calling every day. He'll get around to it when he can. They've had some nasty child murders down here. Guess everyone's busy."

Later that night, I lay in a soft bed with four pillows. Miz Keen liked her comforts, I thought. Outside, a chorus of frogs would be interrupted by the roar and croak of gators and once in a while the wail of cats. All of nature seemed to be in heat. "One big mating hell," I said as I turned on one side and lifted a pillow over my ear. Sometime in the night I woke to the roar of car engines being gunned – mudding again. The midnight rituals continued.

CHAPTER TWO

"Coroner is starting now," said Tony when he joined me at the table for cold cereal and milk. "Coffee?"

"What's happening with the murdered children?" I held my cup for him to refill it.

"Done, I guess. They know who did it. Got confessions."

I shuddered.

"Confessions? He confessed twice?"

"One confession each, most likely. Two pedophiles acting separately."

"Isn't that quite a coincidence in an area this small?"

Tony sat across from me at the small formica-topped table. It was a piece of junk out of the fifties, but would bring quite a penny now because of its retro value.

"This is central Florida. The climate is right. Just about any pervert or jailbird can come and settle here." He sighed. "Evidently two of them did."

We ate in silence. Tony had on a clean shirt, washed jeans, and the hair, as ever, sat thick and combed like a comic book hero's. My own baggy pants and T-shirt top were a match for my short salt and pepper hair that did as it pleased every morning of its life.

"How do you do it, Tony?"

"Do what?" He looked up from his coffee cup, his black eyes a bit swollen.

"Look so neat."

He glanced down at himself and gave a short laugh. "You know, my father always told me to look like a fashion plate because no American would have anything to do with an island Cuban with a thin mustache and pointy shoes."

"You never looked like that."

"People around my father did and got lots of prejudiced bullying for it. And even though we weren't island Cubans—more like Tampa-born Spaniards—he made sure we never dressed like that and that we didn't speak Spanish in mixed company."

"I didn't know you could speak Spanish." He had a Southern drawl and in all the cases where Latino suspects were questioned, he called in bilingual deputies.

"I can't very well. When Daddy said don't speak it, we took it to mean it was taboo. That was when the influx of Cubans came pouring into Miami. We were Tampa Cubans, several generations in the states."

I sighed. Another culture lost in the shuffle so as to become part of the American dream.

"How long will the autopsy take?"

"He said he'd call me tomorrow morning, earlier if anything came up." He switched on the tiny television sitting on the counter. A woman gave a weather bulletin in a decidedly northern accent about a tropical storm in the Gulf. It could come ashore by the next day.

"If that's headed this way, I'd better dive today. Want to call the other diver?"

I stood in the sunshine on the path to the lake, waiting for someone named Wayne Daney to arrive with scuba gear. In the distance, Gulf side, a rolling clump of dark clouds appeared on the horizon. A tropical storm meant business if it crossed directly over you. Worse, it could grow into a full-blown hurricane if it stayed over warm water long enough.

A noisy jeep pulled into the drive as I poked my head around the corner of the house. A stocky twenty-something hopped out and saluted me as I moved to his scuba gear. It looked brand new.

"How long have you been diving?"

"Since my teens," he said, and his cheeks puffed with pride. I wanted to say that must have been all of three years, but I didn't.

"In this lake?"

"Never here, but I've been in lots like it." He stuck out a thick hand. "Wayne Daney, glad to meet you, Miss Fogarty."

Tony joined us and began singing Wayne's praises, knowing, of course, that he had to sell the kid to me. I longed for Vernon's presence.

"He's got certification and hours in the water. Once he finishes school, he could make the sheriff's dive team." Tony patted Wayne on the shoulder.

Wayne ran his hand through blond hair that had been stiffened to his head with some kind of gel. I shook my misgivings and figured he'd be okay.

Inside, we listened while Tony read something from one of his aunt's notebooks.

"I'm not sure there's anything down there, but this is what she says."

After Miss Priss didn't come home for a week, I walked to the other side of the lake where Ferguson's deck is. It's a rickety thing, with nails that need hammering. I can't afford to scratch myself on the rusty things and get an infection. Oh, they'd love to see this old lady in the hospital tied up to tubes, but I won't oblige them. Ferguson's old truck was parked there but he was nowhere to be seen. I brought back a metal box that was sitting next to his truck.

"I spoke to the neighbor," Tony nodded in the direction of the house to the left. "He said his son told him that my aunt stood on the dock and tossed things into the water. They thought at first she was feeding the gators, but she knew better than that. Neighbor's son said sometimes whatever she threw caught the sun and glinted like metal before landing on the water."

"So what are we looking for?" asked Wayne.

"I'm not sure. Maybe there's nothing down there, but if she took something from Ferguson, it needs to be returned. I don't want any lawsuits with this property." Tony closed the book.

"You're the sole inheritor?" I asked.

He nodded. "Her own generation died out before her. She left everything to me. The will is old, except for the autopsy request and the money she left for it. Strangest thing."

"Okay, let's haul scuba gear." I rose and walked toward my Honda parked in front of Wayne's jeep. We dragged the gear to the dock.

"Neighbors will be watching," Tony sighed.

I looked at the sky. The dark clouds appeared closer, but the storm wouldn't begin until later in the night if it actually came ashore. Strapping on a head lamp, I motioned to Wayne that I'd go in first.

"Just keep your eyes peeled for gators," I said. "Stay out of these shallows at the edge. That's where they tend to stake out territory." I stopped to look at Wayne.

"What?" he said.

"You ever dive during mating season?"

He shook his head.

"Keep close and avoid any snugly goings-on, okay?"

The water tended toward murky, then clear, then murky again. In spots, eel grass waved its green stalks, but mostly the bottom was long stretches of mud. Anything could be buried there. All it took was one good stir with your hand to realize that silt ran off from shore so often that a new layer would form in a few days. Keeping Wayne in sight, a yellow blur in the dirty water for most of the time, I skirted the areas where I thought a ninety-year-old might be able to toss something. Finding nothing close to the dock, I pushed into the lake, using a sifter to pull up areas that appeared higher than others. A few feet away, I saw Wayne pull up a pole, creating a line of silt in the water. Its shape dispersed quickly in his wake. I found nothing but bits of rotting tree limbs and a couple of broken oars near the dock. Stopping to look about me, I assured myself no gators were in my path.

I headed around the lake, toward Ferguson's landing. It turned out to be an underwater dump of sorts. Somebody drank a lot of beer. I figured if someone needed to sell aluminum cans to a recycler, he should check out the bottom. Would Miz Keen toss cans into the lake? I doubted it, and I couldn't remember seeing any beer in her fridge. I pushed toward the end of the dock. Not far away, I glimpsed the long leathery tail of a bull gator shifting side to side as he swam near the shore line. That probably meant a prospective mate was in the vicinity. Staying near the dock posts, I swam close to bottom and gently sifted the dirt near the cans. Further out, I discovered a black trash bag full of something and tied with a heavy cord. Shoving it into a mesh bag, I looked back to see Wayne picking up beer cans and loading them in his bag. Behind him, another leather tail whipped gently through the water. I poked my hand in a gesture to tell him to look behind him. His body darted outward toward me as he caught sight of the reptiles above him.

We swam toward the center of the lake. The bottom suddenly tapered off and the water grew colder. I realized there must be an underground aquifer here, feeding the lake with clean cold water. I followed the cold until nothing but a black hole was beneath me. Pointing down, I showed it to Wayne. He swam around the hole and made a gesture that asked if we planned to look inside it. I shook my head and pointed back toward Miz Keen's dock.

When I reached the surface and jerked off the mask, I saw several pairs of bare legs alongside Tony's pants. Raising myself out of the muddy water near shore, I pealed off the tank. Wayne sat beside me, doing the same.

"Who're those people?" he asked as he unzipped his wet suit.

"Beats me," I said but I figured they were curious neighbors.

The two of us sat exposed like caught fish as a large man with a large wife and a large teenager stared at us. All three wore bermuda shorts made from the same red checked material. From their dark eyes and hair, I had visions of a mamma stripping the dining table of its cloth and sewing up shorts for the family.

"These are the Bonos," said Tony. His eyes rolled as he approached us. "They live next door. Mr. Bono is the one who said his son saw Aunt Marta tossing things into the lake."

"Yes, Bono," I smiled in spite of myself and ran my fingers through wet hair.

Sandals, scruffy and well worn, shuffled through the grass all at once. Wayne and I were surrounded by six fat legs, the chubby flesh splotched with mosquito bites.

"My wife, Cara, and son Gil." The man stepped forward and shoved a large hand toward me. "I'm JoJo." He grinned as though he were about to tell a joke. "Actually Joseph is my name, but my school buddies called me JoJo because it rhymes with Bono."

I shook his hand. "Nice to meet you, JoJo. This is Wayne." I nodded toward my diving partner who stood now, his feet spread apart as though he wanted to bolt from the scene.

JoJo and Wayne shook hands, the two men staring at each other for a brief moment.

A sudden gust of wind interrupted the strange pause. Clouds had moved closer to us but still weren't directly overhead.

"That tropical storm off the coast is headed this way, likely," said JoJo. His son nodded.

"Yes, and I need to get out of this suit." I stood up with no help from JoJo who didn't move to give me room.

"You people looking for something?" He made rounded motions with his hands toward the scuba tanks.

Tony moved toward us, his dark eyes darting from us to the man. "Just making sure Aunt Marta didn't toss in something valuable."

"Mmm," said JoJo. "Good idea." He glanced at his wife who smiled a line between chipmunk cheeks. It was hard to tell what she was thinking as her eyes were hidden behind oversized sunglasses. From their shorts and faded T-shirts, it seemed this family hit the second hand markets on a frequent basis.

"Nothing down there," I said, shoving the mesh bag beneath my fins. I grabbed them up and moved toward the house just as another wind gush blew across the lake and made waves that would have rocked a small boat.

Wayne followed me. Tony nodded a goodbye to his aunt's neighbors and led us to the back porch. He turned around when I mentioned we had voyeurs.

"Nosy people," he said under his breath. The Bonos stood three abreast at the edge of the dock, all staring in our direction. "You did find something, didn't you?" He nodded toward the mesh bag.

"Near Ferguson's landing," I said. "Not up here." I shoved the bag toward him with my foot. That's when I felt the soft lumpiness. "You check it, okay?"

Tony knelt and grabbed the cord, jerking the bag toward him. He felt around it. "Oh, boy," he said. "I don't like this."

Wayne and I moved behind him as he took care to untie the cord. Once loose, the bag opened a bit. Something like yellow hair showed through, and Tony jerked back for a moment. He leaned over and used two fingers to pinch some of the bag and pull it upward. A rotten wet smell filled the small porch.

"Kittens!" said Wayne. "Some jerk has drowned kittens."

It was an old practice, as old as farmers and cats had coexisted. Mamma cat breeds and has too many kittens for the number of mice. The farmer needs to get rid of them. Off they go to the nearest body of water. Eventually, gators would get the whiff and take advantage of the food cycle. These were recent. The smell wasn't unbearable yet, and tiny ears and tails were still visible.

"Yellow kittens," I said. "Miss Priss descendants?"

A laugh rose from the yard. The Bonos had moved closer to see what was in the bag. All three chuckled and nodded to each other.

"You know something about this?" Tony stood, his jaw grinding in irritation.

The three shook their heads and shrugged their shoulders.

"Then what's funny about dead kittens?"

"Nothing, really," said Cara. She had shoved her dark glasses to her head, revealing tiny eyes that nearly faded into the flesh of her ruddy face. "It's just that old man Ferguson hates cats and that's what he does to any he finds."

"My aunt loved cats," said Tony. "How did she get along with Ferguson?"

JoJo and Cara looked away, but Gil spoke up. "Not so good. He was like, you know, a polluter, and Miz Keen tried to keep things clean, you know." His voice trailed off in an unsure fadeout.

"Did he ever try to kill her cats, the ones she had here in the house?"

"Look," said JoJo, obviously disturbed, he took the stance of a defending opponent—legs stiffened, feet apart, hands on hips. "You're asking a lot of neighbors who come here maybe once a year."

"From where?" asked Tony.

"From New Jersey," said JoJo. "We own this lake house and come down to see the sights."

"It's the middle of summer, not tourist season." Tony moved closer to the man.

"How come you're asking all these questions?"

Tony sighed, reached in his pocket and pulled out his sheriff's badge. He held it outward where the sun hit the metal. "Force of habit, I guess."

CHAPTER THREE

Television news centered on a tropical storm. It wouldn't move and was tearing up the ocean just off the coast, preventing liners from docking at familiar ports and locals from doing their deep sea fishing, all the while gaining hurricane strength.

Tony had just sat down with a beer, brooding, his eyes glued to the screen. He finally looked up and said, "The coroner never called."

I shrugged. Things went that way. Maybe some other serial killer had surfaced and the medical examiner's office had to put Auntie on hold. I was about to say so, when someone knocked on the door.

"Detective Amado?" A tall man stood in the doorway with his badge ID held open. "Detective Charles Chandler. You may not remember me, but we met a couple years back at the seminar in Orlando. You got me interested in water bodies."

"Water bodies?" Tony stood at the door. When he realized he had a beer can in his hand, he grimaced and put it on a side table.

Chandler grinned at Tony's gesture. "As in dead bodies in water," he said.

Tony nodded, looked at me, and moved aside. He offered the man a chair.

Dressed in khaki pants with a blue shirt and sports coat, Chandler folded up and sat down. He didn't lean back but pushed forward, his knees nearly the level of his waist. He looked my way, nodded and smiled. I knew Tony would be tongue-tied so I introduced myself.

"I know about you already," Chandler said. "Amado told us about your underwater cave discoveries at the seminar."

I looked at Tony, my mouth open. All I could do was raise my eyebrows.

"I conducted a group," said Tony, turning his eyes from me.

"Look, I'm not really here to talk about the seminar, but to bring you up to date on your aunt's case."

"Her case?" Tony and I spoke together.

"Seems she was right to insist on her own autopsy. Coroner gave me the report and asked me to convey it to you." He pulled out some folded papers from his coat. "Her own doctor said she probably had a heart attack since she was being treated for a condition and she was aged—and she did have one. But something else happened to bring it on." He pulled out a copy of the photo of Miz Keen lying in the grass, her face in the green blades. "Here, on the back of her neck, the coroner found finger bruise marks, like someone had maybe knocked her down then forced her face into the ground."

"Somebody tried to suffocate her?" said Tony, his jaw beginning to work in anger.

"Could be. She was a tiny, frail woman and holding her down until she couldn't breathe wouldn't be all that hard."

"Or until she had a heart attack," I said.

Chandler nodded. "That's likely the scenario. She had some dirt in the nasal passages but nothing to indicate suffocation." He let his long body relax and lean back in the chair. "Do you know anyone who might want her out of the way? Was there anything missing from the house?"

Tony stood up suddenly and paced to the door and back again. "The house seemed in good order. I wouldn't know if anything was missing since I didn't know what she had of value. She was just an aunt who talked to me, sent me Christmas presents, and let me know she was still alive." He turned abruptly and stood with his back to us. I sensed he was fighting tears. He shook himself, and faced Chandler again. "Did you check the body for prints?"

Chandler nodded. "Had to use the super glue but there were no prints, other than the finger pressure points."

Tony's jaw ground back and forth. He had turned dark red. "I haven't checked her bank accounts yet. According to the will, I'm the only heir."

"Well, it's a police matter now. I'm handling the homicide." Chandler didn't move. His face turned somber. "We're going to have to search this place, talk to neighbors, whatever." He looked at neither of us.

"We need to tell you about the drowned kittens," I said.

Tony turned around, his face calm again. "And the neighbor kid over there," he pointed west, "said he saw her throwing stuff into the lake."

"You'll work with me on this?" He looked Tony square in the eyes.

Tony stiffened and stared back at him, the familiar dark-eyed glare taking hold. "Of course. When do we start?"

Chandler stood up and put out his hand toward Tony. A good way to gain his confidence, I thought. Tony shook his hand and said, "You want to start now?"

"I've got a man at your neighbor's house now, asking questions. Do we need to get a search warrant?"

"No, of course not. Just tell me when."

Chandler stood near the front window, his full head of graying hair shining in the sunlight. The light was a storm color, one I remembered from my childhood when the elders around me predicted big winds. A dim, yellow glow.

"We need to get going in case the storm blows in," he said.

Tony and I sat still for some moments after the man left. All bets were off now. It had become murder, familiar territory for us both, but too close to home for Tony.

"These journals," I said. "Will they take them away?"

Tony's eyes darted to the stacks on the floor. He shook his head, then said, "Let's read while we can." He grabbed the one he had started.

I joined Tony in the process of skimming as quickly as I could, trying not to miss anything. Lots of Miss Priss antics, new medicines, comments on soap operas, and a few almost poetic bits about how pretty the sunset over the lake played out in Miz Keen's large handwriting. It wasn't shaky like you'd expect from someone in her nineties, but it did have the curvature of the nineteenth century school room.

"Okay," I said. "Here's something." I looked up at Tony who seemed edgy as he ran through a few pages. "Want to hear it?"

I didn't wait for his approval. *Moon set over the lake tonight. Went to stand on the dock to watch it. Ferguson's boat was on the water. He dumped something over the side. Bet he's drowning animals again. Feeding puppies and kittens to the gators. I yelled at him to stop that. Somebody in the boat with him yelled an obscenity at me. Messed up the prettiness of the night.*

"Maybe the detective should interview this Ferguson."

"And maybe I should meet this Ferguson," said Tony. He slammed the journal and tossed it on the "to read" file.

Tony and I walked to the Bono house where another detective was interviewing Cara. Her husband and son had gone to town to

buy hurricane supplies she said. Tony informed the officer that
we'd be out for a while and left a key for Chandler's search.

"We need to get your canoe off the roof and in a safe place,"
he said, pulling open the garage door. "Otherwise, it could fly to
the lake."

I helped him shove it beside his SUV in the packed space.

"We'll take your car," he said without asking and waited for me
to unlock the door.

Tony guided me back to the narrow road that circled the lake.
Twice, tiny rutted lanes led off somewhere to a house. Ferguson's
road was wider with deep ruts cut even deeper by heavy rains.

"He needs to grade this road," I said as I bounced in my seat.
The old Honda managed across the holes and puddles, but it was
no match for a modern SUV.

"Don't they pay you enough at the college to get a new ve-
hicle?" Tony held on with both hands, his well coifed hair nearly
hitting the ceiling as we bumped along.

"I'm not one to splurge on cars," I said. Truth was, I knew it
was getting time to turn in the '84 station wagon that had never
let me down. It would be like getting a divorce.

We finally hit sparse grass and a wide front yard full of oak
trees. Behind the house, giant pines stood straight up to the sky.
Tall front stairs led to a covered porch. The house needed painting, but it was old and charming. Before we could get out, a man
appeared on the steps.

"Mr. Ferguson?"

The stooped body, gray nearly all over, but especially on top
of his head, stuck out a gnarled hand. "Old Man Ferguson, some
say," he laughed. "Got two Mr. Ferguson's here. Which one you
want?"

Tony smiled briefly. "You'll be fine," he said. He pulled out his sheriff's ID and flashed it at the man.

"Oh! You're a new one around here."

"No sir, I work in Tallahassee."

The man's eyes, shiny and a bit watery, stared at us. He hesitated.

"I'm Luanne Fogarty," I said and put out my hand. It broke the impasse, and he offered us battered porch chairs.

When Tony had convinced the man he was Miz Keen's nephew, he had the familiarity he needed. The man began to talk and didn't stop unless one of us interrupted him.

"Old lady was nice most of the time, but she got them cats and they got cats. Too many around. I remember a time when she'd walk clear around this lake. Exercise, she said, but I know better. She liked to look for strays to help. She'd grab a neighbor or somebody with a boat and ask them to bring her home with an animal wiggling in her arms. That woman been scratched so many times, it's a wonder she didn't get a fever."

After several more "I remember a time" episodes, Mr. Ferguson had painted a picture of an eccentric, an ancient lady who lived as she pleased whether it offended anyone or not. She cared nothing for what people said to her about her nosiness. "She gave it as good as she got," said the old man, his laugh a deep throaty sound that invited a cough. His face paled then, and he added, "I sure was sorry to hear she died out in the grass like that. Better to go in your own bed, deep in the night."

"How did you find out where she died?" I said in a gentle voice.

"Somebody must have told me," he said. "Word about things like that travels fast around this lake. We supposed to look after each other, I guess."

"Did you see her the day she died?" Tony shifted on the lumpy cushion someone had placed over the rotting weave.

"Yep, sure did. She'd been to my dock down there. Said she'd found something. Called me a mean old bastard." He gave a laugh. "A bastard! Can you believe that? I ain't no bastard. My parents were married in the Baptist church." He laughed again.

"Any idea what she'd found?" Tony looked up and the man saw Tony's black eyes for the first time.

"You a Cuban?" he asked.

"Cuban descent. I was born in the states."

"That's why old Miz Keen had that black hair and those eyes." The man drifted off for a moment as though conjuring up another time.

"Her hair was quite gray, sir. Almost as white as yours," said Tony.

"No, no! Before the gray. I been knowing her a long time, see. Black hair, black eyes. Like something from a harem."

"More like a Carnival party," I said. I doubt she shared her men.

"Yeah. Exotic like."

Tony's impatience showed in his working jaw and shifting in the chair. His eyes darted from me back to Ferguson.

"What did you say to her that day on your dock?" he said.

"Told her to put back whatever she found. Of course, I never saw anything she had. Don't think she took a thing. Just old lady talk." He hesitated, then looked straight at Tony. "Know what she said to that? No! That's what she said, just 'No' and turned around and walked to the road."

"She could be rather coarse at times," said Tony.

"Coarse? Downright thievery if she took something."

"What was on the dock that might have made her curious?" I asked.

"Can't imagine." Ferguson shook his head, his eyes closed a moment. "Only thing down there are some traps my son keeps."

"Traps for what?" I asked.

"Anything. Squirrels, armadillos, whatever wanders there."

"She'd hate traps," I said to Tony.

"Especially if one had a cat in it," he said, his eyes glaring at Ferguson.

"No, no cats in those traps. Never got one. Never."

"But you *wanted* to get lots of them, right?" Tony's black orbs didn't move from the man's face.

"Tell you the truth? I'd preferred she didn't raise so many. They roamed and got into stuff. But I never killed any. No way!" He held up one hand and shook his head.

"Your son, what did he do about the cats?" I watched sweat pour from Tony's forehead. Even more poured from Ferguson's.

"Cussed a lot. He don't like them. Keeps a hunting dog penned up over there, and stray cats kept that hound barking all night." He gestured to the side of the house. A rusted wire fence with a gate penned off a square. Weeds grew inside it. At one end, a battered dog house stood shaded by an oleander bush.

"And where is the dog now?" asked Tony.

"With my son. Takes that mutt everywhere he goes. No wonder he ain't married. Prefers dog hair to maiden hair." He laughed and broke into coughs again. "Should be back soon. Just took a ride up to Ocala to get some wood."

"Wood?"

"Lumber. Boards. We got some rot on the back porch. If it don't get fixed, the thing is gonna fall in with somebody." Ferguson leaned back in his chair and breathed deeply. Exhaustion had finally won the day. "Here he comes now." Without leaning forward, the old man pointed a finger toward the drive.

A late model red truck kicked up mud from the dirt road as it sped toward the house. Some boards stuck out of the bed across the tailgate, one tied with a red warning scarf. I met Tony's glance. Both of us knew that the friendly chatter of a lonely old man might be replaced with a threatening stance from the son.

The truck came to a stop beside my Honda. The passenger side opened, tossed back by a long arm. A black dog, possibly Labrador mix, bounded from the seat and headed to the steps where he stopped and looked at us, tail wagging in slow motion.

Young Ferguson, who had to be fifty-five if not older, slid from the driver's side. He had the expected paunch, the tattoo on one arm, a rugged appearance. But something wasn't right with this redneck. His skin seemed paler than it should have been for someone who spends hours in the Florida outdoors. His hair, thick without a spot of gray, lay longish over the ears as though the cut planned it to be there. The shirt, well ironed and light blue, never saw a speck of mud, at least not today. But it was the jeans that made me look twice. They were crisp as though ironed and new. Below them, he wore black cowboy boots with silver tips.

"Hey, son. We got visitors. Miz Keen's relatives. Come on up and grab a chair." The old man rested his head on the back of his chair. "Better yet. Go inside and bring out some drinks."

The dog heard the "come on up" invitation, too, and bounded up the steps with this owner. There was no stand offish growling, just a bit of friendly sniffing then a tail wag before he plopped himself in a shaded spot on the other end of the porch. I figured this dog might bark at cats but if he ever caught one, it would be play time.

"Burl Ferguson, ma'am," the son said as he reached the top of the porch. He leaned over and offered his hand. I shook it, introduced myself, and Tony. When he moved to shake Tony's hand, I whiffed the perfume. It didn't smell much like after shave to me.

"Be right back." He opened the screen door and headed for the kitchen.

"He works in town?" I asked.

"On the outskirts," said the old man. "Runs the Fireside Bar. You been there?"

"No," I said, and Tony shook his head.

"Me neither," he said.

I couldn't think of anything else to ask about Miz Keen because of my confusion. He set traps and lived on a derelict swamp patch with a dog in a pen. He drove a truck. But he was clean as a whistle and wore perfume. Or maybe he had just been with a woman and the perfume rubbed off? I jumped when the screen opened again and Burl arrived with a tray. He set it down on a rickety table. I stared. The pitcher was opaque glass, tall and filled with lemonade that had fresh sliced lemons in it. The matching glasses had been filled with ice. No redneck had ever served me something like this. It was either beer or soda pop and in the can.

"Thanks," I said and smiled as Burl poured.

Tony, whose own ideas of what a suspicious swamp rat ought to be and what we were confronted with must have been clashing inside his head, simply nodded when handed the glass.

"I'm so sorry about Miz Keen," Burl finally said after he gave his father a glass and sat in his own chair. He held his glass with a napkin wrapped around it to absorb the condensation.

We chatted a bit, covering some of the same territory the old man had given us. Burl set traps, he said, for moles and armadillos because they ate up the flowers and made a mess. He never set them for cats.

"I don't think the cats were fooled by the traps, anyway. They roamed around and killed their own squirrels if Miz Keen didn't feed them." He took tiny sips of the sweet lemonade.

"And the dog?" I nodded toward the black hairy blob that had stretched on the wooden planks.

"Frankie? He never bothered a cat. Might have chased one or two but never killed one." He smiled in the dog's direction, the affection for the animal lighting up his eyes.

"Do you know anyone who might drown kittens?" I asked.

"Ugh! That's one barbaric act if you ask me," said Burl.

"Any number of old timers around here would do it," said the old man, his eyes closed now. "That's the way farm boys controlled the numbers. Didn't have no spaying and neutering back then."

"They're talking about today, Pop." Burl smiled at us. "I suppose some people still do that. But there might be a law now. Cruelty against animals and such."

Tony, whose silence began to bother me, finally spoke. "How's the bar business down this way?"

Burl's eyes darted from his father to Tony and finally to me. "Does okay." He sipped the lemonade and offered us refills.

"Did my aunt ever go to your bar?"

Burl stopped mid pour. "Your aunt? Not that I ever heard of. Did she habit bars?"

"My aunt was eccentric. She could have habited anything at least once." Tony stuck out his glass for more lemonade. He drank down the refill in two gulps.

"I'll ask the bartender, but I don't think so." Burl sat quiet for a minute, looking at his feet, then gave a quick laugh. He looked up and changed the subject. "That tropical storm is turning into a hurricane. It could come ashore around here but the weather man said it would more likely hit farther up the panhandle."

Tony and I left the two Fergusons sitting on their porch with a sleeping dog. Thunder sounded in the distance as we hit the pond circle road again. We moved through the tall reeds and reached Miz Keen's house just as Gil Bono came toward us, a golden cat sitting on one shoulder.

CHAPTER FOUR

Charles Chandler—who had since earlier in the day become Charlie, grinning when he emphasized the Charlie Chan part—and his two men made a clean search of Miz Keen's place. Clean in the sense of keeping things neat. There was no tossing about drawers or turning over chairs and ripping out cushions. When they did turn over furniture, they patted the bottom with gloved hands and uprighted it, back in its rightful location. I couldn't help but think Chandler was doing this for Tony's sake, a sort of lawman brotherhood idea. I knew he had called the sheriff and got Tony's profile. If he suspected him of anything, he wasn't going to show it like a cop on the warpath.

"We need to read these," Charlie said as he stacked the Keen journals into a box. "We'll get them back to you." He flipped through one that had a marker in it. "Anything interesting?" He said and looked at both of us.

"We didn't get very far," I said. "She seemed to dislike a neighbor, but I don't know who."

Tony shook his head. His jaw worked. He didn't like another lawman taking over where he usually stood, especially now when it concerned his own relative. "Let me know what you find."

Charlie nodded, picked up the box, and stopped. "You want to give us a copy of the will? I can find it elsewhere, but it'd be quicker if you provided it."

Tony turned a dark red. He was the sole inheritor, which made him an automatic suspect. He pulled an envelope from a side table and slapped it on top of the boxes. "I'm surprised you didn't already find this in your search."

"We did," said Charlie, his even-tempered speech gave him an intellectual air. "I just need a copy." He nodded at both of us and headed out the door.

Tony sat in a chair and stared into the growing gloom of the little house. I followed Chandler to his car.

"Look, sir…."

"Charlie, please." He looked down at me, his gray eyes smiling in a strong face. The handsomeness of his stature and grace must have gotten details out of many a female suspect.

"Charlie, sir. Tony is really in a tether about all this. He won't show it, but it's not his nature to sit back and let other people find the culprit." I stopped and smiled in spite of myself. "In fact, he gets uptight when he has to acknowledge I got there first."

"Yeah, I know. I got the scoop from Tallahassee. He's a good man, but he's going to have to wait out this one. Too close to the victim."

Thunder sounded again, and the sky grew darker. Charlie placed the boxes on the back seat and the bag of dead kittens into the trunk. He waved off his officers as they pulled out the drive, and turned back to me. "You two got plenty of stuff to hold you through a hurricane? I've seen only one come through here, but it got that lake up pretty high. Flooded some houses."

"We haven't had much time to think of Mother Nature storms. The human ones have been a bit consuming."

Charlie smiled and nodded. I stood in the doorway until their cars disappeared. A rustling sound came in bursts as the wind moved the tops of the high reeds. In a few hours, they could be bent to the ground.

Before I shut the door, a movement came from the right. Gil Bono jumped from behind a bush, a grin spread across his chubby face. His size made the action look ridiculous. He held up a flashlight.

"You need one of these?" he asked.

"No, thanks. I travel with one in the car."

"Want some oranges? We got a tree and the wind will just blow them ever which way." He held up a plastic grocery store bag with the small fruit.

"Thanks." I looked at the kid. He was nearly as tall as me and pale as a New Yorker in winter. "How long have you been here?"

He shrugged. "We been down twice already. My mom and I came to get the house ready. Then we went back. And now we came again." He stopped the childish sentences to breathe deeply. "I got kicked out of school." He tried to look embarrassed, but I saw pride there.

"Oh?"

"Yeah. I took some beer in my lunch box. Teacher found it and reported me."

I nodded. "Schools wouldn't approve of drinking on campus."

"Not when you shared it with some other people, even some girls!" Gil's grin widened. I expected a giggle at any minute.

"Did you enroll in school when you got here?"

His frown appeared instantly from the smile. He shook his head. "This is the vacation house." The smile reappeared.

"And just how old are you?"

"Fourteen." He held the grin.

I didn't know what else to say to this overgrown child, one who obviously took pride in impressing his classmates with not only free beer, but with expulsion. Our silence was broken by another rustling of reeds.

"Are you all ready for the storm?" I moved out and took a look at the house up the road. I could barely see the front where Mr. Bono was taking in the canvas overhang. He glimpsed me and waved.

"We got stuff we brought in, and my dad bought a generator. It's neat. Cuts on the lights and fridge in case of an outage." He breathed deeply again, and I suspected asthma played a role in this kid's life. "I hope we have an outage. I want to see it work."

"Don't say that, please." I tried to smile back at him. "Your cat? Is it safe?"

Gil shrugged and looked away from me. "Oh, him. He's kind of stuck in a closet on the back porch." His face looked as pained as it could in the tight baby fat. "I can't breathe too good with cat hair in the house, and my mom says it has to stay out there."

I nodded. At least the animal was in an enclosed dark place.

"Did you bring the cat from New Jersey?"

"No. I found it wandering around here. All by itself. It didn't take long to tame it, either. Pop thinks it might have worms, and my mom worries about fleas. I don't think it has either one."

I sighed. "Gil, did you know Miz Keen?"

"Sure. She's had this house since we got ours. She was kind of crazy."

"Crazy fun, or scary crazy?"

He raised his shoulders in a long shrug and frowned as though thinking about this choice. "Scared me. She didn't want me playing on her dock." He pointed toward the lake. "Said I had to leave her cats alone." He looked at me wide-eyed. "I never hurt them. Just played with them. They liked to chase stones down by the lake. I just threw stones and the cats chased them." His face looked as though he saw Miz Keen's spirit hovering over him.

"Okay," I said, deciding not to prod him further with what I thought was the truth—he had thrown stones at the cats.

"I better go now," he said. He looked toward his house. His father had come halfway and stopped. Gil took off. I could hear him telling his father that I already had a flashlight.

Mr. Bono turned and yelled, "Take care!"

I waved back and watched them disappear into the house. The reeds and few hedges were bending further now, but still the wind came in gusts. The Gulf was miles from here, but any hurricane coming ashore wouldn't slow down for a few cattails and a lake. Damage could be awesome.

Inside again, I saw Tony sitting in the dark of the tiny living room. It was hard enough to sort out the death of an ancient relative, not to mention the murder of one. I felt his pain instead of his arrogance for the first time in our acquaintance. But if he wept at all, he never let me see the tears.

"I'm going to the store to get ready for any kind of ill wind blowing this way," I said and grabbed my keys.

"No need," said Tony. He sat on the sofa, looking dejected and lacking energy. "My aunt had preparation down pat." He sighed and stood up, motioning for me to follow him.

The room that served as a laundry center off the kitchen had two sliding closet doors. Tony had to squeeze to get to the one nearest the outer wall, but he shoved it back and revealed stacks of bottled water, canned goods, and unopened cereal boxes. Pulling that door shut, he opened the other one. Flashlights, batteries, first aid supplies, and a ship-to-shore portable radio sat neatly on the shelves.

I stood and assessed the orderliness of this woman. "She was almost obsessed with preparation. I mean, not only for storms... but the autopsy."

"Yeah. My mother said she was always like this. Cut things out for scrapbooks, labeled all the family photos, not to mention the journals."

"But murder? That can't have been in her plans. Think she got under somebody's skin?"

Tony didn't answer. A loud wind blew through the area, reminding us of a higher power about to unleash on the state.

We returned to the living room and turned on Miz Keen's television. An announcer stood in front of a large map, pointing to a disturbance in the Gulf. "Right now, winds have picked up and it will be a hurricane by nightfall. It's headed in a slow northwesterly direction, and could come ashore in the Florida panhandle or turn and hit anywhere from Florida to Texas." He discussed the projection and concluded that we were would definitely get the edges of the storm.

Tony sat frozen in his spot on the sofa. As soon as he had showed me where the supplies were, he seemed disinterested in the danger of the storm.

"I'm going to check around the place," I said and headed out the back door. I crossed the concrete slab patio and opened the screen door, noticing that its small latch was broken. Rounding the house, its weathered sides graced by reeds and high grass that brushed back and forth in the wind, I looked for things that could fall on the roof or hit windows. The few trees, mostly orange and lemon in need of pruning, dotted the wide space. Their limbs wouldn't do much damage if they hit the side of the house. In the distance, I watched Gil and his father pull in furniture from their back porch. Their yard was like Miz Keen's, reedy, grassy, and with a few fruit trees. As I rounded the house, I found nothing that could be a projectile into our sanctuary. It was time to think of my own house up north.

I went into the small kitchen and sat in Miz Keen's chair that looked onto her back patio. The door from the kitchen to the patio was mostly glass. Anyone sitting where I sat could see clear to the lake. I pulled out my cell phone and called Pasquin.

"I got your rockers inside and checked the windows. Can't do much else. Just crossing our fingers no big winds hit this far inland." I envisioned him sitting in his furniture-filled living room with dark curtains. My house, as well as his, was surrounded with high oaks and pines, any of which could shed a branch or even a whole trunk and dump it right on the roof. I had seen entire oaks, years old, lying on a crushed section of brand new structures. But Pasquin, with his eighty plus years of living with the swamp and all its storms, took it as another stride in history. His voice gave me comfort, almost as though he had some magic control over events.

"Same here," I said. "And Plato?"

"Sitting right here. We'll wait it out together."

I punched in Vernon's cell phone.

"The diving has been called off," he said. "The water's too rough and too high. We're going to get a real blow here." Vernon had been standing under a picnic shelter when I rang him. "Body will probably wash ashore somewhere long before we find it by diving. I'm planning on heading home soon. Got to batten the hatches before long."

We talked for a long while, exchanging stories of what needed to be done at his place on another lake where he had a long dock leading from his back porch and out over the water. I wandered the kitchen while we spoke, opening cabinets of neat plate stacks and glasses in matching sizes. The cops searched these shelves, I was sure, but very little seemed disturbed.

"Don't let Tony's moods get to you, okay?" Vernon knew the

underlying resentment that lay in both of us. "He'll be fine in a storm. And he knows you're there to help him out, even if he doesn't admit it."

I felt nostalgic for a moment and fought off a lump in my throat. Danger was blowing my way, and I'd really have liked to huddle down with Vernon. I nodded as though he were there and with a "love you" rang off.

Standing in the kitchen, I thought about houses surrounded by trees, beautiful sights in good weather, but dangerous in storms. That's when I wondered about the Fergusons with their old house, practically engulfed in oak trees. If nothing else, their front yard would be littered with limbs when it was all over. But a storm like this threatened more than that. "Maybe Burl will move his father to the bar," I thought.

I sat down hard in the chair and placed the cell phone on the table. A wind gust reminded me of the present, and I thought it might be wise to move the furniture off the patio. Looking up, I saw the two white chairs with a matching table in the middle, all facing the lake. And I saw a person sitting in one, a wrinkled arm draping nearly to the floor.

CHAPTER FIVE

"I'm Mildred Culley." The ancient voice emanated from a weathered face that looked at least ninety. Thin red, permed hair stood nearly straight up on her tiny head. Her breaths came in short spurts as she leaned her body against the back of the plastic chair. She was miniscule enough to fit into the regular size chair like a doll.

"Are you all right, Mrs. Culley?" I bent over her, thinking I could sit her upright, but she brushed me away.

"Just out of breath. I nearly had to run over here. Was afraid the rain might start." She waved the air in front of her face as though casting off invisible flies. "I got word that Marta's nephew was around." She focused her filmy eyes on my face. "You his wife?"

"No ma'am, I'm not." I introduced myself as a friend and old colleague of Tony's.

"Well, where is the man?" She sat up with surprising energy, hands gripping the chair arms.

"I'll get him," I said. I smiled as I found Tony still sitting in his gloom. He'd need me with this one. "You got a visitor." I motioned to the back of the house. Frowning at the disturbance he stood and followed me to the patio.

"You look like Marta, a little anyway," said Mildred. She had stood when Tony entered the patio and now reached out a hand

50

toward his hair. "Marta showed me pictures of her when her hair was dark as yours. Snow white when she died."

"You hurried over here in an impending storm," said Tony. He lifted his head so that the tiny woman couldn't reach his hair. "Where did you come from?"

"Over there," said Mildred, pointing a gnarled finger across the lake. "I got a boat to use, but don't trust it on a day when the lake is whipping up. Plus, gators are active. I ain't much use as a rower at any time, but I make it all right in good weather."

I walked to the screen where some spiders had built webs and wrapped unsuspecting insects into death cocoons. The entire patio needed a good cleaning. Maybe Mother Nature would do it for us.

"You live way over there? Which house?"

"The white one with the big oak by the porch. I've lived there since I moved out on my sister."

"Have you been here as long as my aunt?" Tony took a chair where he could see both the lake and Miss Culley.

"Longer. I was born here. In the big house right down the road and behind my current house. My sister, Nell Culley, and I grew up on this lake. She stayed in the family house. When I decided to move out, she bought out my share. That's when I bought the big one you see there."

"Does your sister still live there?" I turned back to see a Mildred with a defiant face.

"No! She's dead. Been dead nearly a year."

I started to apologize or whatever it is when we say we're sorry for bringing up a dead relative. Mildred put up one hand and stopped me.

"We didn't depart each other on good terms, and it got even worse when I found out what she did."

A silence moved across the patio in the form of wind that had grown stronger since a few minutes before. Tony didn't notice. He was engrossed in the woman's words.

"Worse how?" he said.

"I figured I'd inherit all her stuff and the old house. I know she was in my will as my only heir." Mildred placed both hands on the arms of the chair that threatened to engulf her. "And I did inherit what she had. The house wasn't hers."

"Not hers?" Tony and I spoke together.

"A few months before she had sold it to Mr. Ferguson. He had the deed signed over to him and everything."

"But you got the cash?" I said after another moment of silence.

"Wasn't none. She spent it all as far as I can tell."

Tony leaned forward, his eyes shining. "How did your sister die, Miss Culley?" He spoke gently, undemanding, a cop voice he must have used on a thousand suspects.

"Fell in her own shower. Hit her head on the tiles and slid down right on the floor with the water still running. She had a broken hip, so the coroner said."

I shot a glance toward Tony who leaned back now and frowned.

"Miss Culley, you came here to tell us something, right?" I asked.

"To tell *him* something," she jabbed her finger toward Tony.

"Tell me," he said, again in a soft voice.

Miss Culley looked toward me, her old eyes flashing anger and questioning my presence.

"She's fine," said Tony. "Whatever you say will stay with us." I knew that wasn't true. If it had any implications on our current quest, he'd share it with Chandler.

"When I found out my sister had sold the house, then died, I couldn't sleep much. She never told me about the sale, but evidently she did tell your aunt. I found that out after we buried Nell. Marta said Nell didn't want me to know since it was the family home and stuff, but Mr. Ferguson was paying high money for the place. And, he said she could live there until she passed away." Mildred chuckled. "Of course that wouldn't be too far in the future. He knew that. She was ninety that year."

"Is that what you wanted to tell me?"

"Well, there's a little bit more and maybe it's just an old lady sniffing dirty air, but after my sister died," she stopped. "Could I have some water?" She placed a hand on her chest and coughed quietly.

I stepped into the kitchen and poured a large glass of water. The woman could be in a bad way herself, I thought.

"Just get these flutters when I talk too much," she said and gulped down half the glass.

"You were saying there was more?" said Tony, still sounding patient.

"After Ferguson made his appearance at the house and let me know it was his, he began sending over young boys to clean out stuff and do up the yard. Things like that. He says he's going to paint the thing and fix some of the wiring." She drank the rest of the water.

"To move into it himself?" I asked.

Mildred shook her head. "I figure he's going to sell it."

"You don't want him to do that, or maybe you want to buy it yourself?" I took her empty glass and offered to refill it.

She put out her hand and shook her head again, her eyes closed. "I'm too old to buy a house. He wants to buy mine now, but I won't sell. I just wanted to know if your aunt said anything about this whole venture." Her eyes opened wide toward Tony.

"Not a word, ma'am."

"Then why is the sheriff going all around the lake and asking people about her death?" The question came loud and clear. It had to be why she came.

"He's been to you already?" I asked.

"Me and the two people who live nearby. I saw the cars over here and I saw a uniformed man go into that house next door." She stabbed at the air in the direction of the Bono house. "I can't stand that boy. He comes around our side of the lake, cutting through property, dropping his candy wrappers."

"Gil?" I asked and looked at Tony. "I can't imagine he'd walk or even ride a bike around the lake."

We both looked at Mildred. "Well, he's there. There's a motor boat hanging around the lake and I guess he comes in that."

I sat down, the empty glass still in my hand. "How did Miz Keen get along with Gil and his family?"

"Couldn't stand them. They're always pushing their noses into stuff, asking to use her dock, and," she leaned forward and lowered her voice, "they drink." She nodded and leaned back again.

"How much?" Tony stiffened.

"Marta, now mind you she'd take a sip of her wine now and then, but she said the Bonos poured it down and got all sing-songy."

"How did she know they did that?" I asked.

"They'd sit out on the grass in those lounge chairs and gulp it down. Had the kid run back and forth to the cooler up on the porch."

"Did he drink with them?"

"Marta never said. I think he ate up everything. Liked to toss rocks at the cats. One time, he even brought their garbage over and stuck it in her plastic can."

Thunder rumbled across the sky almost like the wind was blowing it our way. Dark clouds had traveled the miles from the Gulf.

"Will you be okay in the storm?" I said as I looked around the lake. Even over the wind and turbulent waters, the mating gators roared in their frenzy.

"I sat through a many of them," said Mildred, who stood up and headed for the screen door. "Guess you ain't going to tell me how Marta died."

"Heart attack," said Tony and stood up with her. He held the screen door shut. "You can't walk back in this weather. We'll drive you."

"Gotta go to the ladies' room first." She pushed her wiry body upward, pulled her big shirt close to her body, and headed through the kitchen. "Don't bother showing me. I know the way."

We waited for several minutes until Mildred came strutting out in the way that people who have walked everywhere all their lives do. She followed me to my car that wasn't yet stowed in the crowded garage. Tony climbed into the back seat, not an easy feat for anyone over five feet, after we had placed Mildred in the seat beside me.

"Just go by way of the Ferguson's. You'll see my house right on the lake circle road."

We bumped out of Miss Priss Lane then bumped some more along the dirt road among reeds that blew away from the lake.

Mildred kept her eyes straight ahead, holding onto the dash with one hand. When we reached the turn off to the Ferguson place, she pushed upward and strained her neck to see down their driveway.

"Maybe he'll just blow away," she said.

We moved on until we were nearly opposite Marta's house across the lake. Mildred fished in her pocket for her keys.

"Never locked the place until all these accidents started around here. You know, some kid drowned out there a few years back." She pointed to the lake. "Sheriff said he was trying to canoe and turned over. Couldn't swim." She opened the door just as Tony got out to help her. She brushed him aside. "I don't believe he drowned like that." She stopped and stared at Tony. "And I don't believe Marta died of a heart attack." She walked to her house in long determined strides. Using the wood handrail, she climbed to her porch, unlocked her door, and slammed it without looking back.

"Is this just a cantankerous old lady or did we just hear something suggestive of murder?" I said as I sat in silence. Tony had climbed into the front passenger seat.

"A little of both, most likely." He said and jumped when a loud clap of thunder reminded us of other dangers.

We rode in silence back to Marta's house. Tony's moods were like this. He hadn't changed them much over the years. Forget the hysterical, screaming Cuban like Desi Arnaz. This one sank into his own quiet hell.

"So, what do you make of this whole thing?" I said as I turned off the key in the driveway. Tony made no move to get out. He sat staring ahead of him, into the garage door. "Tony?"

"Sorry," he said and got out to open the door and guide me into the tiny bit of space left. Provided the roof didn't cave in, our cars wouldn't blow away.

A light mist had begun to blow in the winds, feeling almost like damp silk against the face. I'd heard somewhere that this wasn't rain or water from clouds. It was water skimmed off the ocean surface by hurricane winds and blown far inland. It moved sideways, not downward.

"I'm going to check around the house again," I said. "You

want to get something for us to eat while the electricity is still on?"

Tony nodded.

Twilight was closing in. I took the flashlight from the Honda and moved around the side of the house. Nothing looked out of place. On the other side, I could see the lights in the windows of the Bono house, and wondered if they were sorry they came down for the summer. Looking at the flicker of their television set through the side window, I wondered, too, why they came down during the summer instead of the winters like other snowbirds.

I moved to the back of the house where we had met Miss Culley on the patio. We had forgotten to secure the screen. The wind hadn't been strong enough to blow it completely open, but it kept up a steady tapping beat against the frame. I looked around for something to shove against the door. There was nothing, of course. Big rocks weren't a part of this terrain unless you brought them here. Giving up, I made a note to look for hammer and nails inside the house.

Turning to look across the lake, I saw dim lights from Miss Culley's house. The lake water lapped harder now, some real waves washing onto shore. I tried to imagine a full force hurricane here, one that would cover the dock and reach the tiny patio.

"You're scared, aren't you?" said a voice in the reeds.

I jumped, nearly dropping the flashlight. "Good heavens, Gil! Don't surprise someone like that."

The chubby teen appeared near the patio and stood in front of me. He was finishing a popsicle that threatened to melt away with the humid wind before he could shove it into his face.

"It's fun," he giggled. "I like sneaking up on people."

I stared at the boy. He would be the kind you could forget, the obnoxious creature who ate up your food stock and contributed nothing to what one might call the enjoyment of a child. He wore shorts that ended near his knees. The waist and thigh areas looked bound in the tight material. His feet were clad in the latest giant size runners. His shirt may have once been white, but pink popsicle gave it color.

"Do you know Miss Culley who lives across the lake?" I shined the light in his eyes for a short moment.

He turned to face the house across the lake. "Yeah. She used to come visit Miz Keen. They used to sit out on the dock in those plastic chairs and talk a lot."

"Any idea what they talked about?"

He shrugged, but his two glances told me he knew more than he was going to tell. "Old lady stuff, I guess." He sucked off the last of the popsicle and tossed the stick into the reeds. I bit my tongue instead of telling him to stop littering up the place.

"Oh, come on, Gil. You sneak around, you said. I'll bet you sat in those reeds down there and heard every word."

"Did not," he grinned, falling for my flattery.

"Not even *one* conversation?"

He smiled and turned a circle on one of his big shoes. "Guess I heard them talking about Ferguson."

"They didn't like the Fergusons, right?"

He shook his head. "Especially the old man. Said he just about stole Miss Culley's sister's house."

"The old man?" I had understood from Mildred that it was the young Ferguson who had bought the house.

"I think so. They didn't like the son, either. Fact is, them two old ladies didn't much like anybody around here." He took a deep breath, his face glowing in the dying light. "One time my mother asked them over for a spaghetti dinner, and you know what? Miz Keen got choked on some sauce and had to spill her guts in our bathroom." He laughed out loud, said he'd better get inside, and dashed off in his big-sized way to his house.

Back inside, I began talking about my conversation with Gil. Tony stopped me.

"Chandler called. I guess we didn't check those dead kittens well enough. Seems somebody helped them along by slitting their throats before tossing them into the lake."

CHAPTER SIX

The tropical storm-turned-hurricane took a slow stroll up the coastline, tossing its feeder bands inland and destroying what it could. Its slow progress made it even more dangerous.

Coastal homes were pounded, some destroyed if they were flimsy enough. Inland waterways filled and blew over their banks. Silly news reporters stood in rain gear, holding onto railings, and told their stories with Gulf waters slamming the sand in the background.

Tony and I huddled in the tiny block house, turned up the set to overpower the wind and rain outside, and listened to the media tell what was happening all around us.

"We're bound to lose power sometime tonight," said Tony, his only utterance since we pulled in the plastic patio chairs.

We sat facing the television, both with flashlights and cell phones on nearby tables. There had been no calls from Tallahassee. Not surprising that Pasquin didn't contact me. His house phone would be out, and he had no cell. But Vernon worried me. His house was close to water, just like this one.

"I'm going to call north," I said and picked up the cell phone. When Vernon didn't answer his cell, I left a message and turned around and dialed his house phone. No answer there, either. Pasquin's gave the out-of-order signal.

"Just leave it, Luanne. Vernon's most likely outside nailing down

something. Pasquin's phone is gone for the duration of the storm."
Tony didn't look at me. I watched his face, chiseled, handsome, a
nice pale olive color with black eyes. His hair, black too, rested in
its combed place just like the barbershop had done it. Tony had
had one girlfriend that I knew about, but it didn't last long. Who
did he call when he was worried in a storm? I answered myself:
evidently nobody.

We ate tuna sandwiches with bananas on the side. Leftovers
from Marta's kitchen supplies. I silently swore I'd get a big home-
cooked meal when this was over.

"It looks as though the storm is moving ashore slightly." The
news had switched to a meteorologist who pointed to a comput-
erized map that showed the string of outlying storm pushing
against Cedar Key, but with a projected line heading back into the
Gulf and going northwest. "If it continues in its current path, it
could hit shore anywhere from West Florida to Texas."

"I vote for Texas," I said.

"What's that sound?" Tony moved out of his chair and stood
with his ear cocked toward the back of the house.

I sat still. At first there was nothing but I heard something like
yelling into the storm. We moved to the kitchen.

The night was inky black. Only streaks of sideways rain flashed
in the lights shining from the house. Something invisible a few
yards from the house bellowed.

"It must be a gator," said Tony, attempting to shine his light
through the screen without actually stepping on the rain soaked
patio floor. "What do they do in storm, I wonder?"

"From the sound of this one, the same thing he usually does
this time of year. Kind of gives the 'any port in a storm' a new
meaning." I grabbed an umbrella and opened it, and slipped out
of my shoes. Shielding myself at an angle, I moved to the screen

wall closest to the lake. My bare feet sloshed through storm water that was having trouble draining in its usual manner. Holding the umbrella handle under one arm, I shined my light into the yard. Rain shot through the blackness, but the roar got closer. In a sudden movement, an alligator with a large head—meaning one that was also quite long—charged toward the screen, his mouth wide and the sound coming from the depths of his throat. I stepped back, dropping the open umbrella that proceeded to trip me. My flashlight flew off somewhere and went out. Tony's light focused on the gator who had turned away now and slid back toward the lake. His body was so long I thought we'd never see his tail.

"Are you all right?" Tony was lifting me from the floor by pulling on one arm. "Sure am glad you didn't decide to walk outside and confront that thing."

I stood, my left hip and leg feeling a bit worse for the fall.

"The wind is stronger. I'll bet it's whipping up the water and blowing it this way." I braced myself against Tony as he helped me inside.

"You didn't break anything, I hope," said Tony as he handed me a towel.

I stared at him. After drying off, I said I needed to change clothes and limped off to the bedroom. I heard him sit down again in the wicker chair.

I stripped and stared at the damage. An area from the left side of my butt down to my knee was a kind of reddish color. It would turn black pretty soon, and green before it got well. I covered it with another pair of jeans, pulled on a T-shirt and headed back to the living room.

"Only takes a minute to do something dumb," Tony said, not looking at me.

I glared back at him. "You wanted to know about the sound as much as I did."

"I'm not the one who insisted on going onto that wet porch."

My silence didn't bother him. It was what he was used to. Sympathy just didn't occur to him. He had been a loner for too many years to develop a humane streak now. Had I gone outside and gotten into direct combat with that gator, would he have come to my rescue? I watched him as he stared at the news reporter. There was nothing I could do but shrug and towel dab my hair. I stood and went to the window that faced next door.

"Looks like only one light on at the Bono's. Maybe they're sleeping through it all."

"No," said Tony. "I caught a glimpse of them on their back porch. They're watching the storm."

"Watching the storm? You can't see anything but a few feet in front of you and then only if you've got a flashlight." I frowned at his indifference. He never took his eyes from the television.

"They've got at least one. I saw it click on and off while we were on the patio, before you hit the cement."

The man had an eye. That's what made him good at his job. He rarely missed a thing. I whispered to the wall, "and even if he does miss something, he's not going to admit it."

I heard a slam, not like a limb hitting the roof or a flying chair up against a wall, but like a door when someone left in a huff. An outdoor sensor light flashed on at the Bono's, and Gil's heavy body stepped in my line of vision as he trudged toward the back of the house. He had no rain gear on, and his flashlight was tucked into his waistband.

"Where's he going in all this?" I said.

Tony's presence behind me made me jump. He had moved across the room like a mouse darting in the shadows.

"Good question." He stood watching out the window with me. I could feel his breath on the top of my head. "He's coming back."

Gil, soaked to the skin, wrapped his arms around a tarp covered square nearly the size of his own chest. He went to the front door and began to kick at it. A man's arm opened it and for a brief moment JoJo Bono's face appeared. He took the object and said something to his son. Gil screamed over the wind, "There's gators down there!" The front door closed and Gil turned back into the storm. He used both hands to rub the water from his face and tug on his shirt that stuck to his misshapen blubber, forming grooves and valleys over his back and chest. He headed toward the lake.

I could no longer feel Tony's breath on my head. He had moved, and before I could discover where, he appeared from his room in a clear rain coat with a hood and snake boots, his gun tucked into his waistband. "You can follow me if you got boots. Otherwise, stay inside."

The idea of being ankle deep in storm water with swimming snakes that had no place to go gave me a shudder. But in all my endeavors with the sheriff's department, I knew to have those boots wherever I went. I fished them from the closet along with a plastic rain hat, one that little old ladies tied around their new perms on a damp day, and headed outside.

I followed the flashlights. Tony's darted back and forth across a track in front of him. Gil's, farther away, aimed a steady beam at something between the house and the lake. The lake had ventured upward, or more like been blown toward the houses. Before I could see how deep it was, I stepped in nearly a foot of water. Shining the light around me, I waited for the territorial moccasin or the gator in heat. All I got was wind, rain, and darkness.

"Kid!" I heard Tony yell. "What the hell are you doing out in this storm?"

There was no answer but Gil's light began to bounce toward the lake. He was trying to run. Whatever he had to get, he didn't want interference.

The light turned sharply, then seemed to touch the ground. It moved back up again, most likely when Gil picked up another package. His light made a circle as he turned to head up again to the house. When it stopped, he shouted. It was a yell heard above the storm, adding to the wind's constant stream of wet noise.

I couldn't make out the words, but the tone was unmistakable. Gil was in trouble. I ran, forsaking the thought of knocking against a coral snake or stepping flat on a gator's head. Tony's light bounced ahead of me. The three of us finally met in a wet circle of light.

"It's got something!" Gil pointed to the water where an alligator moved near the shore with something in its jaws. The light color suggested a deer.

"Tony, deer must have come out of the woods in the storm. It has to be a deer, right?" Maybe some moss or debris from the storm had caught on the deer's leg, and the bull gator dragged it into the darkness.

Before he could navigate to the edge of the deeper water, Tony yelled that the gator had gone down and was out of sight.

"Whatever he's got, it's dead now." He shined the light onto the lake surface that had white caps almost like the ocean. When a loud thump hit Miz Keen's dock, we all three jerked our lights in that direction. An overturned boat floated bottom up and banged against the pilings.

"It's eating somebody!" Gil shook water from his arms. Had it not been raining, he may have shown tears.

"Who, Gil?" I shouted, grabbing onto the ample arm.

"I don't know!" He jerked away from me and started to run back to his house. He stopped suddenly, went back for his package, then took off again.

I turned to find Tony wading onto the flooded dock and pulling at the boat. He shoved it and yelled at me to pull it closer. I stood up to my knees now, the water pouring into my boots, and waited for waves to move the boat closer. Grabbing it, I pulled hard to get it to shallow water and up a light embankment. With Tony's help, we pulled it to Miz Keen's patio.

"Chandler is going to love this call," said Tony as he shined a light back on the water. The gator and his prey had vanished.

The cell phone worked and the sheriff's department now knew a gator had taken something down.

"Lots of boats come loose in storms like this," Tony said.

"Most people secure them, especially little ones like that one," I added. "Of course, it could come loose, like you say."

We sat in the living room. The weather was hurricane warm and humid, but I shivered, even with dry clothes and a towel turban on my head. With all the emergencies going on, a deputy wasn't likely to be here soon.

"What was that kid doing out in this storm?" Tony faced the television again. "And what parent would send him out in it?"

"He must have forgotten to bring something inside," I said. "Looked like boxes that were getting wet."

"Remind me to ask Chandler if he's done a background check on the Bono's." He sat back in his chair, his well combed hair and dry clothes covering any sign of a nasty jaunt in a storm.

The reporter from the weather service poked a stick at his

map. The eye of the hurricane was headed back into the Gulf and should be gone from our area by morning. From the sound of the wind outside, it had decided to give a roaring goodbye. We heard the boat scrape on the patio cement just before the lights went out.

Both our flashlights clicked on until Tony lit the storm lamp he had set in the middle of the room. It gave off a yellow glow that lit up the room like a haunted ride at the fair. I lit the huge Christmas candle I'd found in Miz Keen's dining room and set it on the kitchen counter. The candle had seen many a season, probably situated inside a holly garnish on her tiny dining table. She never burned it, of course. That would mean buying another one each year. Well, Marta, it's burning now, I thought.

Outside the borders of the two lights, darkness prevailed.

"I'm sure glad it's not cold," I said. "Can you imagine if all this were snow?"

"Could see better," Tony said. "Light off the white snow."

"But we'd freeze. No electricity means no heat."

"Well, I'd think there'd be a fireplace in a situation like that." I wondered if he was grinning in the darkness. For sure he wouldn't be in the light.

"You know, Tony, a gator will grab a live deer from shore—a small one, of course. He'll take it down to drown it, but unless he's got a powerful hunger, he won't eat it right away. He'll often stow it near shore somewhere, in his own territory, to soften the flesh for eating."

"I know that, Luanne."

"Maybe we need to walk the shoreline come morning."

"If there is a shoreline."

Wind forced against the house and windows rattled. I leaned back and closed my eyes. This storm has to leave, I thought. It's paralyzing everything. The television black and silent, the winds in a steady hum, and an occasional thump of debris on the roof. Sitting in a darkened house in the middle of a hurricane made all human efforts futile. The only thing to do was fall asleep.

CHAPTER SEVEN

Sleep doesn't last long if your house is about to blow away. A distant ripping came out of the rain and ran across my brain. I thought of tearing sheets until it got so loud I jumped from the chair. The sheets in my dream turned out to be the patio roof of Miz Keen's house. It was one of those aluminum things you buy from a home improvement store. Nice sun shade and does okay in the rain, too. But wind is another matter.

Tony, who had stretched out on the sofa, rolled off and hit the floor. Before I could go to his rescue, he was up and running to the back. We both knew what was happening.

"Damn!" He said, standing with hands on his hips and gazing out the kitchen door. Even without lights, we could see the gaping hole on one side. The wind had folded about three feet of the roof like a piece of paper. "There's nothing we can do about this. Even if the storm takes off the rest of it."

The screen wall sagged a little from the impact but it hadn't yet broken loose from the support poles. The small boat still rested on the patio floor though it tended to scrape a few inches in a strong gust.

"Tony," I said, trying not to alarm him further, "the water is rising." I pointed my flashlight to the edge of the patio. Another inch and it would wash onto the concrete slab. After that, if it kept coming, we could be in for a flooded house.

Tony stood for a moment. When he ran to the linen closet, I followed. "We'll have to keep watch," he said as he jerked towels from the shelves. "If it looks like it's coming into the house, we'll put these down and hope for the best."

"Shouldn't we raise some things up higher?" I said as I carried a stack of towels to the dining room table.

"Shit!" I heard Tony as something hit the floor.

"What now?"

"Something fell off a shelf. Let it go for now." He followed me with another stack of towels. "Water will come in here first, but we'd better be prepared for the front door, too." He pulled some towels from the top of the stack and rushed back into the living room.

"I'll sit for a while in the dining room. You can relieve me when I get too sleepy."

I nodded. Low lying houses weren't my expertise. My own family home in the swamps outside Tallahassee was built high for river floods that came along maybe every twenty years. Water had come across the road and surrounded me only three times that I could remember. I could stand on the front porch and watch ducks paddle around my front steps. Here, we'd get the damage, but at least the foundation was cement.

I busied myself putting a tapestry footstool on top of an end table and removing books from the bottom row of shelves.

Finishing in the living room, I skirted the two bedrooms and lifted up things there. It wouldn't be easy sleeping in a bed with a wet floor beneath. Unplugging a radio that wouldn't work anyway, I remembered reading somewhere that the electricity should be cut off in case of high water. It wasn't on now, but it could be before the storm ended. On my way to the dining room to ask Tony about this, I stepped on something near the linen closet.

"Teeth?" I opened a small box carved from some kind of stone. Inside, a set of false teeth sat grinning. I poked at them with a finger and realized they were real, not some Halloween joke.

Tony sat at the kitchen table, his back to the living room. He used his flashlight to check the water level every few minutes. The Christmas candle still burned on the counter and cast a glow that reflected off the glass in the back door.

I put the open box in front of him without saying anything.

"Teeth?" he said.

"My question exactly. This is what fell out of the linen closet. I wonder if Chandler found them and just stuck them back."

He held the box but didn't touch the teeth. "My aunt had most of her own teeth still. She had a one tooth plate, I think, but her good teeth were the talk of the family." He shoved the box around so the grinning pearlies slid a bit from side to side.

"Could they belong to her husband?"

He shrugged. "Not sure. I'd have to check to see if he wore false teeth. But even if he did, it's rare the undertaker wouldn't put them in the corpse's mouth."

I took my flashlight and shined it directly onto the teeth. "Shouldn't there be some kind of identification on them?"

"Possibly, but you'd have to take them out and look with a magnifying glass. We'd better not touch them." He closed the lid on the box.

"I had no intention of touching them." I took the box and ran my finger over the carving. It appeared to be jade with graceful water birds carved into the top and sides. "The box isn't cheap."

"My aunt wasn't cheap—more like tight. If she bought anything, it was high quality."

"And this house? How did it happen?"

Tony looked around him. "She'd look at it as a solid house,

one with modern conveniences and sitting on lake acreage. It's big enough for her—meaning she wouldn't be much bothered with a lot of visitors." He smiled in spite of himself.

I sat down at the table. The long night would be one without sleep. Outside the wind rattled the torn roof. "What exactly did the coroner's report say about those finger marks on her neck?"

Tony flashed his light once at the patio floor. The water was still outside. He turned to face me. "It looks like someone held her face down in the grass long enough for—whatever happens to make someone with a bad heart have an attack." He leaned forward, touching the jade box. "I'm not sure that's what happened, nor is Chandler, I suspect. I don't know how, but she could have been in a situation earlier where someone grabbed the back of her neck and left marks. She could have had the attack and fell face in the dirt as we first thought. She didn't necessarily die right away. A few gasps for air would put dirt in her nostrils."

"Then why is Chandler…"

"…calling it homicide? Because it could be and until he rules that out, he has to investigate along those lines." He turned around and flashed the light again when the torn roof slid part way to the ground.

"He didn't seem too eager to search the house?"

"We'd already been in here for two days. I never saw anything out of place, as far as I know. He figured if she was murdered, it was out there in the grass."

"And whoever did it never came inside, not even to steal anything?"

"Seems unlikely." He stretched his head back and moved it from side to side. Eventually his neck cracked and he gave a sigh of relief. "How do you think your old house is holding up?" This signaled the end of the frustrating talk about his aunt.

"Should be okay unless there is a direct hit." I pushed the box with its false teeth to the other side of the table. "Aren't you worried about your apartment?"

"Not much. It's got some oak trees that could mess up the yard with limbs. Of course, one of the old oaks could fall on it, and wouldn't that be a pretty sight."

"Will the manager keep watch?"

"Manager? I'm the manager. Owner, too. It's a four unit building that I bought a few years back. I live in a bottom unit in the front and rent out the others."

I had never known his living arrangements in all these years. "Any women in those other units?" I smiled, knowing he'd not tell me even if he were making whoopie with a neighbor.

"All men," he said. "I had a couple of women there once, but they married and left."

"Never married yourself, did you?"

"Did you?" He handed that back to me .

I shook my head.

After a silence that felt like bricks, he said, "Yeah, I was once. Didn't last long." He waited, probably expecting me to comment but I was in shock from all this new information. "She tried to take me for all I had." He looked toward me and quickly back to the door. "Your Vernon was a big help there."

I remember once when Vernon told me he could pretty much be a free agent around Tony. Tony trusted him. "Besides, he owes me," Vernon had said. But there had also been an oath of sorts, a promise not to reveal anything. And Vernon stuck to his word.

"And where is she now?" I asked. Tony rarely talked. I wanted to get at him while I could.

He shrugged. "I'll tell you about it sometime." He stood and switched the flashlight onto the patio. A thin wave of water washed about the edges.

I opened the kitchen door and stepped onto the cement slab. The wind had calmed some, and torrents of rain weren't pelting what was left of the aluminum roof.

"Tony," I said quietly, "the mating calls have silenced."

He came and stood beside me, listening in the darkness.

"I've heard they go down for as long as they can in a storm," he said. "If it's calm by morning, they'll be at it again."

He went back inside. I could see his outline at the kitchen table. In the wet darkness, I imagined hundreds of alligators huddled on the bottom of the lake, draped across each other in some primeval clasp of safety. When the capacity to hold the breath ran out, they'd have to face the storm after all. "Not unlike humans," I said to myself.

The storm silence was over in minutes. A fierce gust blew against the screen, bringing with it pelting rain. One side of me was drenched. The small boat was caught in the thrust and shoved against my legs. I went down for the second time on Miz Keen's patio, this time landing on the opposite hip and leg.

Tony stood in the doorway and stared at me as I used the bottom of the boat to push myself to my feet.

"You better stay off this patio. How did you get so clumsy, anyway?"

"And thanks for your help, Tony," I said as I stood. "I haven't had much practice standing on a concrete patio in a hurricane."

He stood aside as I headed for my room. I didn't get far. The light from the hurricane lamp didn't reach into the back rooms. I turned back for my flashlight, glimpsing Tony's face. I could swear he showed teeth in his grin.

I stood in the tiny bedroom, my wet clothes tossed on the floor. In the dim light, I tried to inspect my sides. I would most likely be black and blue down each hip and thigh, to the knees. "At least I'll be symmetrical now." Nothing was visible yet, but I shined the light on myself and into the mirror. When I turned, the light hit the window. I could see as much of myself in its glass that I saw in the mirror. It reminded me that the shade was up and I turned the flashlight away. Pulling down the shade, I tried to see outside. A candle glowed from the Bono place yards away. "No fences," I said. It would be easy for anyone to walk across the grass and meet Miz Keen as she came up the path from the lake. I looked back at the Bono house. Maybe Gil was wrong about their generator. It hadn't clicked the house lights on.

"Water's coming in!" I heard Tony shout from the kitchen. "Grab the towels."

Jerking on my last pair of clean jeans and T-shirt, I ran to see him stacking a layer of towels at the bottom of the kitchen door. Through the glass, I could see a rush of shallow water cover the entire patio area. It wasn't enough yet to raise and move the small boat, and if it did get that high, our towels wouldn't hold for long. I left Tony and headed for the front door. The ground here, or at least the walk in front of it must have been a bit higher. The water hadn't reached the level of the door. Perhaps it was the water from the lake that was rising and would have to surround the house before it came in this way.

I turned toward the garage. Rain water streamed across the driveway but no floods there yet, either. Shining my light on my watch, I sighed. It was only two in the morning.

"It's the rain coming in the hole in the roof and the encroaching lake," Tony said as he explained the rush of water on the patio. "If the storm turns back this way or worsens, we're in for a soggy night." He lifted a small wooden table that may have been an antique and placed it on a chair.

"Did your aunt ever live through one of these in this house?"

"Probably, but she was independent to the point of stubbornness. You never knew what she might be thinking, even when you were looking her right in the face."

I smiled. "Like aunt, like nephew," I whispered. The wind covered my words.

"She never needed help on repairs?"

"Not that she told me about," said Tony. "I think I saw some bills for handywork in one of the tax boxes she kept. Nothing big. And there was the addition of that patio roof."

"Maybe you should check out who did the work. See if they had a motive—even it was petty theft—to shove her face in the dirt."

"Yeah," he said and headed to a closet in the guest room.

"Shove her face in the dirt," I said to the room. "Could that have been the intent? Someone angry enough to take vengeance? For what, I wonder."

"Here," said Tony as he returned with a large shoe box of papers. "Let's sit and look at these. Might as well find a motive while the world is blowing down around us."

CHAPTER EIGHT

We cleared off the dining table and sat the hurricane lamp in the center. From here, we could keep an eye on the flood threatening to invade the house while we sifted through receipts.

"All local companies, at least ones in Ocala," said Tony. He stacked the papers to one side. "No pattern so far."

"Here's the one for adding the cover on the patio," I said. "Materials came from a place called The Patio Store. I think that's a chain. Work done by—uh, oh."

"What?"

"A Mr. Stubbs. That's probably the guy I met on the road, the one who guided me to Priss Lane."

"And?"

I shrugged. "How should I know? He needs a teeth job, isn't all that educated, but he could be good at handywork. Said he cleaned up after storms and such."

"Chandler is going to get a list of things to do," said Tony, his jaw moving in anger control.

"You know, Tony, they haven't had much time to investigate this thing. I mean, we have been sitting through a hurricane."

Tony stood abruptly and walked to the front door and back. "Yeah, but if any of the locals have records, somebody's going to have to answer for that."

"For what?"

"For letting criminals loose on little old ladies!" His fist hit the table.

I knew to be quiet now. He had to get over the anger. In another situation, I would have left the scene and come back the next day. I kept sifting through the receipts. Miz Keen had done a good job of keeping everything. She even had one for a bedspread made by a Nell Culley.

"Culley," I said out loud. "Mildred's sister who fell in her shower." I held it up to the light. "Could have been. It's dated over three years ago."

"Let me see that." Tony took the receipt and stared at it. "She made a bedspread for my aunt." He said it like it was some kind of honor.

"Speaking of the Culley sisters," I said, "I wonder how Mildred is faring in this storm."

"No way to know. All the phones are out, and she probably doesn't have a cell."

"Come on, morning!" I said, longing for natural light.

Morning did bring light and a lot less wind and rain. Sometime in the night, the hurricane picked up its eye and toddled off into the Gulf. We still didn't have power, and not being able to make coffee was a strain, but at least we could see.

"Do you have field glasses in your van?" I asked. I could see Mildred's white board house across the lake, but not in detail.

Tony tossed me the keys. Once I had the glasses in my hands, I went outside the back patio. The water had receded but the ground was mushy. I wore the high boots. No sense in tempting some angry snake that had been washed from his hole. There was no way to go onto the landing. That was under the lake now, though the old boards showed through only about a foot of water. If there were no more downpours, things could be back to normal in a few days. I held the glasses to my eyes and focused first on the lake. The alligators had resumed their lovemaking, which consisted of one gator resting his head on the back of a future mate. A few were already in what might be called the gator missionary position where the female had to poke her head out of the water to breathe.

Lifting the glasses, I turned the focus on Mildred's house. A small tree in the front appeared to have fallen near the front steps. The sun shone in at an angle across the porch.

"I think her door is open."

Tony joined me from the edge of the patio where he examined the roof damage. "Let me."

He nodded as he took the glasses away from his eyes. "Wind could have blown it inward. We need to find a way to get over there."

"The road is probably a mess. We'd need a hydroplane." I glanced at the lake itself. The water had risen all around but there weren't any barriers from blown away tree limbs. "I'll go," I said.

"Take Marta's stick in the garage," said Tony, referring to an old broom handle sawed off at the bottom. Just about every Florida dweller I know has something like it to beat off snakes, neighborhood dogs, even alligators if needed. Most of time it's just a security pole—security for the psyche. Just to be sure, I had tucked my gun into my waist.

I sloshed around the back of the Bono house. All three were on the back porch, resetting lounge chairs. They waved and asked if we made it okay during the night. Gil stood staring at me in his doorway, a large plastic soda bottle in his hand. I waved back and trekked on, but a few yards away, I heard the splatter of heavy feet behind me.

"Hey! You got any ice? Our fridge went out last night and I'm drinking hot soda." Gil shook the bottle, held his thumb over the opening and let it spurt into the air.

"Sorry," I said. "We have no ice and no hot water to make coffee." I continued to walk. He lugged along beside me, taking swigs of the hot cola.

"I know. My dad is having a fit over no coffee. Mom, too."

"I'm going pretty far, Gil. Are you sure you want to traipse along?"

He shrugged. "Nothing else to do but work on picking up stuff from the yard." He grinned. "What did you do during the night?"

Coming from a teen I thought for a moment he was asking a smart aleck sex question. When I thought about it, I realized he meant it the way a child would—what did we do to occupy ourselves in the rain and darkness.

"Listened to the wind blow off the patio roof, for one thing."

"For real?"

"Gil," I stopped to slosh water on my boots to remove a heavy layer of mud. "What was all that stuff you were toting inside?"

His smile vanished, and his eyes darted toward the lake and back to me. "Just some stuff my father had ordered. I was home when the delivery came and told the man to stack it out back." He looked down at his feet. "Guess I forgot about it." He sighed. "And my father got pissed."

"I guess so, especially if it was something valuable."

"Just his card tables." He ran ahead and jumped with both feet into a puddle, streaking mud up his bare calf.

"He plays indoor games, then?" I followed at a distance.

"Yeah." He found another puddle and splashed again.

"Think you could stop doing that? These are my last pair of clean jeans and the washing machine won't work without power."

He shrugged. "Okay." He came back and stood close. "Could you do me a favor and not ask me about my father's tables?"

I just looked at him.

"He doesn't like me to talk about it. And don't tell him I told you what was in the boxes, okay?"

I nodded. If Gil wasn't going to talk, he could tag along behind as long as his energy held out. He trotted a few yards away, tossing sticks into the lake, picking up frogs and shoving them underwater. I had visions of the kid-who-sticks-pins-in-butterflies syndrome. He finally stopped to fish up a piece of unusual drift wood that had washed in from the lake. I had nearly lost sight of him when I stepped in a soft spot, sending me reeling butt first into soaking grass.

"Damn!" I managed to raise myself on one arm when I realized I was in a cove that had been hidden by all the excess water. But it wasn't the cove that gave me the biggest surprise. It was Mildred Culley's face staring up at me through broken reeds and mud.

I staggered backwards until I hit more or less solid ground. From there, I leaned forward to be sure I had really seen the old lady. Her clothes were torn, her arms showing signs of wounds. The same wounds showed up near her tiny waist. They might have been taken for stab wounds but something else came to mind—alligator teeth. "This is what that gator had hold of last night." She lay in the shallows, a perfect little territory for the gator's food. "At least he hasn't eaten her." I got on the cell phone. Tony would get someone out here, even if it had to be in a helicopter. When I yelled at Gil, he came running, his big shoes slamming water out from all sides.

"I'm going to stay here," I said. "I'll have to slam this pole into any gator that tries to reclaim his territory. You run to Miz Keen's house and guide Tony to this spot."

Gil stood frozen, his face a ghostly pale. He couldn't move his eyes away from Mildred.

"Gil!"

He looked at me and started to whine, clasping his arms around his full chest.

"Don't flake out now, Gil. I need your help. Can you get to the house?"

He blubbered out loud but he nodded and turned to run like he'd never run before. I heard water splashing for a long time.

Turning back to face the cove, I tried not to get too close. I decided not to touch Mildred. The alligator could be nearby and any suggestion that I might be taking away his food supply could bring on aggression. But I couldn't let him go away with her. I stood like a native with a spear, ready to clobber the leather head should it swim anywhere near the woman.

What seemed an eternity of staring into muddy waters ended when Tony came running, Gil beside him and pointing in my direction.

"Jesus Christ!" said Tony as he bent over the woman. "How did this happen?"

"Gil," I said, "what does Mildred's boat look like?"

The kid, again bug-eyed at seeing a real dead body, looked at me and puffed out breath. "It's a little thing. No motor. She rows it like a canoe."

"Is it kind of battered, like it needs painting?"

His head bobbed up and down.

"That's her boat on your patio. I'll bet on it. Could she have been on the lake in the storm?"

"She knew the dangers in that, said so when she walked over." He had taken my pole and was lifting one of her arms from the grass that half hid one side of her body.

"She couldn't walk in that storm, and, if she needed help, maybe she risked the boat."

"The gators were submerged in the worst part of the storm, or at least we think they were." Tony stopped to look at teeth marks down the woman's arm. "Do you think this is what we saw last night? What we thought was a deer?"

A great gasp came from Gil who stood some feet away. "I knew they were eating somebody! I knew it!" He threw one hand over his mouth.

In the middle of the lake, the mating roars began again, and alligators dived and surfaced, laying their heads across the backs of potential mates. For now, they ignored us, and the one who owned this end of the cove hadn't decided to feed.

"Can't we move her, Tony?" The thought of touching her frail body with all the wounds came me a chill, but seeing her lie there in the grass made me nervous.

"Gil," said Tony turning to the boy, "go back to the house. In the corner of the kitchen is a coat tree. There's a plastic raincoat there, the kind you can see through. Grab it and bring it back here. And try not to drag it in the mud or otherwise get it dirty."

The boy hesitated, but either his thrill at helping or his fear at standing there with a dead body jarred him loose. He nodded and took off again to the house.

Gil nearly bent double from lack of breath when he returned with the plastic raincoat. It had been a long time since he'd had this much exercise.

"We need to get the plastic beneath her and just drag her onto shore," said Tony.

I waded into the water on Mildred's left side. Tony, on the right, knelt and slipped the plastic under the water. I took my side and together we slid her onto the grass. She wasn't heavy at all.

"Three dead ladies, Tony."

The three of us formed a kind of circle around the body, somehow paying homage to an old dear who had really come upon a hard time.

"Yeah. And no telling what time the sheriff will get here."

Providence intervened. Across the lake a truck with a boat trailer stopped in front of the Culley house. Two men in uniform pulled off a small air boat and shoved it into the water. Tony's cell phone rang.

When the men had located our position, Tony stuck the pole in the air and waved. The noise from the boat engine startled everything. Birds flew, and gators submerged. Flying just inches off the surface of the water, the two men stopped a few feet from the cove and shut down the boat. That was when I realized they were in wet suits, a sheriff's logo stamped on the right chest.

"Good gravy!" said one of the men. "Miss Culley, how did you get yourself in this mess?" He dropped into the water up to his knees. "We got the call from Chandler. Deputies are all over the county rescuing people. Some of us got dispatched to the coast. Lots of destruction there."

"Will a coroner or scene techs be able to make it?" Tony helped the second deputy pull the boat nearer shore.

"Our orders are to secure the body and transport it to the coroner. The roads around here aren't passable. We got the truck through one lane that's been cleared on the other side."

The first deputy removed a camera from a black case and took shots of the body on the grass. He asked where we'd found her, and he took shots of that space, too. The two of them, gloved and with a dark blue body bag raised Mildred Culley inside it and zipped it closed.

As they left, the noise of the air boat drowning all other sounds, I felt I should wave or say something, but she couldn't hear me or the engine.

CHAPTER NINE

Volunteers were pouring into the county from all over, even other states. Some guy with his own road scraper got busy and cleared the dirt road around the lake. Stubbs had the kindness to lay boards over the deep puddles in Priss Lane. We could finally get the cars out.

I circled the road, its old ruts now a smooth ride in spite of the storm. At the Ferguson turn-off, I slowed. Someone, maybe Stubbs again, had placed planks on their drive, too. I backed up and pulled into the lane. Many of the tall reeds lay on their sides, batted down by nonstop winds. At the sight of the house, I stopped. Old man Ferguson was stooping in the yard, lifting broken tree limbs and tossing them into a wheelbarrow.

He stared at me until recognition set in. "Ma'am! How'd you get through this mess?" He leaned on one handle of the barrow, his bowed legs threatening to give way.

"Just a little patio roof damage. I dropped by to see if you're okay." I scanned the area around the house. The truck wasn't there.

"Just got all these tree limbs, and that sorry son of mine thinks his bar is more important. He stayed out half the night while the winds were blowing through here."

"He's at the bar now?"

"Far as I know." He leaned down again with a moan.

"I'll help for a while," I said and turned off the Honda.

He didn't protest, and before long, he said, "More help coming."

A familiar battered truck pulled to the edge of the grass. A female, looking much like Stubbs even to the missing tooth, slid from the driver's seat.

"You all right, old man?" The voice came from a gray face whose bone structure had been messed with, probably with a fist.

"Yeah," said Ferguson. "This here's Betty Stubbs. Luanne." He hesitated with the last name.

I held out my hand. Even with the residue of oak limb on my palm, I could feel the roughness of Betty's skin. Her sad eyes nodded my presence.

"You want some help?"

The three of us filled up the barrow in no time. I began stacking limbs in an area that appeared to have been a leaf burn. "Your son can do what he will with these. Maybe you can use them in your fireplace."

"He don't like that thing. Says it's too much trouble to clean out the ashes. Stuck a little space heater inside to keep my toes warm."

I looked at the house. It had been built at least a hundred years ago, probably longer. Familiar with old houses, I knew it would have faulty wiring.

"You must have redone the electric system in order to run a space heater."

"Yeah, some years back. Burl and a friend of his came in here and did over the whole place. He's got all that computer equipment and stuff in his room upstairs. We even got a generator out back. Came on during the storm."

"You had power during the storm?" It wasn't really a question, but an admiration.

"Yep. Helps out." Ferguson's forehead dripped sweat. His shirt soaked through, he called it quits and headed for the porch. He sat in a wicker chair and fanned with an old hat. For a moment, I pictured Pasquin on my own front porch in a rocker, fanning himelf with his battered straw hat.

Betty Stubbs had worked quietly while we chatted. She kept a distance from us, glancing up from time to time. With Ferguson off the yard, I moved closer.

"You're Mrs. Stubbs, right?" I had visions of a drunken husband punching out his wife after a night at the local bars.

"No. I'm his sister. Took back my maiden name from that bastard I married. Been living with my brother now for two years."

"I see." I wanted to know more but Betty leaned over to pick up small limbs. She offered nothing else and asked nothing of me.

A few more limbs, and the front yard looked clean again. I swiped sweat from my face on my shirt hem.

"Any chance of a glass of cold water?" I asked the old man.

"Inside. Straight back to the kitchen." He waved me in the direction of the front door.

Betty swiped her face with the edge of her shirt and sat on the steps. I opened the screen door and stepped inside. A cool drift of air came through a vent somewhere. Young Ferguson had also installed central heat and air in this old place. The living room sat in stately darkness. What Burl had done in modern wiring, he had not done in furniture. The sofa and two heavy chairs were old, the upholstery nearly bare in spots. Antique end tables and a buffet packed the walls. At one end, the large brick fireplace appeared like an insulted giant with its tiny space heater on the hearth. Heavy curtains closed off the outside. "What is it with old men and blocking curtains?" I asked, again remembering Pasquin with his dark green curtains and heavy furniture.

Passing down a hall, I paused to look into a dining room. It had been grand in its day, long and narrow with a table to sit twelve. At one end, a hutch nearly covered the entire space of the wall. It would draw a fortune at an antique show. I stepped quietly into the room and gazed inside the hutch. There were dishes, maybe some expensive gift to a grandmother when she married in the 1800s, a few other pieces of bric-a-brac, and one whole shelf with nothing on it. I swiped a finger across it and it came off clean. "Somebody dusts around here."

I closed the hutch door and went into the kitchen. It was neat except for a half eaten bowl of cereal on the drain. Burl had added the conveniences of a dishwasher and a fridge with an ice maker. I grabbed three glasses from a cupboard, filled them with ice and ran tap water.

Back on the porch, I handed one of the glasses to Ferguson and one to Betty who nodded her thanks. The old man sipped loudly and ran his cold hand from the glass over his face.

"I'm too old to work in this heat. Damn boy!"

"He runs a business, right? Maybe it's just too much and he needs to hire someone to help out here." I took a seat.

Betty looked back toward us from her seat on the steps, a yearning in her eyes.

"Not too much. He's got other business here and there. Stays gone too much." Ferguson's eyes glazed over for a moment. He looked like a sad old man wondering why his son didn't take care of him in his old age. "He does hire somebody once in a while. Young men who need the money but got no sense when it comes to a big old farm house."

"Never hires women, does he?" asked Betty. Ferguson seemed not to hear her.

"He bought Nell Culley's house, didn't he?"

Ferguson nodded. "Got it for a song, he said. Let the old woman live there until she died. He's been fixing it up since. Stays over there all the time, too."

"And did he buy the contents of her house, too?"

The old man pulled up some life and chuckled briefly. "Now that was a fight. Sister Culley said the antiques were her things, she being the next of kin. But it wasn't so. Burl had the bill of sale in writing, house and furniture."

"Men get it all," said Betty in a whisper.

"When Nell died, she must have left her sister the money from the house. That should have made up for the contents."

Ferguson shook his head. "Never understood that. Guess old Nell spent it all before she died. Only a few hundred left to Mildred."

"What could an old lady spend a lot of money on?"

"Who knows. People come around here sniffing at our old heels for donations and investments. Somebody got to her, I suppose."

"I guess real estate and a bar keep Burl pretty busy."

"Ha! Not to mention them other things he does." Ferguson took another sip and showed no sign of telling me the other things. "You know he just came back here five years ago. Been running all over the country doing this and that."

"What exactly is this and that?"

He stared at me, he watery eyes angry and pained from the humidity. "Damned if I know."

"Think he'll stay around or go running off to another state again?"

"Can't never tell about that boy. Always did just what he pleased. Sure don't do much around here."

I wasn't convinced. The place was neater than most houses where two males lived. The house appeared to sit on at least five acres of lakefront property. If Burl was interested in real estate, he was sitting on a gold mine.

"Would you like more water?" I asked.

He nodded and handed me the glass.

"Betty?"

She shook her head and sat her empty glass on the top step.

"I got to get going. Promised to help clean up in some other places." She stood as though her hips hurt and turned back to the old man. "You call should you need a cleaning lady, okay?"

Ferguson nodded and waited for her to leave in the truck before speaking.

"Poor woman. She's kind of lost. Been beat silly by some man she moved in with and now she's relying on that poor brother to take care of her. She's not quite right in the head. Maybe that man throttled her once too many times. She tried cleaning here once, but couldn't even see the dust." He closed his eyes and leaned back in the chair.

Inside, I refilled his glass after leaving my own and Betty's sitting on the sink. For a moment I wondered what it would be like to go from an abusive man's house to brother Stubb's and that was all there was to one's universe. I shuddered.

"Will you be okay out here in the heat or would you like to go inside where it's cool?"

"Better sit here until I cool down some. Not good to walk into a ice bucket."

I left old man Ferguson trying to cool down not only from the heat but also from his son's indifference. Was it really that, or just an old man who magnified things and interpreted it as negligence?

As I drove the lake road back to Miz Keen's house, I met Gil

walking toward me. He held his gigantic soda in his hand and
sipped on it when he stepped to one side. He looked like a big-
sized cherub emerging from the reeds.

"You need a ride, Gil?"

"Nope. I've got a job at the Ferguson house. Get paid to pick
up limbs."

"Oh you're a bit late to do that in the front yard at least."

"But Burl said he'd pay me!" The boy frowned and swiped his
forehead.

"Well, go on. I'm sure you can do the back yard and keep the
old man company."

I drove off and watched Gil move back to the center of the
road, maneuvering his big shoes across the boards set across the
ruts. Could this overweight kid really spend a hot day cleaning a
yard?

I was back at the house only a few minutes when Chandler
drove up. He got out of his car with the load of journals.

"We got a mess all over the county," he said. "Water damage
mostly, some wind. But nothing like what they have down on the
coast. I've loaned out most of my men to them." He sat down
next to the stack of journals. "Which brings me to these. I've
skimmed through them and can't make much sense out of the
old lady's writing. She talks a lot about how she feels about something but rarely mentions exactly what that something is. Now,
mind you, I haven't had much time to concentrate." He looked at
Tony. "Technically you're a suspect, you know. But your alibi
checked out, and I trust you. Think you can take these journals
and read them closely? Let me know if you suspect anything?"

He was one lawman making a request of another. Even if
Tony was related to the victim, Charlie knew he was an expert in
his field and a resource he needed at the moment.

"We'll both look at them," said Tony, volunteering me without asking.

Chandler nodded and smiled at me. "I may need you for something else. You and that Wayne kid you had out here. Like I said, I'm short of people after this storm. I'm not sure what we're looking for, but we need to search the lake. At least parts of it."

I looked at Tony. He seemed as perplexed as I was.

"You see," said Chandler, speaking in his slow commanding style, "when the deputies brought the body in—Miss Culley's body, the medical men looked her over pretty good to count the teeth marks. One mark right in the middle of her back was about the same size but it wasn't made by a reptile tooth. Somebody shot her."

"In the back?" I don't know what made me ask that unless it was the old cowboy tales I'd heard as a child. Only a coward shoots someone in the back. "Somebody shot an old lady in the back?"

Chandler nodded. "And with her own gun. She kept a rifle in that old house of hers. We found it leaning against the wall. One shot fired. No prints."

I leaned back in my chair. That feisty old lady with thin red hair had been gunned down like an animal.

"If she was hit in the back and the rifle was at the door, could she have been running from someone?" I asked.

Chandler nodded. "We think she may have gotten into her boat and onto the lake before the shot hit her." He pointed to the patio. "That's why I've got to take that boat in as evidence."

"Then it wasn't the alligator that grabbed her and drowned her?"

"Didn't drown at all. I figure she either fell out of the boat when she was shot or the waves tossed her out as she drifted this way. She was probably coming here, you know. Looking for safety any way she could."

"And my aunt?" Tony had remained quiet during the report on Mildred. His olive skin was about as pale as it had ever been.

"We have to rule that as homicide for sure now. These two women were friends. They may have known something that got them both killed."

Silence fell across the living room. We could hear JoJo Bono yelling at his wife about sweeping water off the porch.

"Those teeth you found," said Chandler. "I'll have to take them in, too. Funny we never found them when we did the search."

"Tony," I said, remembering Mildred's visit, "Miss Culley had to use the rest room." I looked at Charlie. "She said she knew the way. We let her go back there. Do you suppose she slipped that box into the linen closet?"

Chandler frowned and nodded. "Won't rule it out. Would explain why my men never saw it."

Tony went to the kitchen and brought back a paper bag. He used a towel to lift the box and place it inside as he would any piece of evidence.

"Thanks," said Chandler. He couldn't look at Tony directly. The idea of one lawman investigating another didn't sit well with him.

"And what do you want Wayne and me to do?" I tried to break the embarrassment.

"I need you to search the lake bottom just in case Miss Culley had something in that boat with her. Might be nothing there. It's a goose chase but as Tony here will tell you, we have to cover all the bases. I'm not holding out hope for finding anything, but we have to do the search."

"You realize the storm might have churned up the bottom pretty good. If anything is there, it could be buried."

"Or knocked loose," he said. "I want to do it now before the dirt settles."

I shrugged. "Good idea. The bottom of that lake is gathering silt from the shoreline on a daily basis."

"I may have one diver to help you out if they don't need the whole team elsewhere."

"You have any people on loan from north Florida?" asked Tony.

"Not yet."

"I know a diver. I'll do my best to have him take orders from you temporarily."

I looked at Tony and mouthed "Vernon?"

He nodded.

"I don't have much experience in searching lakes—doing grids and all that stuff," I said. "But I take orders. Can't say what Wayne will do."

"He'll take orders, too. You can count on that." Chandler rose and stretched as though he had been through an ordeal and was glad it was over. He said directly to me, "I doubt you're going to get grid equipment. Maybe some underwater metal detectors, but you'll have to rely on your own wits more than anything else. Everything is on hurricane relief and state-of-the-art is on the coast."

"You know," said Tony, standing with him, "I can't stay down here forever. I took just enough leave to clean out the house and bury my aunt."

"Yeah," said Chandler. "Let me know when you leave. We'll cordon off the area as a crime scene and get a watch on the house. This whole area is part of a scene now." He swept his arm to include the remote section of lakeside where Mildred's body had been found.

After he left, Tony and I stood in the living room, surrounded by stacked furniture and the prickly feeling of death.

Without looking at me, Tony asked, "Do you think we can find two more places for people to sleep in this house?"

"You know where Vernon will sleep," I said. "Who else?"

"I'm going to try and get Marshall Long down here, too."

CHAPTER TEN

Everyone arrived at once. Vernon showed up with Marshall and stashed his small suitcase in Miz Keen's room alongside mine.

As two men settled in, a delivery truck showed up at the Bono house. The tiny road filled up with cars and vans.

Vernon and I stood in front of the window, watching as two men lifted boxes the size of refrigerators off the back of a truck and carried them inside the house. "What's he taking out?" I said to him.

"Ever been in there?" Vernon said. He kneaded my neck, a familiar gesture that felt pretty good about now.

"No. They aren't hospitable like that. I've talked to the kid, but the parents just wave from time to time. They stood on their porch when all the hullabaloo with Mildred Culley's body was happening."

"Chandler interview them?"

"Yes, I think so. But he's Mr. Silence. You can't even tell from his expression if he got any info from them."

"You know," he turned toward me, the tanned face that reached all the way over his bald head making me melt a little inside, "Tony can't run a check on him since he's at the center of this mess." He took my face in both hands and kissed my forehead. "If Chandler doesn't, then I can."

As quick as I could write down the names of the Bono family

and their vacation address, Vernon was out the door and on his cell phone. He strolled to Miz Keen's dock while he talked.

"Okay. I got somebody to run the check, but they have to call my cell. No other phone."

I nodded. Vernon was what he called "between" right now. Tony was technically not his boss, though he was the one who had the authority to lend him to Chandler, but he wasn't yet under the command of Chandler who would deputize all of us prior to doing a search. He had taken a chance running the check.

A rain squall blew over in less than half an hour. It managed to further soak the ground, but scene tech Marshall Long was determined to check out the watery and temporary resting place of Mildred Culley. I figured he was working on "between" time, too. Chandler hadn't shown up or given any orders yet.

"If I get stuck in this stuff," said Marshall as he trudged through grass and water mixed with mud. "You'll have to get a crane to pull me out." He wore untied running shoes that threatened to come off and find a home in the bog at any minute.

"Is the white coat necessary?" I asked. He had arrived with the lab coat on and hadn't taken it off yet.

"Shall I remove it?" He jerked it open and faced me. A chest with forty-plus years of accumulated hairless flab stared at me. "Don't get personal, Luanne."

"Geez! Why no shirt?" I tried not to laugh.

"I got the call before I could do my wash. Power was out in Tallahassee, too. Vernon said get in the car. I did, with a bag full of laundry."

"You'll do it yourself, Marshall Long. You aren't giving it to me because I'm female."

"But you're familiar with the machinery in that house!" He whined but closed his lab coat and continued through the slosh.

"Then it's time you got acquainted."

I pointed to the inlet where the gator had left Mildred. Marshall skirted the area, his eyes peering from fleshy folds like a robot honing in on a target. Suddenly, he turned his head back and glanced down the lake.

"Who the hell is that kid?" He looked straight at Gil Bono who stood a few yards away. "He's followed us here."

"Yeah, the neighbor kid. He's seen it all—the gator, the body, and the airboat pickup. Scared him silly, but he's curious."

Marshall gave a grunt and turned back to the scene. He bent over, a move that always scared me. Many times he had nearly tumbled his great bulk into a body of water when his balance shifted. If he ever fell, I wondered if I could pull him to his feet.

"Lots of reeds and grass here. Just the shallow spot for a gator to claim territory and stow food." He lifted his eyes to the surface of the lake, but did not stand up straight. "Don't see any out there now."

The lake had a slight breeze blowing little waves against the shore.

"The season must be over," I said. "We've had reptile orgies here for several days."

"All pregnant and barefoot now, I guess. Bulls can return to basking in the sun." Marshall pulled on a bag he carried. He moved about slowly clipping plants and placing them in separate specimen bags. He collected a water sample in a vial. The mud beneath the water, he put in a large plastic cup with a seal. "Just in case we have to identify stuff in the body."

Marshall took one more look at the scene then straightened with a loud moan. "Damn! I'm too old to do this."

"You're too big to do this," I said.

"Watch your tongue, woman." He pulled his feet from the mud with a loud sucking sound. "What's for dinner?"

"It's not like anyone cooks here. Tony and I have survived off tuna and stuff from his aunt's pantry."

Marshall gave a louder grunt at this but offered no solution.

We reached the patio where Marshall sat his evidence collection in one corner. He eased his backside into one of the plastic chairs. I held my breath it would hold. It did but his hips and thighs ran over the edges like dough getting ready to bake.

Vernon joined us on the patio. "Where's Tony?" We both shrugged.

A voice sounded from the living room, "I'm here."

"Come back to Luanne's room for a minute. Those people are still at it next door."

Tony put down the journal he had been staring at with glazed eyes and followed Vernon. I followed both of them and stood in the doorway, while they watched at the window.

"Been unloading boxes for a while over there. Whatever is in them gets emptied and the boxes tossed back on the truck." Vernon held the drapes to one side.

"Are you sure they're the same boxes?" Tony leaned toward the window. "Nothing written on the side of the van."

"Nothing on the boxes, either," said Vernon.

Both men acted as if they didn't know I was there. They stared at the van, the workers, and JoJo Bono. When the workers sat down to drink some sodas Mrs. Bono brought them, Tony turned to Vernon.

"Looks familiar, doesn't it?" He nodded as though remembering something painful.

"Yeah. Boxes and boxes." Vernon put his hands on his hips,

dropping the curtain back in place. Both of them stared at the drape in silence.

"What boxes?" I asked and the two sheriff's men jumped liked I'd fired off a shotgun.

"How long have you been there?" Vernon said.

Tony looked at Vernon and nudged him slightly with an elbow. "Tell her. I've already said I'd tell her sometime." He left the room. I heard him shut the front door.

"He said he'd tell you?" Vernon looked perplexed and sat on the edge of the bed.

"He never said anything about boxes. He said he'd tell me about his marriage one day. I never knew he was married." I stacked some pillows against the headboard and joined him on the bed.

Vernon sat for a few moments looking at his feet. He smiled and squeezed my knee. "If he said to tell you, okay. I had a pact with him to keep quiet. I figured it was forever."

"You said one time there was something between you that kept him from giving you the rough house like he does everyone else."

Vernon laughed now. "Nothing like getting a man out of a jam that involves a woman." He lay back on the bed, his head near my waist. I massaged his bald crown.

"Talk," I said.

Vernon closed his eyes. "Tony was married to a woman named Ethel Moorhouse." He stopped to laugh. "A name like that should have warned him before he ever took the vows. She was a little ditsy in the head and smiled a lot. Couldn't cook worth a damn, but Tony didn't require that. She worked in a wholesale store warehouse out on Highway 27. Not sure what her title was, but she had a key and the run of the place. They hadn't been married two months before boxes started piling up in that storage shed he has in back of his apartment building. Then nice stuff, like perfume and jewelry still in the packaging showed up in their bedroom. When Tony started checking her dresser, he found several bras with double D cups. Ethel was more like an A minus. Then there were the dresses, blouses, underwear, things women wear, all tucked into a drawer with the labels still attached. Tony guessed what was happening."

"Shoplifting from her own employer. She stuffed the clothing into those bras, right?"

"Yeah, familiar story, right? Only the lifter was the wife of an up and coming sheriff's detective. Tony's panic was visible when I went to his place one night to report a body found in Lake Jackson. He wasn't able to concentrate on that job. When we were alone, I asked what the trouble was. That's when he told me to return to his apartment with him. Ethel wasn't there. She worked until eight some nights."

"He confided in you?"

Vernon nodded. "He knew I was divorced and that's what he asked about first. Wanted to know what the steps were and who my lawyer was. When I asked why he wanted a divorce, he told me."

Vernon pushed himself up and sat against a pillow beside me. He folded his arms across his chest as though protecting himself from what he was about to reveal.

"Tony showed me the boxes he'd found inside the shed. Ethel had told him they were empty, but they weren't. Full of merchandise like toasters, lamps, shoes, whatever Ethel could lift. All of them were sealed except the two boxes Tony opened to satisfy his curiosity. This is where I came in. I helped him reseal those two boxes. We put them in Tony's truck and carried them in the middle of the night back to the warehouse. He got Ethel's key after one big fight with her and told her he'd have her arrested. Tony, with his sheriff's uniform on, pulled the night watchman to the front of the building to ask him about the robberies they'd had lately. I drove around to the back and unloaded those boxes in high speed time—with gloves on. I had also managed to disable the cameras."

"Nothing like being a deputy to know how to do that," I said.

"I left things in good order and reset the cameras. I don't know if anyone noticed they had ever been off, but the next day, the company called the office to say someone had returned some stolen goods."

"Did Tony make Ethel take back the other things?"

"No. He just said it was divorce time and she'd best not make a fuss because he'd have her in jail in a flash. She packed and left. Tony declared 'irreconcilable differences,' and that was the end of it."

I breathed deeply. "And that's why Tony has treated you like you're Mr. Perfect?"

"Could be," said Vernon. He smiled and wrinkled his forehead at the same time. "He owes me and he knows it."

"It's not a crime to return stolen merchandise," I said.

"But I covered up one."

After some silence, I turned to Vernon and put my arms around his neck. "I pardon you, Mr. Criminal. I'd rather have you here than in jail."

Vernon's smile turned to a grin, his arms reaching around my waist. "And if you ever tell, I'll say you helped me." He tousled my hair for a moment then stopped cold. "Look, don't bring it up to him, okay? It bothers him to no end."

"You mean I can't tease him about Miz Ethel," I said in the best Scarlett O'Hara I could manage.

"Don't you dare."

"Where is she now?"

"Moved out of the state he says. I don't think they're in contact, but you can count on his knowing where she is. He wants her a long way from him."

We heard the front door open. Marshall Long called from the patio. "Anyone around here?"

"Just coming in," said Tony. "You want a beer?"

Vernon and I joined them. "You see anything over there?" asked Vernon, motioning toward the Bono house.

"The road that runs past their house gets pretty muddy and narrow a few yards away. Looks like nobody lives beyond them."

"And the boxes?" I said, trying not to look into Tony's eyes where I just knew I'd see Ethel.

"Whatever was in them is stashed inside the house. Nothing on the front or back porches." Tony walked to the refrigerator and yelled back, "Only one beer left."

"Look," I said. "The road goes almost all the way around the lake. It runs right past the Ferguson house and continues past the Culley house and a couple of other places. It must peter out after that, just like it does past the Bono place."

"What's your point, Luanne?" said Tony.

"No point. I just had an idea. Why don't we all go to the bar that Burl Ferguson owns?"

The three men stared at me.

"How did you get from a lake road to a bar in one thought process?" asked Marshall.

"It's a female thing," I said. "Has to do with cycles and stuff."

Vernon laughed while the other two blushed.

The Fireside Bar really was beside a fire, a barbecue fireplace set up beside a rambling make-shift building. The sign, a marquis, sat beside a marshy hole of cattails and offered spirits and bull, the bull being ribs along with the bull you'd get if you drank too much spirit. The outside had a fake front of pine railings and carved cowboy boot designs. In spite of the isolated location on a state road, it appeared neat and cleaned of dust and mildew. The aroma of barbecue sauce and sizzling meat filled the humid air.

Before we went inside, I thought about Burl's attire. In an area where people wore grubby T-shirts, he was clean and well coiffed. I wondered if this was a gay bar but I wasn't going to mention it to the three men with me. Besides, Marshall's taste buds were dancing a jig.

"Not bad, Luanne. Better than tuna for sure."

"I don't know about the food, but we will…"

"…partake? You bet your little bitty butt, we will." He pushed ahead of Tony and Vernon, his weight creating creaks and moans across the wooden porch.

Inside, after our eyes adjusted to the darkness, we saw a large room filled with individual tables and a long bar at one end. Only a few customers had ventured out after the storm. One was a lady whose silver hair and lined face appeared to put her in her eighties, at least. She sat on a stool, leaning her frail frame over the bar. She smoked until she saw us then tossed it into her drink. Smoking was no longer allowed in public places in Florida, but this lady seemed to have privileges.

A voice came from my side. "Why hello there, Miz Keen's nephew," Burl said to Tony. "Nice for you to join us."

"Got a good sturdy table?" said Marshall. He wore a double X large T-shirt that hung over his hips but couldn't hide the stomach rolls.

"Are you kidding?" Burl pointed.

From the position near the rear of the dining hall, I could see other customers drinking beer and watching baseball on a television attached to the ceiling. Except for one table where a man and woman ate ribs, they all seemed to be men. But, if these were gay men they surely weren't the kind I'd seen in the gay pride parade in Orlando. These were dirt farmers or the like, maybe something like Ma Barker sons.

CHAPTER ELEVEN

Burl stood over us with shiny menus. His face was shiny, too, like he'd been working up a sweat. His silk shirt with beige and brown diamond shapes looked hot. At the bottom of creased beige trousers he wore white cowboy boots with silver toes. He smelled a bit like burnt wood.

"Ribs right off the 'cue," he said. "Lownde's been working all afternoon in this heat." His eyes darted from the door leading to the outdoor barbecue to the old lady at the bar and back to our table.

"Lownde?" I asked.

"The man who does the 'cue for us. The recipe has been in his family for two hundred years since they were slaves,." Burl dealt the menus like cards. "We got baked beans and slaw to go with it. Nothing else."

"Lownde do that, too?"

"He and his helpers do it all," he said and glanced at the elderly woman at the bar who was attempting to slide off her stool without breaking something. The bartender hurried around the counter and took her arm.

We all ordered the same thing: the 'cue meal with tea. Marshall said he may have a beer later. "Depending on how full you can get me," he added with a grin.

"You look pretty full already," said Vernon. Before Marshall could shoot back with a joke about baldness, Vernon added, "Which makes me wonder what the sleeping arrangements will be tonight."

Tony gave Vernon a hard glare. "I'll take the wicker sofa. Marshall can have the guest bed."

Marshall saw his turn. "And Vernon, you'll be in LuLu's bed? I wonder how that's going to look in court. Yes, judge, our dive team sleeps together.."

"Dive team?" The alarmed question came from Burl who was still standing at our table.

Tony frowned. "We got two deaths on that lake. We need to see what's there."

"But the rumors around the lake is that Miz Keen had a heart attack in her yard, and Miz Culley drowned in the hurricane." He held the menus tight under his arm.

"Drowned after falling out of her boat, most likely." Tony would say no more. No one, not even the Bono family, had been told about Mildred Culley's shooting.

"Well, this is going to be a sight for a bunch of lake dwellers whose only excitement has been gators mating and high winds." Burl turned away and ran smack into the lady from the bar.

"Oh!" She giggled like a school girl, raising a blue-veined hand to her wrinkled face. It was made up mostly with powder. The white hair had been curled recently and teased in the style of forty years ago. Her figure was trim and the pants suit expensive, but it was the jewelry that stood out like beacons. Diamonds on both hands made me wonder if she hadn't been married more than once. The necklace was fit for a ballgown yet sat on the crow's neck that had sunk to her collar bone. She smelled of Chanel Number Five.

"Burl, darling, can you drive me into Ocala? I need some

things." She gave him a coy smile.

"Now, Miz Rosie Quinne, you know I got a bar to run." He patted her tiny shoulder. "Just wait until I get things going here and I'll run you into town."

Rosie Quinne smiled and rubbed Burl's cheek. He looked embarrassed and headed out the door to fetch the ribs. Rosie turned to us. "He's such a sweet man." She giggled again when the bartender brought her purse to her. "I keep forgetting this thing."

I watched Burl disappear out the door. His dress and slight effeminism was just the kind of prissiness an old lady would find charming. I brushed off the idea of a gay bar. Burl could most likely turn on good-ol'-boy macho when it suited him.

When Rosie left us, I decided to check out the place. Excusing myself to go to the ladies' room, I skirted the dark walls and went into a hallway where the doors to the restrooms had boards engraved with HE and SHE. Past the doors, the hall became darker. Glancing around me, I passed the SHE door and stepped onto a floor tiled in maroon and gray. I found myself in a small area with a few dining tables and a fireplace. I figured it was for private parties until I heard the sound coming from the dark red bricks. The fireplace was covered with one of those folding glass doors, but this one had latches on the top and bottom. From inside came a constant rustling sound of urgency, the kind of sound that would send me into a cold sweat in the swamp. I pulled out the pen light I carry on my key chain and shined it through the glass doors. The rattlesnake must have been four feet long, and he had been aroused by my motion and body heat. He had coiled, his tail rattling nonstop. The head moved backwards in a pre-strike manner. I moved back and stood for a few moments, until my blood warmed up again.

To my right, was a door that reached all the way to the ceiling and was wide enough for people in wheelchairs. There was no sign to indicate this was a handicapped restroom. I turned the handle and found the door to be locked.

Inside the SHE door, were two toilets and an antique dresser that had been converted to a vanity. The mirror above it was flush to the wall. The cleanliness made me think the maid had been there earlier in the day.

"There's a rattlesnake in the fireplace back there," I said as I returned. All three men stared at me. "If you don't believe me, go take a look. It's in that private room off the bathroom hallway."

The bartender sat the tea on the table. I was pretty sure that he hadn't heard my comment. Vernon stood up and headed for the bathrooms. By the time Marshall had gulped his entire glass, both Vernon and the bartender had returned to the table.

"Do you know you've got a snake in your fireplace back there?" asked Vernon.

"That thing again," said the bartender with a sigh. "It's an old fireplace and can't be used anymore, but Burl hasn't had it closed up the way it should be. That damn snake crawls down there off and on."

"And crawls out again?" asked Tony.

"Must do, because he's not always there." The bartender left a pitcher of tea on the table, smiled and walked away.

"No way," said Marshall. "They got that thing in there to entertain people. Bet they drop mice and stuff down the chimney to feed it."

I cringed. Could someone who dressed as natty as Burl really be super redneck and keep a pet rattler?

The door to the barbecue area burst open and slammed against the wall. Vernon and Tony both pushed back and put their hands on their guns. I figured shooting would start any minute and flinched behind Marshall's shoulder. He just sat there, his eyes rounded in a round face.

But it wasn't the local ornery cuss who burst through the door; it was one of the biggest black men I'd ever seen. Kind of like a basketball player with triple the weight. He wore a sauce streaked white apron over an undershirt and jeans. His hair, gray at the temples, was the only thing that indicated he might be over forty. He carried a pan of ribs with both hands.

Marshall smiled when Lownde took long strides toward our table. He set the pan down in the middle and grinned, all teeth accounted for. He pulled the bottom of the apron up and wiped his face.

"Sorry about that, but that dumb ass helper of mine ain't nowhere to be found today. He's supposed to bring in the ribs. I done had to kick the door to get inside." He grinned again. "Beans and slaw is coming."

"Oh, we've found the glory hole!" said Marshall as he shoved his pudgy hands into the rib pan and tore off a long one. He studied the bottles of sauce on the table and chose the one with the sweet hickory flavor.

The bartender appeared with bowls of baked beans and slaw that must have been put together in a kitchen somewhere behind the bar. "You really planning on searching Lizard Lake?" he asked.

"And how would you know that?" said Tony. The rest of us stared in disbelief.

"Word gets around." He nodded and turned away. "I hear there's a sinkhole in the middle."

"Burl can't keep a secret, I guess," said Tony. "What about a sinkhole, Luanne?"

"I didn't search the entire lake. Just the bit between the Ferguson landing and your aunt's. I did see an aquifer. Fresh water is coming up constantly. Could be a sinkhole down there, too."

We ate ribs until our own were nearly at the breaking point. The tender meat fell from the bones. Bits of meat had been used to season the baked beans, heavy on brown sugar. The slaw came from somebody's own recipe, grated cabbage, a little mayo, a dab of sugar, and grated Vidallia onions. We didn't stop until Marshall asked for his beer.

"This place is filling up," said Vernon as he pushed his plate away. "Must be hopping at night."

"Funny," I said, "I see one bartender who serves as a waiter and one cook. Burl isn't around, and no waiters. I guess there are people in the kitchen."

"Wonder if anyone reserved the snake room for dinner?" Marshall wiped the foam from his lips. "Jolly place to bring a lady friend, I'd say. Right off the bathroom hall and a rattler to boot."

While we waited for the bartender to ring up our bill, Burl returned. He had changed shirts, a white embroidered thing from Mexico, to match his white boots. He smelled of after shave when he reached our table.

"Lownde treat you kindly?" he asked.

"So very kind," said Marshall who slapped his big tight stomach. "Won't be able to row a canoe for a week."

"Marshall!" I laughed. "You won't even get into a canoe."

"Still won't be able to row one." He took the last swig of his beer.

"When you people going to dive in the lake?" Burl asked, turning our faces somber again.

"Don't know yet." Tony stiffened, letting us know not to give the man any more details. "Not sure even if we have enough divers."

Burl glanced at me. "I see. Well, when you do it, don't be surprised if half the county don't come out to watch. Operations like that are kinda unusual around here."

We stared at him in silence until Vernon shoved back his chair. "Time to go. Thanks for a great meal." He stood. We followed.

"Nosy bastard!" said Tony. We had packed into his van.

"Speaking of canoes, Marshall, I think I'll drag mine out to the lake and skirt it before it gets dark." I checked my watch. "Sun goes down late these days. I've got another two hours of light."

"Forgive me if I don't join you," said Marshall who closed his eyes and stifled a burp.

Vernon helped me move the canoe to the edge of the water. He had given me this vessel as a sort of making up gesture in one of our few rocky moments in the relationship. He had painted the name "Peace Offering" over the red color of the canoe. He climbed in, facing front.

"I can do it, Vernon," I said.

"I know that, but I'd like to see the lake, too." He took up an oar and shoved into deeper water. I took the other one and followed his rhythm.

We moved to the right, following the shore a safe distance from the clusters of cattails. We passed some old posts where landings had long since rotted in the sun. The first intact one belonged to the Ferguson place.

"We found the drowned kittens near here," I said. "Actually, kittens with slit throats who had been tossed into the lake."

"Think Ferguson did that?"

"His father says no but after seeing that snake at his bar, I don't know."

"Where's the aquifer?"

"I think it's almost directly out from this landing." I pointed to the center of the lake.

We rowed slowly, staring down at the water that seemed to get a little clearer as we moved. At one point, a slight bubbling hit the surface.

"It's probably here, unless that's some turtle about ready to stick his head up."

"See any turtles in the lake?" Vernon dipped his hand in the water to test the temperature.

"None. But there's been a storm. Nothing is quite normal right now." I put my hand in the water and found it cool to the touch. "Pretty sure this is where I saw the aquifer."

We moved back closer to shore and continued the circle. We followed the road but could only see it once in a while when the reeds and cattails thinned or someone had built a boat landing. We were on the exact opposite side of the lake when we saw Mildred Culley's house. It sat near shore, the front lawn only a few yards from the dock. She had had steps with a handrail built on the bank that led to the landing, something you'd expect an elderly woman to have. At the bottom of the steps, a strong post rose from the water. Rope marks scarred the area where she had tied up her little boat. The landing was for bigger boats, ones that had motors and would dock at the end in deeper water.

I looked at the big imposing white house. Somewhere behind it in the trees was the family home, the one her sister inherited then sold. Mildred's house had a front door in proportion to the building. The oval window above the door made it seem higher than it was. Right now, yellow police tape crossed that door.

"I can see her running out the front door. Not running exactly, but walking hard like she did when she came around the lake. Scared, because someone is in the house and after her. She scuttles down the path, grabs hold of the railing, gets down the steps and into her boat. Somewhere along the way, she's able to remove the tie from the post. She takes up an oar and heads into stormy waters." I sighed. "She must have been terrified to risk her life like that."

"She was hit in the lower back." Vernon held the canoe steady with his oar.

"Which means she was standing in the boat or near it." I tried to imagine Miz Culley sitting down. She was too short. The gun shot would have hit her in the upper back. "Maybe she didn't reach the boat at all. She was shot and tossed into the boat. The killer then untied the boat, shoved it into the water. The wind blew from this side that night. Water came up to the house. Her boat would have been shoved our way."

"I wonder if Chandler got any crime scene stuff done over here. The storm would have obliterated a lot of it." Vernon edged the canoe around the landing and close to the steps. He leaned in to check out the wood. "Nothing that looks like bullet chipping."

We rowed into the wilder part of the lake. Houses hadn't been built on this side, except for two beyond the Culley place. Cattails grew thick and hid bird nests, turtles, and most likely a few snakes and gators.

"Mating season must be over," I said. We had seen only one large reptile swimming in the area, and the deep croaks had turned into higher pitched frog choruses.

"That's the Bono house, right?" Vernon pointed to the house with the long back porch in the distance. It sat on an incline, noticeable from the water. It rose off the ground as many houses did in the area to protect it from flooding. But the area beneath the house was closed off with lattice work. My own house had this feature. It was intended to keep out critters. The incline of the Bono house wasn't only on the water side. The side facing away from Miz Keen was also a rising slope.

"Someone is in the yard," I said.

"He disappeared beneath the house!" Vernon held the canoe steady.

"There must be a door there."

"Hang on," said Vernon. He placed the oar across the canoe and took out his cell phone.

I held the canoe in place while he talked to someone about the background report on the Bono family. Just before he rang off he said, "Okay, hold the written stuff for me. Don't send it here unless I call you." He stuck the phone back into his pocket.

"Anything exciting?" I asked.

"The old man has a record. So does his wife. He has been arrested a few times for business fraud. His wife put up a ruckus when the cops served a warrant on their house in Jersey. She got violent enough to be arrested."

"Recently?"

"About four years ago. He did time, paid a fine and went home. No trouble since then."

"What does he do for a living now?"

"Mail order, whatever that means. And, the kid got expelled from school for passing out beer to his schoolmates."

"He admits that, is a bit proud of it, I think."

"Like father, like son?" Vernon picked up the oar again.

CHAPTER TWELVE

Charles Chandler stood on Miz Keen's landing with Tony when we had finished the tour of the lake. The two men, nearly the same height, presented a distinguished picture as they watched us pull the canoe onto shore.

"You find anything unusual?" said Chandler who looked tired up close. There were signs of beach sand on his uniform and a couple of unidentifiable stains.

"Have you done any searches around the Culley house?" Vernon said as he stowed the canoe oars.

"Some. We found her front and back doors wide open. Must have been that way during the storm because the floors were wet. House is too high for any flooding that night. No prints, however."

"But you know it was her own rifle that killed her?" I joined the men on the landing.

Chandler nodded. "Pretty sure. Ballistics hasn't reported yet, but the gun had been fired that night, and the bullet in her back matched the caliber."

"You think she kept the gun in plain sight?" asked Tony.

"Most old ladies around here keep it either by the bedside or by the door. She probably learned to fire it when she was younger. It might have knocked her to the floor if she used it now. It was to scare people." He smiled. "We got lots of old ladies in this part

117

of the world. Oh, nearly forgot." He turned to face Tony. "Did your aunt know anyone by the name of Paulette Henderson?"

Tony shrugged. "She never mentioned the name to me, but then she never mentioned any names to me. I wouldn't know her best friend."

"That was the name on the false teeth. We'll check it out soon as we can."

We moved inside the house just as the sky turned purple. Marshall was signing a credit card slip at the door, while a delivery boy held two large pizza boxes.

"I figured we'd be busy tomorrow, and I ain't eating tuna fish. We can refrigerate these and heat them in the microwave tomorrow." He carried the boxes to the kitchen before anyone could say anything. When he let out a groan about not having enough room in the fridge, we laughed.

"Foil is in the cabinet above the sink. Wrap the pieces separately," I yelled. "And don't eat it all while you're doing it."

After a few moments, we heard Marshall drone, "One for foil, one for me."

"Look," said Chandler, "I haven't been home since five this morning. The mess down at Cedar Key is going to keep me busy a long time. I'm trying to run this and a few other investigations and using the security team to find missing persons at the same time. Whatever you guys can do to clean up here, I'll appreciate." He looked at Tony. "Just let the others do the searching, okay? You're not a suspect in my book. Your alibi for when your aunt died is solid. But the courts could try and say you had her killed." He held up one hand, expecting a protest from Tony. "I'd rather not have to tell the courts that you found evidence."

"Your office called me down here, remember? You're the one who told me my aunt was dead." Tony's stiffened jaw began to grind.

"Yes, and like I said you're no suspect in my book."

"Who's coming from your dive team to help out?" Vernon intervened, giving Tony a chance to get up and walk to a window.

"Retired diver. Amos Tindall. And Wayne Daney, of course. He's helped us some before. Let Amos set up the plan. He knows this lake fairly well."

Chandler shook hands and bid us farewell. He would go home and sleep a few hours and head for Cedar Key again. From the television news, several people had gone missing there, and mobile homes were in shambles. They had no power, and only the main road had been cleared into the damaged areas.

We hit the bed before midnight. Tony stretched out on the big square pillows his aunt had provided for the wicker sofa. He was reading one of her journals when Marshall shouted "Night all!" and closed the door to the guest room.

Vernon and I slid between the sheets and listened to the faint hum of the air conditioner. Just his closeness gave me solace. We would dive together tomorrow, in water darkened by silt and bottom grasses. He would look out for me, and I for him. Tired and full of ribs, we fell asleep in each other's arms on a dead woman's bed.

Dawn brought the smell of reheated pizza. Marshall was up before all of us. He made coffee and put cereal boxes on the table. We were eating in silence when Amos' truck stopped in the driveway. Wayne was with him. They towed a small trailer that held the scuba gear and maybe some other supplies.

"I got sodas in a cooler. I figure Mr. Amado," he nodded toward Tony, "you and Mr. Long can stay on dock and assist from there."

Tony nodded. "I'm used to that."

"Assist?" Marshall stared at the man. "I don't stand on docks."

"Have you got a land metal detector?" I asked.

When Amos said he had, I suggested Marshall walk the shore line and use it there, and maybe even in shallow water. I knew Marshall would be grateful not to have to stand on something that could collapse and send him into deep water.

"Now we don't have anything to make a grid. I think we can work it out this way." Amos took out a paper and pen. He began to draw lines. "Here's Miz Keen's dock. Here's the cove where the gator left the body." He made two large dots. "And here's the direction we think the waves came across the lake during the storm." He made an angled motion with the pen above the paper. "If we line ourselves up, we can search back and forth within a makeshift grid pattern."

"We'll be able to see each other?" I asked.

"Yes, just be sure your head lamp is on. We'll use the aquifer hole as a limit. No use trying to search the entire lake. We'd wear ourselves out in such a big space. I got underwater metal detectors, but we don't know what we're after. Could be something that won't make them react. However, don't stir up too much silt." Amos put his pen down. The paper looked like swimming lanes in Olympic trials, four of them.

"Luanne takes the first section near the Keen dock. Vernon, you're her buddy and will do the next section. Wayne next. Then me. I'll cover the gator cove. I've settled on ten times each, five out and five back. Won't hurt if we overlap a little bit of territory."

It was a session of respect. Amos Tindall had run the local dive team in the old days, taking care of details that could save his divers' lives. Even with his white hair and leather-skinned face, he still had the alertness of a search diver. Wayne's eyes showed nothing less than awe as the man talked. He had been temporarily deputized and put on the Sheriff's payroll. An adjunct, someone I felt akin to.

In two hours, we had suited up and were standing at the edge of our areas. Marshall was fiddling with his metal detector, while Tony laid out the sodas and towels on the dock. He grabbed another cooler and packed it with more sodas and dragged it to the cove end of the lake. This would allow Wayne and Amos to grab a drink without having to swim to the dock.

Someone had called the neighbors. The Bono family sat in patio chairs on their back porch. Gil tried to run toward us, but Amos told him to stay clear. He retreated to the steps of his house. On the road between the houses, two trucks stopped. Stubbs had brought some friends. They sat in the truck beds with binoculars. Betty climbed out and shoved herself onto the front hood. She kicked off her thong sandals and swung her legs back and forth against the side of the truck.

"All we need are reporters now," I said.

I placed the metal detector headset on my head and waited for Vernon to do the same. He was used to the instrument. I had only used one in practice. He nodded, and I nodded back. We entered the water walking until we reached waist high and then went underneath from a squatting position.

With dive lights shining from our foreheads, we lowered to the floor of the lake. I held the detector arm in front of me and gently moved it from side to side, making a sweep of the silty bottom. A few yards away, I could track Vernon. His head light swayed with the movement of the detector. I expected the process to be tedious and slow, picking up any number of metallic objects tossed into the water over time. I had to listen for the detector beep, watch the lake floor for nonmetal objects and keep in a line as I moved toward the aquifer. The signal went off a few laps from the end of the dock. I held the detector steady and, with my other hand, raked into the silt. I found a long nail, the kind that would be used in the dock itself. Tucking it into my evidence bag at my waist, I tried the detector on the same spot. No signal. I moved on.

As I came closer to the aquifer, the water cooled and became clearer. The opening was no bigger than a ruler, both in width and length, but fresh water flowed constantly from it. I turned and moved over a body length and headed slowly back to shore. Nothing came up, not even a beer can.

At the edge of the dock, just before I pulled myself out of the water, I glimpsed something in the sand. It was in the area where I had started. I swam there and used the detector. Nothing happened. Sifting through the sand and grass, I found a notebook, the pages warped and nearly falling to pieces. I left it, swam to shore and handed over the detector to Tony. When I swam back, I was able to lift the notebook with both hands, careful to check for any pages that had come loose. Even in its warped state and blank pages, I knew it was one of Miz Keen's. The woman bought the same brand every time she started a new journal.

There was no time to study the notebook. I handed it to Tony and with the detector back in my grasp, I made another tour to the aquifer. The lake, at least in my area, appeared to be clear of metal products. It was, after all, a private lake and the residents most likely wanted it clean.

Traveling back to shore, I felt the tedium of the process take over. I wanted to see the lake from beneath, to touch its beauty and listen to the light bubbling of the aquifer. Once, I spied an alligator in the distance, its powerful tail swaying back and forth to propel it toward the shore where it would lie in the sun to warm its blood. Its reptilian feet hung in the water, barely moving as it disappeared in the distance. It wouldn't bother us. We were too near its size.

"Enough sightseeing, Luanne," I told myself. I needed to get the job done. I arrived on shore again and lifted myself to a sitting position at the edge. Vernon was doing the same not far away.

"Drinks?" Tony offered me an orange soda and walked toward Vernon with another.

The cool soda went down fast, and, in spite of myself, I let out a huge burp. No one heard me, unless you count the snake that slithered near shore, not five feet from me. I winced and tried to move sideways. The scuba tank was too heavy for this kind of subtle movement. Instead, I remained very still and prayed like crazy the thing would go somewhere else. I didn't dare remove my eyes from it, and it didn't appear to be going anywhere.

"It's just a water snake, Luanne," said Tony.

"Why is it I'm terrified of them on shore but not in the water?" It was a rhetorical question. Most likely someone had told me, mistakenly, when I was little that a swimming snake won't bite. That psychological suggestion remained in my brain even though as an adult I knew it wasn't true.

Just before I picked up the detector and headed back into the water, I saw Amos and Wayne come on shore.

The search in my part of the grid produced nothing more. Vernon found more nails and some fish hooks. Amos pulled up some kind of fish trap that had been down for a long time. It nearly fell apart as he raised it to shore. But it was Wayne who got lucky. Besides more nails, he had located a watch.

"I found it pretty close to the middle of my section," he said, wiping his face with a towel. "Looks like it hasn't been in the water for too long."

Tony twisted the elastic type band back and forth. It gave easily, like there was no water damage. He held it up against the sunlight. "There's an engraving on the back." After squinting and moving it close then away from his eyes, he read, "Nell Culley."

"Mildred's sister," I said.

We stood on the grass, our tanks and fins stacked like a bonfire in the middle of our circle. Marshall joined us with his detector still in hand. He had a handful of nails and nothing else to show for his trek around the shore.

"Maybe Mildred had the watch on, or better yet in her pocket, when she got dumped into the lake," I said. "The watch showed up here." I pointed to the middle of our grid. "Her boat ended up at the Keen dock, and she ended up here thanks to an alligator."

"Did she wear a watch the day she visited you?" asked Vernon.

Neither Tony nor I could remember.

Amos put his hands on his hips. In spite of his years, his body was strong with very little fat. He was a lifetime swimmer.

"Maybe she wanted to show it to you," he said.

"Okay," I said. "Mildred shows up here after walking around the lake just before the rain starts. She leaves some teeth that belong to a stranger in a jade box in Miz Keen's linen closet. Then she gets into her rowboat in the middle of the storm at night with a watch that belongs to her dead sister."

"And gets blown away doing it," added Marshall. His face poured sweat and his untied running shoes were the color of the mud he had waded in for a couple of hours. "Pun intended."

After changing, we sat in the Keen living room and sipped iced tea that Marshall made. Amos placed all the articles we found inside a box with their own evidence bags. It looked like a large box of picnic lunches. Tony had placed the notebook on a towel on the floor.

"Too bad it's unreadable," he said. "If it's the only one in the lake, it must have had something to say."

"You know," I said, "that Bono kid told you your aunt was tossing something into the lake. You thought it came from the Ferguson's dock, but maybe it was this notebook. Maybe?" I shrugged. Motive was lacking in this discussion. Whatever reason Marta Keen had for sending her notebook to a watery grave, or the appearance of false teeth and a watch, weren't making much sense. It did seem that they connected to two women's deaths.

"The lab might find a way to bring up the writing in the notebook. It might tell us something but if it's like her other ramblings, we won't have much. Now, I think it's time we had a talk with that Bono kid," Tony said. "Anybody know where Chandler is?"

CHAPTER THIRTEEN

"I'm not sure," Gil Bono stammered when he spoke to Chandler. It wasn't everyday a kid his age had to answer to a sheriff, but I suspected Gil knew what it was like. "I just saw her go out to the dock and toss stuff in the water." His eyes grew wider, trying to evoke an innocent look that came out more of an ignorant one. "Maybe it was just bread for the fish."

"My aunt knew there were gators in the lake, son. She wasn't going to attract them by tossing food out there. She had cats, remember." Tony's jaw moved in agitation.

Chandler darted a look from Tony to the Bono parents. They sat on either side of their son on their back porch. Vernon, Tony and I stood. Marshall opted for an iron patio chair in the yard at the bottom of the stairs.

"What about you, sir," he looked at JoJo Bono. "Did you ever see her tossing stuff out there?"

"Not a thing, but I didn't really watch her much." He turned to his wife who didn't wait for Chandler to ask her.

"Nor I. But our son was out and about. We prefer to sit here and watch our section of the lake. He roamed about, meeting people, doing odd jobs. I'm sure he's telling you what he saw." She leaned over to pat Gil's fat thigh where the sun had burned his fair skin. He wore cutoffs, and today he had chosen flip-flops instead of his running shoes.

"Honestly, I don't know what she was tossing." He shook his head as he spoke.

"Well, something the size of a notebook wouldn't be that hard to see from here," said Vernon. He had turned around to look at the Keen dock. "Maybe she didn't toss it in herself—or did it when you weren't watching." His eyes darted toward mine.

"Did you watch her a lot?" I asked.

"I—no!" Gil's eyes widened again and he looked to his mother for support.

"The cats, Gil," said Tony, trying to speak softly but chewing his jaw at the same time, "did you and my aunt see eye to eye where they were concerned?"

Gil shook his head, "I don't know what you mean. I like cats. I got one that comes around here a lot. I even kept it safe during the storm."

"The one riding on your shoulder?" I asked.

"Yeah, that one." He grinned, proud of his ability to train a cat.

"Did Miz Keen give it to you?"

"No, the cat started coming around our porch. I gave it some food and it kept hanging around here." Gil pointed to a cracked saucer at the end of the porch. It had remnants of cat food clinging to the sides. Flies had found it delightful.

"Look," said JoJo as he moved closer to his son, "we never really had much to do with Miz Keen. She never chatted or asked for any help with yard work."

"I thought she had dinner at your house once," I said.

JoJo glanced at his son. "Once, only once."

"Who did her yard?" Tony asked.

"She paid Stubbs," said Gil. "I helped once, picking up limbs and stuff. He paid me." The boy looked up at his father and gave a slight flinch.

"That's about it," the man said, glaring at his son.

Chandler stayed a while that evening. Marshall brought out his pizzas and heated them in the microwave, piece by piece. He couldn't settle for warmed over cheese and pepperoni, but embellished the slices with some baby shrimp he found in the freezer. When he had filled himself as well as rehashed the day's events, Marshall said he'd like to see the bodies of the women. He left with Chandler and Tony.

"I'm going to flip through some of these," I said and took up one of the notebooks Tony had stacked by his makeshift bed.

"I'm going to walk around a bit," said Vernon. He took a large flashlight from his suitcase and headed out the kitchen door.

I sat in the peacock chair and put my feet on an ottoman. The journal I had picked up was dated a few months prior to Miz Keen's demise. It was in an old lady's handwriting. She had been trained to make large curving movements on her esses. After a few paragraphs, I could see why Chandler gave up. There was something here but he had neither time nor, I suspected, patience to find it.

That Stubbs girl came back to live with her brother. What a mess her face is. Brain not much better. Keeps asking for a cleaning job, but she isn't too clean herself.

Had to fasten the screen in case the wind blows it back again. Banging nearly scared me silly. Miss Priss hid under the bed until the man left. He's okay I guess but I don't want him around too much. Nell didn't care for the kid in her yard. Mildred neither. He's okay. Just a bit lazy about clearing the place.

"What man?"

Saw a coral snake yesterday. Yellow bands running through the grass. Must get that cut back. Mildred took the wagon back to Ferguson. He said I could have it but I don't want to be beholden to him. Old man invited us to play cards. We'll go just to keep him company. His son is back for good, I guess. Keeps a dog.

"So they did socialize with the Fergusons, at least with the old man," I said. The journal went on like this. Miz Keen didn't much like anyone, including her Bono neighbors.

They come down for six months and run a business on computers they say. Never saw that. Woman doesn't look too clean. Kid is even worse. He ate nearly a box of cookies the first time I invited him inside. Never again.

Then the old writing referred to something familiar.

That kid has a playhouse under the house. He's got it blocked off so nobody can see inside. I peeped yesterday. Couldn't see a thing. It's boarded up just inside the lattice. Kid takes in boxes. Must be using them for furniture. Never see the father go in. Mother did once, with food.

I slowly realized that Miz Keen snooped on her neighbors. She didn't much like anyone and she showed it with her suspicious tone.

What kind of name is Bono? I think of that Hillside Strangler case in California when I hear it. I'm going inside one day.

Marta ended her discussion of the Bonos and rambled on about her days with Mr. Keen. He hadn't been all that good to her, demanding she cook all the time and not go out to visit friends. She 'put him in his grave' with resolve to make a new life however short it may be.

I was a bit out of sorts for a while after he died. Mildred cheered me up just after I moved here with a little gift of jade.

I sat up in the chair. A little gift of jade? How little? I looked around me and wondered if it could still be in the house. Maybe it was the jade box in the linen closet. But that wasn't little. Not big, but big enough to hold teeth.

I went to the kitchen and began to open drawers. If the jade hadn't struck a suspicion in a deputy's head, he would have left it here. It could have been anything, a pin, a box, a spoon, whatever. Marta didn't say.

In one drawer, Miz Keen had placed odds and ends of knives, lids, paper clips and measuring spoons. A few rubber bands flopped about as I rummaged through it. I did this all over the kitchen and nothing jade surfaced. Heading for the bedroom, I pulled open all the drawers along the way. In her dresser, I searched underneath knotted hose and dressy slips. The cops had done this, too, I was sure but did they find the jade?

By the time I had exhausted all the spaces, including the lady's jewelry box, I decided the jade was gone, maybe stolen by the person who held her face in the grass.

I heard the front door and Tony and Marshall arguing about something. From the window, I watched Chandler's car back up and pull away. He had dropped them off and likely headed back to whatever catastrophe from the storm had surfaced in the last few hours.

"There was evidence of water in her lungs," said Marshall. "Not much, but enough to choke her."

"Who?" I asked. "Marta or Mildred?"

"Nell," said Marshall. "I read the report on her accident. Cause of death is probably the knock on her head from the shower fall, but she had enough water in her lungs to choke her."

"Coroner finally ruled it an accidental death from a fall," said Tony. His face was tense and he stood with hands on his hips.

"Coroners have been wrong before," I said.

"Oh, God!" Tony sighed and plopped in a chair. For once, his hair seemed to have come uncombed.

"I've told Chandler he needs to reopen that case," said Marshall. "Especially in light of these last two women."

"Did you see the other bodies?"

"Pretty messy the one in the water. Teeth marks and a bullet hole. Old lady skin tears easily."

"I can't stay down here another week," said Tony. "I've got cases pressing in Tallahassee." He stared into the darkness of a window.

"Me too," said Marshall. "And Vernon's got a bundle of problems."

"Vernon!" I just remembered he was outside, wandering around the lake somewhere. He hadn't come back. I turned to the patio and stared into the night for his flashlight. I wanted to call out but didn't dare.

"What's the matter?" asked Marshall from the kitchen door.

I waved him back and grabbed a flashlight from the counter. Outside the frogs sounded a chorus loud enough to be on microphone. Anything disturbing them would shut them up for a few minutes. That wasn't happening right now, and I felt a tiny bit of relief.

"Is he out here?" Tony appeared at my back.

"I don't know where he is. He said he was going to look around a little."

We headed for the dock, shining our lights into the reeds and hoping no coral snake was on a nightly hunt. They wouldn't rattle in warning. In the distance, car lights danced on the lake road, appearing then disappearing amongst the cattails. It rushed past, probably headed for the main highway.

On the dock, I aimed my light into the water. The pitch darkness just made it reflect back at me. Tony went eastward and I went the other way, our lights darting the lake shore. I walked past the Bono house, darkened except for a porch light. They must have gone out for the evening. There was no moon and suddenly no sound. I stopped just before running smack into a warm body.

"Luanne!" Vernon said in a loud whisper. "Couldn't tell it was you in this darkness. Who's that other light?"

"Tony is looking for you, too. What the hell is happening? Where is your light?"

He clicked it on and shined it around him. A frog jumped into the water.

"Just did a long walk." He turned me around and with his arm across my shoulder, walked me to the dock. Giving a signal to Tony, we waited for him to return.

"Find anything?" said Tony.

"Did a lot of thinking," said Vernon. "What if the Bono family are fronting for something? What if that stuff being delivered isn't really being sold on computer but has another use?"

"Like what?"

"Not sure. Just a lot of card tables are appearing off the trucks."

We headed back to the Keen house. I kept quiet. Vernon's cryptic speculation told me something. From past experience, I knew his intuition was good.

"I have to go back tomorrow. I'll drive Marshall. Maybe you could stay another day with Chandler?" Tony sat at the table with the other two men. Marshall passed around iced tea.

"That's fine, but next day I've got a job lined up. I need to get back, too." Vernon squeezed my hand.

"I need someone in this house," said Tony. He glanced in my direction.

Sometimes ideas pop up at the best times. I nodded. "I'll be glad to stay, but send Pasquin down here to keep me company."

"That old man?" Tony knew the friendship but to him an octogenarian would be more trouble than it was worth to have as a companion.

But I knew Pasquin was never just a companion in times like these. He had age and experience on him. We decided to call Pasquin in the morning. We'd have to figure out a way to get him here.

Vernon and I lay side by side in the quiet of the mid-Florida night. A breeze had picked up and sang through the cattails and high grass. If not for the frog chorus, we could have been on the prairie somewhere.

"You went under the Bono porch, didn't you?" I spoke to the ceiling.

"Locked up tight."

I turned to him and brushed his cheek. "This house isn't exactly soundproof, is it?"

"Hell, the woman's bedroom door won't even close properly." He turned to me and kissed my neck. "You want to make a scene?"

I flopped on my back and breathed out a "no." Mad passionate lovemaking with Marshall and Tony in the adjoining rooms might be a disturbance neither could take. I had visions of both running into the room to investigate a strange noise.

We held hands in the dark, both too tense to sleep. I didn't want him to go. I shuddered slightly when I thought of him in the dark, circling the lake and peeking into the Bono house. We didn't need to be together every minute, but the thought of losing Vernon sent chills down my spine.

"You did go under the Bono house, didn't you?" I said once more.

"Go to sleep, Luanne." He patted my hand and turned his back.

CHAPTER FOURTEEN

Getting Pasquin to come south was the topic of discussion. Marshall figured he wouldn't come at all. "Too attached to that house of his."

Tony said he'd have to find a car to bring him down. "He can't drive, remember?"

"Maybe he can take a boat into the Gulf and weave around to Cedar Key where Chandler can pick him up." Vernon laughed out loud at his own suggestion.

"He'll get here. You'll see." I acted smug, knowing that Pasquin was like a wizard of the ages. And he did get there all on his own. I had to drive to Ocala to pick him up at the bus station.

He sat inside the air-cooled station, a small bag at his feet and his familiar straw hat on his knee. He hadn't straightened his hair after removing the hat. It formed a kind of white rooster plume on the top of his head. He fit right in with the assortment of humanity sitting beside him who were wearing funny hats, tropical shirts, and some even had missing teeth.

"Ain't traveled like this for years," he said. "Wasn't even sure the buses ran down here anymore, but it did even after the storm."

He hadn't asked why I wanted him there, but he knew somehow that it wasn't just companionship.

"I got Edwin looking in on the houses. Maybe Vernon will do the same."

"No trouble at all from the storm?"

"Not a bit. Lots of limbs on the ground. Some floating on the river, but no damage. Nothing other than ditches flooded." He fanned himself with his hat as though he needed to move the air conditioning inside the car.

"Wish I could say the same about here. There's a man coming to do temporary repairs on the roof this afternoon."

The others had left for Tallahassee. Pasquin would get the guest room tonight. I had spent the past evening doing laundry after Vernon left. Being alone in a strange house, and one where women hadn't fared too well, left me with an eerie and empty feeling.

I settled Pasquin in his room, and he immediately insisted on a nap. The bus ride was long and noisy, he said. Too many little kids squealing like pigs. I closed his door and opened the front one to Stubbs and two younger, but just as grubby, helpers. Betty stood in the background, her sad eyes trying to see inside the living room.

"We're here to put the roof back on the patio," he said. He grinned, and the teeth reminded me of our first meeting. "Saw you in that diving suit. You guys find anything?"

"A few old nails. Meet me around back with your stuff."

Stubbs set up his tools and ladders next to the patio. Betty sat beside it like a guard. Once in a while she would hand him something light, but they never asked her to do anything bigger. He did his best to straighten out the bent aluminum and to reattach it to the frame. It looked a bit crooked, but it would keep out the rain.

"Won't last through another wind storm, but hard rain won't hurt it."

I gave him the check Tony had left and walked with him to the front. His helpers placed the tools back on the truck and leaned against the cab and smoked. Betty climbed into the truck bed with the tools and sat upright like a kid ready for a fun ride. The only thing missing was a smile.

"Are you acquainted with the Bono's next door?" I asked.

Stubbs glanced at the house. Mr. Bono was sipping beer on the back porch.

"JoJo?" He dragged out the name the way a child would for a stuffed toy. "He's a peculiarity around here. Plays cards sometimes with the men in the area. Never bets much. Guess his old lady don't want the family jewels to disappear in a poker game."

"He plays here?"

"Nah, of course not. We got places we play. Ain't pretty but we like 'em." He grinned, and I was close enough this time to get a whiff of chewing tobacco breath. He leaned and looked into the front window. "You staying here by yourself?"

Even if I were, I would have told him otherwise. "No. An old friend has arrived from Tallahassee."

He shrugged. "Good. Ain't nice for a woman to stay alone. I was going to offer my sister to stay with you if you needed somebody."

"That's really nice of you," I said, sure that he just wanted to get her off his back for a while. I moved toward his truck to signal I wanted him to leave. He wasn't too dumb to notice.

"You give me a call if you need anything, hear?" He got in and revved the engine, and three men in desperate need of baths headed away from the Keen house with a mute Betty in the back. Her scraggly hair was too greasy to blow much in the breeze.

When I went back inside, Pasquin was up and in the kitchen making coffee—his brand of Cajun strong.

"You got me here to cook for you ma'am," he said and chuckled to himself. "This old lady who lived here sure had a lot of pots and pans. You buy any groceries?"

I had laid on a new supply that morning before picking him up at the station. I opened the fridge to show a jam-packed stock of meat and dairy.

He nodded. "Now, tell me what's happening here."

We sat down with mugs of his strong brew laced with lots of milk. He closed his eyes a couple of times as I related the events surrounding the two ladies who had died here recently and the one who died a few years back. He nodded at some points, letting me know he wasn't asleep. Once he made a rocking motion then gave his chair a frown for not having rockers. We would usually have conversations like this on my front porch, long into a hot summer night, keeping rhythm with the wooden rockers on the floor boards.

"You planning on asking me for help?" He said this after a silence when I'd finished the briefing.

"Maybe we could go around the lake, see people, talk to them. You might discover some things I'd never see."

He smiled, his leathery face pushing all the lines upward. "Old people, right? You want me to talk to old people about backgrounds around here."

I blushed. I could feel the blood hit the skin of my face. "How do you do that?"

"I know you, ma'am. Now, if I've got to galavant around meeting new people, I better get some sustenance. You buy any sausages?"

Pasquin pulled out the largest frying pan he could find and filled it with peppers, onions, and sausage. Whatever oil and spices he used didn't matter. It smelled like heaven and tasted even better. I made rice and we ate the concoction until it was gone.

"Tuna fish never quite did it," I said as I leaned back in the dining chair and sipped more heavily laced coffee.

"Don't look now, but somebody just pulled into the driveway," Pasquin said as he stared through the living room. Car lights hit the ceiling.

"Tony said to keep an eye on you," said Chandler as he stepped into the living room. "From the aroma, you don't seem to be doing too badly."

I introduced Pasquin and the two of them talked about Cajun food. Chandler had spent some time in Louisiana when he was in the military. Food and mosquitoes were about all he remembered. "And I don't care to recall the skeeters."

"You know these old ladies that got done in?" Pasquin asked, long after he had built a rapport with the man.

"I knew them, yes. Not well, but they had their moments of calling law enforcement. Mildred Culley raised quite a ruckus when her sister died. She went silent when she found out the dear old girl had sold the place without telling her."

"And Marta Keen? Did she call the sheriff?" I asked.

"More than she should," he answered. "Any little disturbance next door, or maybe Ferguson sitting on his dock and fishing. She'd accuse people of hitting her cats with rocks. Even called the animal shelter once to try and get the Bono kid arrested for just that. They called us, of course. The sheriff's office gets called for everything—even for a teen the mother can't control."

"Something had to be wrong," I added. "Now that the coroner has found suspicious events in all three deaths."

"Yeah, that's the trouble. You get these," he hesitated and shot a glance at Pasquin, "um, people who call the sheriff all the time, it becomes like the boy who cried wolf. Nuisance calls that pan out to nothing. When something does happen, nobody wants to listen."

"Do you think the old lady called for help that day?" Pasquin grinned and emphasized the old lady part.

Chandler looked embarrassed. "No. She had quit calling. So had Mildred Culley."

"Maybe they decided to take it on themselves," I added. I'd had my frustrations with officers who didn't want to listen. If Marta and Mildred could get no satisfaction from deputies, they were just the tough old broads to nose into things.

"They did something for sure." Chandler rose. "Tony comes back on the weekend. You people will be all right here alone?"

"Yeah, but, sir," I added, "please come if we call."

Chandler looked down at his feet, and smiled. "We'll come by when we can to check on the house." He squeezed my shoulder when he left, a gesture I found a bit too familiar.

"Now tell me about this old man Ferguson," Pasquin said. He sipped out loud from his hot coffee full of milk and sugar.

"He grumps about his son not being home during the storm. There was something about him going away a few years and coming back to live with the father. The boy doesn't drown cats, however, so the father says."

"I think we ought to pay him a visit. What do you think, ma'am?"

It was the Southern thing to do, but I still felt odd about just showing up at the Ferguson place. Pasquin didn't seem to have any qualms. He cooked up some more sausages, peppers, and onions and put them in a covered dish.

Ferguson was on his front porch when we pulled into his cleared road. Burl's truck was nowhere in sight.

"Boy has gone to his bar, of course. That place is more important that his old man." He stood, leaned against a banister and eyed the dish I carried.

I introduced Pasquin as an old friend and neighbor from Tallahassee and handed over the dish. "I'm not sure how you like Cajun food, but I made him keep it mild, not too spicy."

Ferguson removed the lid and took a whiff of the warm dish. He smiled and nodded. "I'd eat this even if it had fire coming out the corners. Wait here a minute."

Pasquin and I pulled up two old chairs to make a little circle on the porch. I sat where I could keep an eye on the road. Ferguson returned with a pitcher of iced tea. He had to make another trip to the kitchen for the glasses and a box of graham crackers.

"I'm not much of a cook myself. And that son of mine don't see fit to bring any ribs home from the bar." He sat in his chair. I poured.

Pasquin began his *ray-par-tay* as he called it, establishing a friendly and common ground for old man talk.

"You live here long?" He slowly fanned his face with his straw hat and leaned back in his chair. Ferguson took the bait and started rambling about how his ancestors had settled swamp land, cleared it and for a while raised cattle and had a garden. Pasquin would drop in a word here and there to ask about a particular kind of fruit grown in the area or to ask about the Ma Barker gang. I sat, listened, and nodded off a couple of times. Ferguson didn't seem to notice. He kept talking, his ancient gravel voice like a steady saw on old boards. I had lost track of what he was saying when I heard him mention the Culley sisters.

"Now Nell. She was the pretty one. Had lots of marriage offers but just never gave in." He chuckled. "I think the old man decided she was the more helpless of the two and left her the family house. Left Mildred some land. Mildred worked for years down at the post office. Never married either. She lived with her sister until she got enough money together to build her own house. Right proud of that place, she was."

I figured she must have been quite independent for her time to do that. Women like Mildred had paved the way for the women's movement in later years.

"Mildred didn't have much to do with menfolk, but Nell, she'd go with men right up to the time she died. Had them over for meals and stuff. Mildred called her a silly old spinster, still holding out hope."

"Did she take pills of any kind?" I asked.

"Oh, yeah. We all do. You live long enough, you'll take a pill for just about everything." He turned to Pasquin. "You on blood pressure pills?"

Pasquin nodded. He never told me exactly what he took, and I wasn't about to hear it now. He turned the subject back to Ferguson. "What are yours called?"

Ferguson droned on again about trying this pill then that one and finally coming up with a couple that kept him from having strokes.

"Did you happen to know if Nell took any medications?" I asked.

Ferguson looked at me. I saw a flicker of distrust in his eyes, but it must have been the addition of a younger voice from another generation that annoyed him. Pasquin shook his head slightly when I glanced at him.

"She was an old lady. Her bones were fragile. Falling is a problem, and, if we ain't careful, we'll slip in the shower." Ferguson took a big swig of his tea.

Pasquin took over asking the questions. His voice and demeanor were catalysts for talk, and Ferguson rambled on about the dispute over selling the house and how Mildred and Marta had become close friends.

"Mildred, she'd walk around this lake like a school girl. Once in a while she'd stop in here. Said she needed a glass of water, and she probably did. Brought me homemade jelly once in a while. But, you know..." He looked toward the sky. "I always got the impression she wanted to snoop along with her generosity."

"Snoop?" Pasquin sipped his tea.

"Yeah. She came here when Burl wasn't here, but that was pretty much all the time. She'd always tell me she could get the glass herself. I followed her inside once when she took too long. Caught her looking at the bric-a-brac in the china cabinet."

"Just admiring it, I suppose?" Pasquin spoke softly as though making for a small talk comment.

"Nope. She was rummaging. Pushing things back here and there. Said she was rearranging stuff to show it off better, but I don't believe that. She was looking at what we had."

Pasquin and I sat in silence, waiting for Ferguson to tell more. "I told Burl about it later. He said not to let her inside the house ever again. I think he got into it with her, too. They were always fussing with each other over Nell's house and the stuff inside. Mildred never did come back here after I told Burl."

"Did Burl get along with the sister?"

"Oh, yeah. He and Nell were 'chums' he said. He learned that word chums when he went to live up in Trenton. Uses a lot of Yankee words he never learned around here. He played cards with Nell. Took her places when she needed a ride. Even had her over to the bar when he first opened it. He got right upset when she died. Said he'd lost a friend."

"And he owns his friend's house now?" Pasquin used tact when he said this.

Ferguson nodded. "He'd bought it a year before, but he said she could live there for as long as she wanted. I think she'd about had it with fending for herself and wanted to move into assisted living somewhere. That's what he told me."

"Those places can cost a pretty penny," Pasquin said. "Might be worth it if the food is good." He grinned and waited for rest of the story.

"Old Nell looked into a place. Burl even took her over there. She was going to use the money from the house to pay for it." Ferguson frowned and shook his head. "Didn't work out. She fell in that shower. Never did get to the assisted living place."

"And her sister inherited the money," Pasquin chuckled.

"Nope. Weren't none. She got the money out but nobody ever knew where it went. Maybe old Mildred found the check and stashed it. Who knows?"

Ferguson took a long swig of tea and closed his eyes. Fatigue had rendered him silent for now. Pasquin and I stood up, said our goodbyes, and eased down the steps. I turned as I opened the car door. "I'll drop by tomorrow for the dish."

"Now let's go find us a rib dinner," said Pasquin.

"It's a little early, don't you think?"

"Not for a feeble old man who likes to go to bed when it gets dark."

"Feeble, my eye! And you stay up with the owls." I turned the car toward the highway and headed for the Fireside Bar. "You know, I just realized something, Burl has a dog. A big old friendly thing. I didn't see it at the house. I wonder if he keeps it at the bar."

"You said he keeps a snake in the fireplace?" Pasquin slapped his knee and laughed. "If he has a dog inside that bar, too, there's gonna be lots of barking. Ain't no dog going to like a live rattler in there."

We turned into the driveway. The parking lot was nearly empty, too early for after-work drinkers.

"Just back up a minute and go around the corner," said Pasquin.

I backed and pulled to the side of the building where car ruts led to a large, tree-covered area. People parked back here, too. Tire tracks had worn down several spots under the trees. This part of the building appeared newer than the front. It began at the chimney and extended to the edge of the trees. A door opened in the middle of the back wall. Above it, a sign read, STAFF ONLY.

"Must be for storage," I said. "Place for Lownde to keep the ribs. I'll bet that locked door I tried leads into the area."

"Sure seems a big area for a little country bar," said Pasquin.

We drove back to the paved lot in front. Smoke rose from the back side of the building. Lownde was cooking for the evening crowd.

Two men sat at the bar. Their uniforms gave them away as people who worked on septic tanks. The bartender chatted with them, and from the looks of the bottles, they were working on their third beer. Two women sat at a back table. Their jeans and T-shirts from Disney World let their little circle know they'd had a nice vacation once in their lives. The haggard eyes and stringy hair indicated there weren't many more than that one good time in their lives. They nursed beers, too.

"Dark place," said Pasquin. "Never did trust a dark place. Where are the windows?"

One window opened at the side of the bar. The only thing anyone could have seen would have been the rutted road to the back part of the building. The only other window was a little glass square in the middle of the main door.

"I never noticed this when we came before. It's like what my father used to call a honky-tonk bar. There's a juke box over there." I pointed to the modern compact disk version of the old juke boxes that played hits for a nickel. "And if they shoved back some tables, there'd be room to dance." The floor was wood, same brown texture and color as the walls.

"Not big on decorations, is he?" Pasquin looked around him. The only color came from neon beer signs over the bar.

The bartender came our way with menus. "You liked it so much you came back," he said, staring at me without a smile.

"I wanted to treat my friend, here." I nodded toward Pasquin who tipped his hat to the man.

We ordered a rib plate each and sipped on iced tea. I expected a giant Lownde to come bursting into the room again, loaded down with ribs right off the grill. Instead, I heard him shouting in a voice nearly as large and frightening as he was.

"Get that away from the fire!" he bellowed.

"I can't pick it up! It's too hot!" A young voice screamed back in anger.

"Sorry about this, folks," said the bartender as he rushed to the side door. "Lownde got new help and neither one is a happy camper." He jerked open the door and shut it behind him.

Voices mumbled and sometimes shouted until Lownde said, "Just take these into the bar." The door burst open in anger, slamming against the wall. Chubby arms and legs carried an oversized pan of fresh ribs. The carrier didn't look at the tables. Instead, he headed for the bar and slammed the pan on the surface hard enough to make the top ribs bounce and threaten to hit the floor.

"Gil Bono! Whatever are you doing here?" I said.

CHAPTER FIFTEEN

"Oh, gosh," said Gil. He looked from me to the door and back again like he wanted to be anywhere but there.

"Relax, kid," I said. "Are you working here now?"

Gil scuffed his running shoes on the wood floor as he walked over with his head turned downward. Guilt seemed to shine like a halo all around him, but guilt for what?

"Yeah, Mr. Ferguson needed somebody to help Lownde." He breathed heavily and looked around him. "My father offered me."

"Figured you could earn your summer money yourself?" Pasquin chuckled and winked at me.

"No! Well, yeah, I guess so. He thought this would be a good place for me to be." Gil's forehead dripped sweat even in the cool air conditioning.

"You got a penchant for running around and getting into trouble?" Pasquin made his query only half-serious, something Gil couldn't grasp.

Gil shrugged. "I don't get into trouble. I just needed some spending money." He nodded a bit too long.

"Spending it on girls, I'll bet." Pasquin was having fun now. "Too much on Sally and not enough on Sue." He chuckled.

"I do not!" Gil's chubby cheeks blushed from anger. His silly haircut appeared to stand on edge. "I don't even know any girls around here." He turned and stumbled off to the outside door.

"You insulted him," I said, trying not to laugh.

"Boy doesn't even know what a girl is," said Pasquin and grinned when the bartender brought over our meals. "Not sure he's all that good with rib delivery, either."

We pulled off the tender meat that nearly melted in the mouth with the pungent sauce, leaving only a clean bone, all the while watching a few customers come in for drinks at the bar or a rib dinner.

Gil came in twice more with a huge pan of recent barbecue, huffing from the weight and slamming it on the corner of the bar. Each time the bartender shot him an evil glance and said something under his breath. Gil hadn't been his choice of help.

"Place does good ribs," said Pasquin, wiping off the last bit of sauce from his chin. "Slaw is unusual, but good. Beans, too."

"This seems to be it for the place," I said. "No other choices. Not even barbecue sandwiches."

"Not all that many customers either." Pasquin looked up and stared at the front door. "Now looky that!"

I turned in time to see Rosie Quinne stroll inside, Burl close behind her. Her white hair had been done in the latest elderly lady pouf, making her thin hair look abundant. She wore a red safari suit.

"She come here often?" Pasquin took hold of his straw hat that had rested on an empty chair and placed it on his knee as though something might come along and grab it from his sight.

"I met her the only time I was here," I said.

Rosie took a spot in the center section of the bar seats and flipped her fingers toward the bartender. "You know, dear!" He smiled and fixed one of those drinks you put in a martini glass with a red cherry. It looked expensive.

Burl patted her shoulder and strolled among the tables when

he spied me.

"You two enjoying the food?" His face was red, maybe from sun or maybe from drinking. I couldn't tell.

I introduced Pasquin and told him we'd visited with his father. Burl frowned.

"My father went out?"

"No, we visited with him on his own front porch," I said.

The red face appeared to get redder. "I see." Burl sighed. "It's just I don't like him walking around the lake or getting rides with neighbors I don't know. He's not young and gets tired easily."

"Maybe getting out would strengthen them old bones a little," said Pasquin.

"His old bones are strong enough," said Burl. He put both hands to his collar and pretended to straighten it. This was another of his colorful shirts, this time a tropical blue and green thing with yellow and red parrots. He tucked it inside brand new blue jeans. He wore another pair of silver-tipped cowboy boots.

"Did he socialize much with the Culley sisters?" I asked.

"Nell, yes. She was an old dear. Mildred was another story. Nobody socialized with her. And your friend's aunt, Miz Keen, hated his guts. As far as I know, they had nothing to do with each other." He turned to see Gil walk through the outside door with an empty pan. "Excuse me." Burl met him half way, took the pan and disappeared behind the bar, passing a dimly lit display of old photos and a greasy license.

"It's still light out, right?" Pasquin tapped his arm as though an imaginary watch encircled his wrist. I'd never seen one there.

He suggested we take a ride around the lake to the Culley houses. He wanted to see where the woman had run out of her house and into a boat. "Seems a bit worse than just killing, to shoot an old lady in the back," he said.

"Don't you want to see the snake first?" I smiled and pointed the way to the restrooms.

While Pasquin walked to the hallway, I scanned the dining room and was again surprised at how few people ate there. There was no sign of a band coming in or even a place for one to sit. It was just a slow, lazy, dark room where a person could brood in silence for hours.

Rosie Quinne was on her third fancy drink and feeling little pain at the moment. She scooped up the cherry by its stem and lifted it in the air, waved it about and slowly lowered it to her open mouth. "Just like a mother might do for a baby who didn't want to eat," I thought. Her purse sat on the stool beside her. Burl appeared again from a door behind the bar. When he sat on the stool, he held her bag in his lap.

"Damn right there's a snake in the fireplace!" Pasquin tried to whisper but it came out like rolling gravel in a well. "Got little bolts on the glass screen to keep people out." He laughed. "Or maybe to keep the snake in."

We left, Pasquin tipping his hat to the bartender and Burl as we went out the front door. As we left the driveway, Pasquin leaned forward then back and said, "Stop a minute." Looking to my left toward the big storage area behind the main bar and restaurant, I saw at least eight cars parked under the trees.

"Weren't eight people inside that place," he said.

"Maybe they belong to Lownde, the bartender, and…."

"And who? That Gil kid?" Pasquin shook his head. "I'd sure like to know."

We drove the rutted road away from the Fireside Bar and headed to Mildred Culley's house. It stood large and white and was visible from almost all parts of the road. When we pulled into her drive, crime scene tape greeted us across the door.

"We'll have to ask Chandler if we can get in sometime," I said.

"Any scene tape around back?" Pasquin smiled. "Promise not to touch a thing."

"They've done the fingerprint stuff already. But it was all a hurried job. Most of the scene techs were needed at Cedar Key."

Pasquin took himself from the car in the manner of an elderly person saving his back. He held onto the door until his legs steadied.

"Nice old place," he said.

"She had it built back when she left the family home her sister inherited."

"How could she afford to build this place?"

I didn't know the exact answer to that. Maybe she sold some Culley land she had inherited. Or worse. Maybe Nell felt obligated to donate money to Mildred to erect her own house. "Could be a little jealousy between the two," I said.

"Always is," he added and walked toward the house. He got to the bottom of the steps and inspected them, even taking hold of each one and trying to shake it. He leaned over, balancing himself on the end of a step and gazed beneath the house. For a few minutes, he stood staring at the closed front door with the crossed yellow tape secured over it. He took one hand and drew an imaginary line from the door to the dock, turning himself toward me in the gesture. He pointed to the side of the dock.

"She ran down here—or most likely walked fast down here," he smiled. "And I would imagine went up on the dock to the other end, or, if her boat was at this end, she climbed in and began rowing."

"She was shot in the lower back," I said. "Wouldn't that mean she'd have to be standing? She was short. Sitting down, the shot would have entered her between the shoulders."

"Or in the head." Pasquin closed his eyes and stayed silent for a few minutes. "If it had been me—and we're about the same age—I would have trotted down here from the house and been out of breath by the time I reached the boat. Now, assuming the boat was at the shore tie, I'd wade and get in that way. Might've been a little hard to push off with an oar, and I'd have to slip the rope off the post…"

"What is it?"

"The storm is raging. Doing all that with rain pelting your face is a little hard for an old bitty, even if she is a hellion. You know, I think I'd try to hide. Maybe she was climbing into the boat to hide there but the shooter got her in the back."

"Then he would have to come down here and release the boat and shove it off, with his victim inside."

"Would have been a lot of blood," said Pasquin.

"The wind blew from this direction toward us. Between that and the rocking on rough water, she was dumped out and the boat overturned by the time it reached the Keen dock."

"Blood would have been washed away," he said, nodding.

"Everything was washed away," I said. "Footprints, blood, whatever she was carrying with her, except maybe that watch."

"If she grabbed that and put it in her pocket while running for her life, that watch meant something," he said.

Pasquin took another look at the house and motioned for me to follow him. At the back door, there was no scene tape. He tested a narrow wood step and walked onto the porch. It had a screen, torn now perhaps by the storm, perhaps by an intruder. He knocked on the kitchen door after peering into the square window.

"Think it's okay?" He didn't wait for an answer, but turned the handle. It opened with a little nudge. "Door frame is warped."

"We shouldn't be here," I said.

"We ain't," he added, looking around at the white wood cupboards.

Mildred had a portable dishwasher with one of those Clean/Dirty magnets on the outside. Clean was up. Pasquin hooked a finger under the door and pulled it open. Shiny clean dishes waited for someone to put them on the shelves.

"These washers can be noisy. Old lady might not hear somebody coming into the back door if it was running." He turned to look out the window again. "Plenty of trees back there to block her view. What's behind those trees?"

To my relief, he headed out the kitchen door and into the trees that bordered Mildred's house. After a few steps through what could have been the edge of a forest, we stepped into a clearing. Here we could go no further. Someone had erected a chain link fence around a wide expanse of lawn, oaks and an ancient house. The fence had a gate with a padlock.

"This has to be the family home, the one Nell inherited," I said. "Mildred built her own beyond the trees—or maybe planted the trees to put a blinder between her and her sister. Burl Ferguson owns this place now."

We stood gazing in wonder at what the place once was—a grand manor in the Southern sense. It had three storeys, the top one most likely an large attic for storage or for the children's rooms. The old gables at that level were boarded up now, blinded eyes that no longer looked down on graceful, moss-draped trees. The most glamorous part by far was the wrap-around porch with a wrap-around balcony that served as the roof. The storm had left limbs and leaves strewn about the lattice-like bannisters. Below, the bottom of the porch sagged a bit near the front steps. The steps themselves stood the test of time since someone had replaced the old wooden ones with concrete.

"Car's coming," said Pasquin and moved back into the cover of the trees. I followed him.

Burl's truck pulled underneath a large oak. He let down his windows a crack as though he would be parked there for a while and didn't want the truck to get too hot. A passenger moved from the other side and removed a push broom from the bed of the truck. Burl got out and lit a cigarette. He moved about the yard and finally came to the gate.

I placed my hand over my mouth when I saw Gil Bono head for the porch.

"Do the balcony first," said Burl, following him and unlocking the door. "I'll be back to pick you up in about two hours."

"You said twenty dollars for each, right?" Gil's early teen voice sounded nervous.

"Get on with it, then." Burl got into his truck and backed out, disappearing into another group of trees that lined the driveway.

Gil pushed the front door open and moved inside without closing up behind himself. Moments later, a door opened just above the front entrance and Gil stepped onto the balcony. He looked around, decided to begin right where he stood, and began shoving the long broom from wall to balcony edge. Green leaves dropped to the ground as he steadily made his way around the second storey.

"Let's go around front," Pasquin said and scooted off next to the fence. We ended up in the driveway and made a short walk to the front of Nell's old house.

"Door's open," I shrugged and followed Pasquin inside.

We found an entryway made of lovely oak floors and beadboard walls. There were shelves of all sizes on the walls as though valuable pieces of art or even family portraits sat there once. There was no rug on the floor but there must have been, and for a long time, because the floor was darker in the area that received no sun from the windows. The lower doors were closed, but that didn't stop Pasquin. He opened each one.

"Big living room empty. Parlor empty. Not even a curtain, a rug, nothing."

We looked up the staircase, a grand thing wide enough for an antebellum skirt to float down to waiting suitors. I chuckled when I reminded myself that both Culley sisters were old maids in their time.

"He's outside. Let's go up," Pasquin took hold of the railing and pushed his old legs to the second floor. I gazed behind me and then followed him.

Another oak floor expanse surrounded the landing. It was large enough for tables and maybe etageres to be pushed against the wall. Now only their shadows told where they stood. At one end, a glass door led to the balcony. Most likely, the bedrooms had doors that also led to the balcony. Gil had left this one ajar.

We stood looking over an expanse of trees to the east and the lake to the west. Beyond the narrow grove we could see the top of Mildred's house, but not the back door. At night her upstairs windows would have been like beacons. A soft breeze swept through the treetops, swaying their limbs in soft rhythms. For a moment it was tempting to sit here, to feel the old South wrap around me.

"Damn!" Gil's voice sounded from the side. "Stop blowing!" He shouted at the wind that was pushing the leaves back onto the balcony.

"Having problems?" I said as he rounded the corner and came face to face with Pasquin and me.

"What the hell!" He turned pale and dropped the broom.

"You left the front door open. We came in to see if anyone was squatting or maybe trying to rob the place." I smiled at my own lie.

"Back where I come from, hobos—what you call homeless today—got into old places like this. Made cook fires in the living room and sometimes burned down the place." Pasquin nodded.

"I've got a job! Mr. Ferguson wants the leaves cleaned off." Gil stooped with a grunt to retrieve the broom handle.

"Well and good, but lock the door, okay?" I said. I looked about me, hoping my face would convey wonderment. "So this is the Culley family home."

"Yeah," Gil shoved the broom back and forth, making his labor more intense than it should be.

"You ever see it when it was full of furniture?" Pasquin didn't wait for an answer. "Must have been a grand old place with valuables like you couldn't imagine."

"Yeah, I was over here once or twice when Miss Nell was alive. She had lots of things, breakable stuff. I guess it was valuable but I don't know about glass and such. Had some paintings of old people and great big tables and chests. Things stuffed with all that glass."

"And Mr. Ferguson owns all of it now?"

"Far as I know. She died and a big moving truck came to take it all away."

"I wonder if any of it is for sale at the antique markets in Ocala," I said, giving Gil an opening.

He grunted and finished the balcony. "I got to do the porch now. We have to go downstairs."

"You'll lock this door?" Pasquin said as we entered the landing.

"No key. At least I don't have one." He trudged downstairs,

the heavy broom pounding each step.

"Well, you better not tell Mr. Ferguson you left the front door open," said Pasquin as he tipped his hat to Gil. "He sure won't like any hobos taking up residence inside."

"Ain't telling him nothing," said Gil as he shoved the broom across the damp boards.

"Physical labor doesn't agree with that child," said Pasquin as we walked the tree lined driveway. "He won't say we were here. Doesn't want the wrath of Ferguson."

It was nearly dark when we reached the front of Mildred's house again. The black water lapped gently against the shore.

"Something happened here, Pasquin," I said as I unlocked the Honda. "Who could have been inside Mildred's house?"

"Ferguson, the kid, a stranger, a hobo even," said Pasquin. He sat hard on the front seat. His breathing told me he was exhausted. "Anybody got a reason to shoot an old lady in the back?"

"That's the crux of this, isn't it? A reason. We know Mildred and Marta didn't get along with everybody and there was a rift of sorts between the sisters."

"Ferguson doesn't like his own son, and this bratty teen will do anything for a buck," Pasquin fanned himself with his hat.

"Damned if I can see a motive for shooting somebody in the back, or holding an old lady's face in the dirt until she dies, or shoving someone in the shower. That's pretty drastic for just not liking your neighbor."

Pasquin leaned back on the seat. "Ma'am, people have killed for less."

"Then what is the less?" I asked. Pasquin grunted and stayed silent for the rest of the ride to the Keen house.

I pulled into the driveway behind a marked sheriff's patrol car. A uniformed deputy got out from the driver's side as he saw my lights.

"Luanne Fogarty?" He nodded toward Pasquin. "Chandler says to bring you down to the department."

CHAPTER SIXTEEN

"Vernon!" I was relieved to see him.

His wide grin and bald head sat at a computer in the local sheriff's department. Chandler stood behind him, and offered Pasquin and me chairs.

"I never got back to Tallahassee," Vernon said, brushing my arm in a gesture of affection that only I knew. "After I left, I let Chandler know about what I'd found on Bono, and he ran a more extensive check." Vernon tapped his finger on the monitor and Chandler leaned over to read something on the screen. He nodded as he read, his lips moving.

"Man has a record, all right." He nodded again, and Vernon hit the print icon.

"Let's go for coffee," said Vernon. "I spent last night in a fleabag motel near Gainesville, about the only place left with a room."

"Why didn't you come back here? We aren't all that far from Gainesville."

"I needed to check something there, a warehouse."

"Furniture? Card tables?" I figured he'd seen what was in Bono's storage under the house.

Vernon smiled. We sat in Chandler's office. It didn't look much different from Tony's, even down to the clutter of file folders on chairs and in stacks on the floor. Maybe in the final analysis this was how detection was done, order out of chaos.

Chandler poured coffee for all of us. Pasquin loaded his with milk and made a face at the first sip. It wasn't strong enough, something I knew from years of being knocked off my chair when I sipped his brew.

"Bono makes a living, so he says, from selling furniture whole-sale and retail on the internet. It's dining room furniture," Chandler said.

"Depends on where and how you want to dine," Vernon smiled. "Not too many card players want food all over the table."

"So it really is card tables he orders, just not the kind we used to sit the kids at when there were too many people at family dinner," I said, remembering Gil pulling in the heavy boxes the night of the storm.

"Gaming tables is more like it," said Vernon. "He's got a stock of them under that house."

"Must have some solid walls to keep the water out down there," said Pasquin. He had set his coffee cup, still full, on Chandler's desk and didn't pick it up again.

"Yep," said Vernon. "Inside the lattice work is a solid wall of cement. Floor, too, and the door is tight, too tight for water to seep in. But Bono was taking no chances. All the boxes are piled three feet off the floor on cement blocks covered in tarp."

"It must have a good lock," I said, eyeing Vernon who I knew had broken into the place.

"Ah, yes. A great lock in fact. However, one must actually close the door for the lock to catch."

Pasquin and I looked at each other and nodded. "The kid left it open," we said in unison.

"Left it open to chase a dog away. The parents weren't home, and I figured someone could be breaking in. I investigated."

Vernon grinned even wider.

"And did Gil catch the dog?" I laughed.

"I heard a loud cry, like a dog being beaten, so I guess he did at least catch up with the mutt. That's when I knew I had to leave."

"Okay, here's the stuff on this guy," said Chandler after a deputy handed him the printouts. "Bono has records—three it seems—of consumer fraud. Like promising merchandise but never delivering it or delivering less than was ordered, less in quality. He got off with fines twice and a fine and some jail the third time. When computer shopping came along, he set up a business that's mostly mail order. He can do it from anywhere."

"You don't see much of the Bonos, do you?" asked Vernon.

"Except Gil, and we seem to be running into him constantly."

"Yeah. The kid doesn't handle the business. We figure JoJo and Cara are sitting at computers most of the time." Chandler ran his finger down a printout page. "Or at least that's where they want us to think they are."

"Guess you don't need a big city to run that kind of business," said Pasquin. He wouldn't use a computer but he understood their convenience.

"And buying a lonely house on a lake in central Florida could do it," added Vernon.

"And is he into fraud now?" I asked.

"Not as far as we can tell," said Chandler. "He gets these boxes in from a warehouse in Gainesville, then sends them out. We haven't had time to do the computer checking on the sales. Got somebody on it right now. If we can steer the hurricanes in another direction, we may be able to solve a few crimes around here."

"We had a power outage that night," I said. "Gil Bono mentioned a generator, but if the house had one, they didn't turn on the lights."

"I didn't see any signs of one," said Vernon. "Maybe they shut down the business."

I sighed and drank the rest of the lukewarm coffee in my cup. Lownde's ribs sat uneasily on my stomach.

"Will you be staying with us tonight?" I asked Vernon.

He turned away and shook his head. "I'll explain later," he said in a whisper.

"As long as you're in the Keen house, we'd like you to log the comings and goings of the delivery trucks," said Chandler. "We think the same ones deliver as turn around and mail out stuff. We'll get a better idea of where they're going as soon as our tech does the computer search."

"Might be nice to search the Bono computers," I said.

"Can't do that now," Chandler said. "All in good time."

Vernon drove Pasquin and me back to the Keen house, or at least to Priss Lane. The sign had weathered the storm and still hung from its two hinges. We had to walk in the dark the few yards to the house.

"You must be tired, old man. What say we have some grits and hit the sack?"

"I'll make them," he said. He rattled a pot from the cupboard and boiled the white corn grits, tossing in some sharp cheddar just after they were done.

The warm grits went down easy, soothing on top of the heavy rib meat. Pasquin made strong coffee and sat in a wicker chair without turning on a light.

"I thought you'd be sleepy by now," I said checking the clock. It was after eleven.

"This old Cajun don't normally go to sleep before midnight," he said. "I got to thinking about these poor old ladies. They knew something, or had something on somebody. Must have been pretty serious to get them killed."

"And the first two deaths might have been taken for natural or accidental deaths. Assuming it's the same person doing it, he must have been pretty desperate to shoot one in the back."

"I'd say so." He leaned forward, his gnarly hands gripping the mug of coffee. "Can that kid shoot a gun?"

It wasn't a question I wanted to hear. The thought of chubby Gil, who gave beer to his classmates, pulling out a rifle and blowing away an elderly woman gave me chills. Gil might kick a dog and throw stones at cats, but kill a person? I shuddered.

"I wonder if Miz Keen found out something about these game table orders." I looked at Pasquin. His eyes closed and he didn't seem inclined to comment further. "I'm off to bed."

I lay on my side in bed, my eyes glued to the window for any sight of a light, whether from a car or from inside the Bono house. I wanted to know what went on there. Mrs. Bono evidently never invited Miz Keen for coffee. In fact, it appeared they hardly ever invited anyone to their house. But it was the Bono family who found Marta dead in the grass. I slept fitfully, seeing unlocked doors and Gil floating in and out of them.

CHAPTER SEVENTEEN

"I want to check out some antique shops," I said as I ate the sausage, egg, and pepper omelet Pasquin had made. I washed it down with cool orange juice and thanked my stars for it. The Cajun sauce had roused me from a groggy morning. "You want to come along?"

Pasquin nodded and grinned silently at my quick sips of the juice. "You got some place in mind?"

I didn't, but I called Chandler's office. His secretary suggested Old Hill's, a large warehouse that got top dollar for a lot of locals. Pasquin, keeping up his friendly contact, called the Ferguson house in hopes of talking to the old man. He chatted nearly ten minutes before asking about antiques in the area.

"Old man said I might could offer myself up for sale," he chuckled as he put down the phone. "Said the only place he knew about was Old Hill's. Not a hill in sight around here. Wonder what old hill they're talking about."

We rode the miles into Ocala and wandered around on some side streets before coming to a place that rested between the last of the car lots and open woods. The sign atop the Quonset hut-like building had faded, but you could just make out white letters on a maroon background. The portable marquis at the driveway was easier.

The hill in Old Hill's turned out to be Mr. Junior Hill, long dead. The current owner had bought the name and the business. Coolers blew atop the high curved ceilings, and their air was further spread by a series of fans high above the crowded cement floor. A short man greeted us with a cocky smile. He stood rigid with his head tilted toward us. His hair cut was right out of the early sixties, before the long stringy stuff became the fashion. He wore sideburns. His shiny tie tack matched the shiny ring that weighed upon a small hand. I was reminded of a country gospel singer when he opened his mouth and spoke in a high tenor.

"Sonny Hobbs. Nice to meet you folks." He stuck out a hand. I shook it. Pasquin nodded and tipped his hat.

"We'd like to wander for a minute, if you don't mind," I said.

Pasquin had already moved away and ran his rough finger down the edge of a bedstead. Sonny smiled at me and frowned about the same time at Pasquin.

"My card," he said. "Just let me know if I can help. I kind of stick around this end unless you see something you like better down there." He pointed to the far end, which appeared to house more *avant garde* stuff.

I drifted to a dining set and ran my fingers across the top. Not a speck of dust. Sonny followed a few steps behind.

"I suppose you get lots of local stuff in here when people move or die." I pretended an interest in the crocheted doilies resting in a pile on top of the table.

"Oh, yes. Lots of local stuff." Sonny moved closer to me and bent over to see something beneath the table. "I'm pretty sure this one came from an old house in town." He squatted, almost disappearing underneath. "Yes, the Baker residence."

I moved the chairs that sat nearby. The cane bottoms were torn.

"These would need replacing," I said, and pressed a palm on

the top of one.

"We've got men who do that," Sonny nodded his head.

"Do you have anything from that grand old house out near Lizard Lake?"

Sonny thought for a moment. "Ah, yes! The old Culley place. Sad place. I heard her sister drowned in the hurricane."

I stared at him. The word must have gotten out that Mildred had drowned. Relieved that no one outside the Sheriff's Department knew she had been shot, I nodded at Sonny.

"But the stuff we got in here is from her sister Nell's house. Lots has already been sold, and I think the new owner kept a lot, too." He stood like a tiny groom and motioned for me to walk with him. "Most of it is right up here." He led me to a group of sideboards and chairs with cases of glassware behind it. One side was sectioned off with a dark red velvet rope. "This is what's left."

I nodded to Pasquin who had followed at a distance. The smell of the old wood was stifling even with the ventilator fans running above us. We opened doors, looked at the backs and undersides of the big furniture. They had marks, as did the chairs, but I only lifted my eyebrows. I didn't know a Chippendale from a Montgomery Ward. Pasquin looked with me, nodding as though he could read quality. I made my way to the shelves on the wall behind the sideboards. Fragile looking teacups, miniature figurines, and a few plates made up all that was left of poor Miss Nell's pretties. I picked up a plate and actually recognized the Wedgewood mark. On the top shelf, some odd assortment of really tiny animals sat like the forlorn lot left behind at the local pound. I reached for a rather odd one and pulled down something that looked like a small island with a water bird standing atop it.

"It's real jade, you know," said Sonny. "Miss Nell had a huge collection of it. We sold the other pieces we had."

"Real jade? And why didn't this piece sell?" I ran my fingers over the graceful bird. Someone had done a clever job of carving his long legs, bending one as the beaked head searched for a fish in the water. On the base, I hit a tiny snag, a little broken spot. "Oh, I see."

Sonny looked at the spot, too. "Yes, it is still pretty but marked way down."

I bought the bird for ten dollars and probably was overcharged, but it had triggered the thought of Nell giving Miz Keen a piece of jade as a gift. And the jade box with the teeth—also with water birds.

We drifted to the other end of the building, feigning interest in small tables and lamps. Dust was rising from one section where a woman used a broom to sweep the concrete floor. When she looked up, she seemed confused, but gave a quick smile and a nod. Before I could speak, a salesman approached her.

"Betty! You don't sweep while there are customers here. It makes people sneeze." The man took the broom and headed away from the woman who stood looking first at him and back at me.

"How are you, Betty?" I said.

"I got a job here," she said, almost whispering. "I clean."

"That's good." I watched her run towards a door that led outside and wondered how long she'd last.

"Whoever knocked that woman in the head did a thorough job of it." Pasquin smiled.

We rode back to the Keen place with my jade and Pasquin's antique spittoon with a striking cobra on the side. It was for Edwin, his swamp friend who had an on-going relationship with the reptile world, both living and dead.

"Wonder what Edwin would say about the snake in the fireplace."

Pasquin whooped. "Ha! He'd like it. Wouldn't be able to pull him away from that hallway." He chuckled the rest of the way home. Edwin pretty much had algae for brains, but he knew his snakes.

We made a stop at the local Publix for groceries, especially fresh fruit. Pasquin picked out some greens and potatoes along with more peppers. As we left the store, thunder sounded in the distance.

"I need to contact Tony tonight. He wants to be updated before he comes back this weekend." I glanced at Pasquin whose eyes were shut. He made no comment but I still wouldn't swear he was asleep.

At the last moment I decided to turn into the Culley place to see if there was any activity. Ferguson's truck sat in the driveway, but there was no sign of him. I had an eerie feeling he could be inside the upstairs landing, watching us looking at his house. I backed out and rode to Mildred's house. Nothing but the scene tape, still in its place. Thunder rumbled as I headed around the lake. Passing the Ferguson place, I sped up then slammed on brakes around a bend of reeds. Pasquin's eyes flew open as he braced himself on the dash board.

"Woman! What are you doing?" He jerked the seat belt as though testing its strength.

"It's Mr. Ferguson," I said.

Right in the middle of the road where the strip of grass grew, the old man stumbled along, making as much progress sideways as he made forward. I turned on the hazard lights and hoped someone would see them before slamming into my rear as they rounded the bend. Pasquin moved faster than any other eighty-year-old would move removing his seat belt and heading out the door.

"Come in the car," he said as he took the man's arm.

Ferguson followed him. I held the back door while Pasquin got him seated and belted.

"You're not feeling so good?" He leaned into the back seat and frowned at the man whose eyes appeared tired and glazed.

"Maybe we should take him to an emergency room," I said. "His son is back at the Culley house."

He looked back at Ferguson and turned the volume up on his voice. "Do you want us to take you to your son?"

Ferguson blinked and focused on Pasquin's leather face. "No," he said in a barely audible voice. "I don't want nothing to do with that kid."

"What about a doctor? Can we take you to a doctor?" Pasquin had his hand on the man's shoulder now, shaking it lightly.

"Doctor Johnson," he said.

"Come on, Pasquin. It's the emergency room." I returned to the driver's seat and waited for Pasquin to buckle himself in again. "He may have had a heat stroke from walking."

"More like a regular stroke if you ask me."

I stared at Ferguson in the rear view mirror. The glazed eyes weren't the same. One leaked tears and drooped slightly. So did one side of his lower lip. I'd heard of mini-strokes in the elderly and this sure looked like one to me. I stepped on the gas.

Not far from the lake turnoff, there was a sign that pointed toward a hospital. I followed the highway until I reached a three storey white building. Aiming toward the emergency room, I slammed on brakes and honked the horn.

"This is our neighbor. He may be having a stroke," I said, breathing hard though all I'd done was drive and move out of a seat.

The orderlies removed Ferguson and sat him in a wheelchair. Without saying anything, they rolled him into the room and out of our sight. The administrative clerk took over. Before answering her questions, I pulled out the cell phone and dialed Chandler's number. His secretary said she'd try to find him.

"Tell him somebody needs to go by Nell Culley's old place and bring the son with him." I put the phone away and sat down with Pasquin to answer the perturbed clerk's questions.

We had no answers, or at least not the ones she wanted, like insurance coverage. When we mentioned Doctor Johnson, she shrugged. "There are several Johnson's in medical practice in this county. Can you be more specific?"

We had already explained what we knew of Ferguson, yet the clerk wanted more specificity from us. I sighed impatience. "Look. The sheriff is bringing his son over. Can't you wait? Better yet, wouldn't you have a record of such an old man. He must have been in here once or twice in his life." My voice was turning into a hiss.

The clerk shot me a knife-like glance and turned her side to us in order to hit some computer keys. She didn't say anything else while reading the screen and typing in some data. I looked at Pasquin. We both shrugged, and he grinned.

The clerk asked us to sit in the waiting area and give over our chairs to another distraught family who had brought in an old lady with a nonstop bleeding nose. I figured that poor family would get the same run-around, insurance first, medical help second.

We sat in hard chairs for half an hour, watching a steady line of smashed heads from motorcycle accidents outdo all the other maladies combined. Families followed, the mother gritting her teeth in anger over the purchase of such a machine; the father looking guilty and worried. No one was coming out to tell us anything about Mr. Ferguson.

Another hour and Sheriff Chandler showed up, with Gil Bono in tow.

"He was at the Culley house, raking up the backyard." He gave the boy a deliberate frown. "Seems he drove Ferguson's truck over there himself."

Gil turned his terrified eyes to the floor and mumbled something like, "He said I could."

"And where is Burl?" I asked. "His father is still in there." I pointed to the drawn curtains.

"I called his house and the bar. Bartender says he's pretty sure he took a trip to Tampa or somewhere. Said he'd call his cell." He looked again at Gil. "Man is going to have to answer for more than one thing."

"Where are your parents?" I said to Gil.

He looked up at me, his baby fat jowls shaking slightly. "They went out somewhere. I'm not sure..." He shrugged.

"That's why he's here with me," said Chandler. "No one at home, no Ferguson, minor left alone with a big old truck to drive." He put a big hand on the boy's shoulder.

Chandler pulled another chair over and placed it between Pasquin and me. He gently pushed Gil into it and told him not to move. He headed toward the clerk's desk. After a brief conversation, a nurse in full operating garments came from behind a curtain to speak to him. She nodded once in a while. Chandler took out a small pad and wrote down some things. They parted with smiles, and I thought what a great weight a badge carries.

"He's had a TIA, a small stroke not uncommon in a lot of people. They've done a scan on him and will run more tests, but he's going to have to stay overnight. Soon as they get him in a room, we'll pay a short visit. Any idea what he was doing on the road?" Chandler watched Gil as he spoke.

"None," I said. "He said something about not being able to stand that boy. I figured he meant his son since he'd said something like that before. I think he hates being alone and feels it's his son's duty to be there."

Pasquin cleared his throat. "And for sure he'll need somebody now. I got an acquaintance who's had them kinds of strokes. Can't stay by himself, no siree!"

Gil stared at Pasquin.

Chandler pulled up a chair and sat in front of us, or mostly in front of Gil. Clearly he wanted to intimidate the boy.

"How well do you know old man Ferguson?" he asked.

Gil shook his head some moments before getting the courage to answer. "I just met him when I did some work at his place. The other Mr. Ferguson hired me."

"To do what?"

"Same as at the Culley house. Clean the yard and some things in the house. I only did it to make some spending money." He gripped the chair beneath his heavy thighs.

"Do you ever do jobs for your own dad?" Pasquin asked.

Gil's head turned quickly toward him and back again to Chandler. "All the time, but he doesn't pay."

Pasquin chuckled quietly and nodded.

"What do you spend the money on?" I asked, knowing there wasn't much in the way of arcades around the lake area.

"I save it," he said. "Sometimes, I buy shoes or something I want, but mostly I save it."

"In an account?" Pasquin asked without looking at him.

Gil shook his head. "Just in a box in my room."

Chandler turned his head to hide a smile. Seeing the kid sweat was probably the only punishment he'd get for driving a truck without a license. Burl, on the other hand, would be in for a sermon and maybe a fine if he really had allowed Gil to drive the truck.

We sat, walked around, went to the restroom, and listened to families cry in torment over slashed faces and broken arms. Chandler went outside four times to make calls. After the fourth one he came back and nodded for me to follow him. We met at the side of where the automatic doors opened for stretchers.

"Vernon called. He's got some data. Like I said, those teeth belong to a Paulette Henderson. She disappeared from her home outside Clinton, New Jersey, over four years ago. The sheriff up there says she owned lots of land in the area. Most figured she had money, too, but her bank accounts were just about empty. And no one is going to be able to inherit until she's been declared dead."

"And when will that be?"

"Not for a while. They're doing all they can to track her, but have come up with nothing. Vernon used Public Records to find a Henderson who wears false teeth."

"So she may be in this area, or at least her teeth are. Have you tracked the dentist?"

"Sheriff in Jersey is doing that now."

I looked through the doors. Pasquin was waving his straw hat in my direction. Back inside, he told us we could see Ferguson for a short time. Chandler motioned for Gil to follow and the four of us entered a private room near the trauma area. The old man wasn't in ICU but he was close to it.

"You feeling better now?" Pasquin said as he leaned into Ferguson's face. He didn't have a breathing tube in his throat, but he did have the nasal oxygen tubes and an IV in his arm. Other hookups made lines on a monitor above the bed. A steady beep kept rhythm with his heart.

Ferguson's eyes moved to Pasquin's face. They rolled slightly as though he had little control over them. He gave a quick half-nod and squeezed them shut.

"Mr. Ferguson," I said. "We found you walking the lake road. Were you trying to get somewhere?"

Chandler put his hand on my arm and nodded toward the nurse that had entered the room.

"Your—your," said the voice that came from a drooling mouth. "Our place?"

He gave the quick nod again. "Keen house."

I looked toward Chandler, hoping he would step in and ask something. He shook his hand and motioned for me to keep talking.

"Your son, Burl, will be here soon," I said. I placed my hand on his arm.

"No good—no good!" He shook his head, causing the oxygen tubing to swipe back and forth across the sheets.

"Why no good?"

"Too much stuff," he said, the word "stuff" coming out with spittle. "Can't keep it."

"Stuff?"

He tried to nod, his eyes wide, not blinking. One still drooped and leaked.

Chandler, who had stayed in the background, moved toward the bed. "Mr. Ferguson, I've contacted someone who will notify your son that you're in here. Meanwhile, you need to rest. Is there anything you'd like the Sheriff's Department to know?"

Ferguson didn't answer. He didn't even look at Chandler. His gaze focused now, on the area just inside the door. His eyes went from a squint to wide open terror.

I turned around and followed his gaze. Gil Bono stood in frozen silence. He stared at the old man, and his young jowls continued to shake.

CHAPTER EIGHTEEN

Chandler followed us back to the Keen house. Gil rode with him and would be deposited into his parents' custody.

"Wonder what spooked old Ferguson?" said Pasquin. He had remained fairly silent after seeing the old man in his bed, attached to all sorts of tubing. It must have been too close a reminder of what people his age had to suffer.

"That kid scared him somehow," I said. "Don't you wonder, too, how come he's always here and there, but his parents aren't?"

Pasquin took long moments to answer. "Just where are the parents?"

"I don't know. They don't socialize, didn't even offer condolences to Tony about Miz Keen."

"Well, they just don't have the Southern tradition of neighborliness," he said.

"You mean people in New Jersey aren't neighborly?"

"Must not be," he smiled.

"I don't exactly think that's the case. The father has a record. So has the kid, if you count being expelled for passing beer around to his classmates. And the mother's violent."

Chandler passed us to turn into the Bono drive.

Pasquin headed for the kitchen to put on some coffee. I was restless. Something was going on with Ferguson and this kid, and I could make no sense of it. I wandered about Miz Keen's little house. The wicker furniture, the standard lamps and rugs, the prints on the wall—mostly of cats—even the table runners, all gave the impression of a comfortable but far from flamboyant home. I stared at a group of cats someone had painted in acrylics. "Where are all the cats?" I wondered aloud. Maybe they had been blown away by the storm. "And where is Burl's dog?" Before I could make a guess, I heard a knock at the door.

"Kid's parents are on their way. I told him to stay put." Chandler moved inside the cool of the house.

"Coffee?" Pasquin appeared with the pot and a carton of cream in the other hand.

We sat in the twilight, sipping and talking about the Bono family.

"Do dogs and cats disappear in hurricanes?" I asked.

"They can, but most try to find shelter. Why?"

"It's just that a lot of strays around this lake are no longer around. Nor is Burl's dog. The day we met him, he had the mutt in his truck."

Chandler shook his head, unable to offer an explanation. "Chalk it up to hungry gators?"

I shook my head. That was too simple.

Around dark, car lights headed past our door to the Bono place. Chandler was about to call a deputy to check on the kid when he saw them coming. He drove the few yards and parked behind them. I watched him talking to the couple when they got out of their car. Most likely it was a warning to keep their kid out of the driver's seat until he was old enough for a license. Minutes later, Chandler's lights headed away from the lake, their beams casting eerie colorless light on the reeds by the roadside.

Pasquin went to his room earlier than usual after we ate. I could see a light beneath the door and knew he was reading something, probably the newspaper. In my own room, I kept checking the Bono house. Lights were on in the kitchen and living room, and the Bono van sat in the driveway. Outside, the sky was clear and a full moon cast a light over the grass and water, almost like a street lamp. A gentle wind blew the reeds, bending the tops slightly and keeping up a faint hum. The lake remained silent, its female gator population impregnated and content.

The phone startled me from my uncomfortable quiet.

"I'm in Gainesville. Bono owns this warehouse himself. He stores his merchandise here, even comes to see it once in a while." Vernon sounded tired. He had spoken to Chandler and would stay another night in his seedy motel near the warehouse.

"He's paying you, right?"

"Somebody is. I'm still deputized to Chandler."

"Can you run a check on Mrs. Bono?" I explained why I asked. When he said he would, I mentioned the disappearing animals to him.

"That night," he began and hesitated. "When I checked out the open door to the Bono basement, I knew Gil had run after a dog. I heard the dog yelp, like it had been hurt."

"Do you think the kid hurt the dog?" Even though he hurt the cats, I found it strange. Most boys liked dogs.

"Did you see Ferguson's dog after that night?"

I had to admit I hadn't, and goose bumps raised on my arms.

Vernon clicked off, saying he still had to call Tony. I placed the phone on the hook, and slipped on my boots. The light still burned under Pasquin's door, but I could hear him snoring. I left by the back door.

Moving down the narrow foot path toward the Keen dock, I could hear the soft but urgent lapping of water against the shore. The wind blew toward the west, carrying the clouds out to sea.

The black lake water sparkled in places where moonlight was able to shine through cattails and lily pads. In the distance, I could see a faint white outline of Mildred's house, its paint reflecting the night light. Off in some trees beyond the Bono house, an owl took up its vigil for rats, hooting a mournful warning. Frogs, quiet at first, began their songs again as I stood still on the wooden dock. At times, it was almost deafening. But it didn't drown out the sudden yelling coming from the Bono back porch.

I couldn't make out the words, but the voices were both male. Was JoJo on his son's case for driving without a license? The answer to this felt like a no to me. I didn't think the man would care.

The door to the porch slammed hard. Gil turned on a dim light and moved around to the furniture storage area. He appeared again in the light with a bulging plastic trash bag. His feet hit the steps in anger. After reaching the lake shore, he turned and headed the other direction, swallowed up by darkness. I couldn't hear his footsteps from that far away, and he didn't return for nearly half an hour, I guessed. I left the dock and took the shore path in his direction. Before I got ten feet away from the Keen dock, I saw him coming back along the shore. He suddenly turned and ran up the embankment toward his house. His anger hadn't abated. The foot stomping and door slamming continued until he was inside the house.

I walked slowly beside the lake, using a small flashlight. Stepping on a gator wasn't the worst of my worries. I wanted to try and follow Gil's footprints. Stopping at the Bono landing, I listened for more angry voices, but the house was silent now. I moved on, tracing the deep and large-sized running shoe prints. They disappeared in the remote location just before the place where Mildred's body had ended up—the gator holding hole. The grass ran all the way to the water line here, but it was covered in mud as though someone had trudged through water and back again. I shined the light on the area, moving it among the cattails and lily pads. Nothing showed up but I could bet something was there. If the Bonos left home tomorrow, I planned to go for a swim.

On my walk back, I shined the light on anything that looked like a mound or clump. I was jumpy and not at all sleepy. Reaching the Keen house, I pulled my canoe from the garage and took it to the water. Trying not to make a sound, I shoved off toward the Bono landing. The water was too dark to see if Gil had dropped anything into the deep, and I didn't want to use a powerful light. I marked the spot in my mind.

Rowing not far from shore, I made my way toward the Culley house. No one else had the inclination to ride the lake tonight. I rounded the bend and headed for the Ferguson dock. To my surprise, someone had tied up a rowboat here. It rocked in the small wake of my oar as I passed it. It was nearly the same size as Mildred's boat. Not much room for more than one person really.

I grabbed the side of the boat and pulled my canoe closer. Inside, two oars rested on the bottom along with a small blanket, kind of like those used for babies. I reached over and grabbed one end, pulling it straight up. A thud hit the bottom of the boat. Shining my light closer, I saw the grimy fur of a cat, stiff and dead. The stomach appeared distended, dotted with full teats. The mouth was open in a sharp tooth silent howl. There was a gash from the skull to the throat.

I turned toward the lake and took a deep breath. How does one slash the life out of a furry, cuddly animal? "It would be no problem for someone shoots an old lady in the back," I whispered to the winds. I thrust the blanket back at the cat and rowed away quickly. Car lights were coming from the Ferguson house.

I moved to the darkness in the middle of the lake and waited.

Burl parked his car, moved to the boat and held it steady as he stood upright. I couldn't hear him, but I thought I could see his lips move. He had rested a large lamp on the dock. I guessed he was re-wrapping the cat. He finally stood up straight and held the blanket away from his chest. He seemed to be weighing it by moving it up and down. He moved to the end of the boat, held the blanket over the water and let it unwrap again. The cat's body hit the water. He wadded up the blanket and tossed it back into the boat.

I sat frozen in my canoe, daring not to make a sound. I had no idea Burl would pick up his flashlight and shine it around the lake. It was too late to duck. I may have been too far away, and it may have been my own case of nerves, but it seemed he slowed the light in my direction. At any rate he would know the canoe. As soon as the light moved on, so did I. I rowed toward the Keen house. Once there, I dragged the canoe back to the garage and covered it with a tarpaulin.

Inside, I took a deep breath.

"Where've you been?" said a voice out of the dark.

"Pasquin! You scared the hell out of me."

"You need to tell me you're heading outdoors. I just about took up a chair when I heard the back door open."

"It's that kid next door. He's been dumping in the lake."

We sat in the living room with only the light from the kitchen. It cast an eerie dimness across our faces. I told Pasquin what I saw and heard from the Bono house.

"You want to dive now?" he asked.

"I thought I'd wait until tomorrow morning."

"Kid or his parents might be hanging around all day."

I looked at the wise old man. "I'll be diving alone."

"You want me to wait on shore?"

I didn't answer him. The urge was too great, greater even than the rule of always diving with a buddy. I rationalized that I'd be fairly close to shore and in familiar waters. I left my chair and gathered my tank from the garage. Slipping into a bathing suit, I grabbed a face mask and head lamp. Dragging all this and my fins, I headed for the Keen landing. Pasquin followed with two flashlights, one a large police issue that Tony had left. He had picked up a wicker stool from the patio and placed it on the dock near the stairs.

"You think it's better to swim over there instead of just going into the water at the shore?" He leaned over to talk to me as I edged into the cool lake from the stairs.

"I don't want to attract attention and the lights might do that. As it is, anyone near the shore might spot this head lamp if I'm close to the surface." I saluted him and shoved away from the dock.

The water deepened a few feet into the lake. Without the lamp, I wouldn't see much of anything. I used it and a compass to head toward the dump area. It was night, and snakes and gators could be on the prowl, but I'd take my chances. With black water all around me, I followed my beam over the bottom grass that grew from the sometimes sandy areas and across the smooth flat mud in other spots. I wasn't too deep, maybe fifteen feet, in most places. Where it really dropped off, I could see no bottom at all, just a black abyss. I passed the Bono dock, its wooden posts standing like lonely sentinels in the dim light. Moving beyond that, I came to an incline in the lake bottom. It was sandy in most places here, and grassy. Small fish darted among the blades that waved with the movement of the water. Beyond, closer to shore, the grass grew thicker until cattails took over, and the depth wasn't enough for a swimmer, much less a diver. I figured it was about here that

Gil had waded part way into the lake and tossed the bag into the deeper area.

Swimming close to the bottom, I felt the water grow colder as I descended. Blackness surrounded me, but the narrow strip of white sand on the bottom stayed bright in my light. It didn't take long. Wedged on the side of the slope against some long grass blades sat a plastic garbage bag. My light cast eerie silver flashes across its blackness. Its edge at the opening waved a bit in the water and it appeared to slide as I swam toward it. It dislodged just as I grabbed it with both hands. It felt soft and hard at the same time but not too difficult to carry in the water. I headed back to the Keen dock, knowing that if I had waited until tomorrow, the bag would have been in the depths, out of sight and maybe out of reach.

"You're right, old man," I said as I lifted the tank off my shoulders. "Tonight was the best time." I removed the fins and lamp and joined him on the deck.

"So this is what he tossed into the water?" He stood looking down at the garbage bag that he had grabbed from my hands when I surfaced.

"It's what was in the water where he tossed something. I guess we can't say for sure it's the one he tossed, but I didn't see anything else down there." I took the large flashlight and lay it at the opening of the bag. "You ready for this?"

Pasquin pulled the stool closer to the bag and leaned over with his pocket knife to snip the cord that wound around the opening. With the tips of two fingers, I grasped part of the bag and lifted it. An odor, not quite foul but not pleasant, filled the night air.

"I don't like this," I said. "Wait here." I went to the house and brought back the old broomhandle that Miz Keen used to kill snakes.

I knelt on the dock a few feet away from the bag. Pasquin still sat over it. He had poked around with his foot.

"It's hard here and soft here," he said.

I lifted the opening with the stick, the flashlight still lying where it would illuminate the contents. The odor flew out and both of us covered our noses.

The stick hit the hardness of cement. The light shined against a common block, the kind you buy at any home improvement store.

"This is what kept it down," I said and shoved it to one side with the stick. I had to use both hands. The odor assaulted my senses.

"Dead animal," said Pasquin. "Black and been dead a little while, I'd say." He pointed to the neck area, getting past the open mouth where tongue and teeth exposed the throes the poor animal had when he died.

I shined the light closer. On top of the animal's head, a nasty gash made the black hair appear copper.

"He's either been hit or run over," I said. "Okay, I'm going to try and do this." I slipped my diving mask over my head and pulled it down across my nose, hoping it would act as an odor barrier. Holding one of my fins at the tip, I lifted the tag upward to the light Pasquin held in place.

"Ferguson," I said. "This is why we haven't seen Burl's dog around lately."

"Think the kid killed it?"

I remembered then the incident Vernon spoke of when he went into the open door of the Bono cellar. Gil had run after a dog, and Vernon had heard the animal cry.

"He may have. Wonder what Ferguson would say about the kid tossing it into the lake?"

"And weighting it down. Seems like if he just wanted to be rid of it, he'd leave it for the gators." Pasquin used his foot to shove the bag back over the animal.

"Those cats, Pasquin, the ones Wayne and I found on our first dive. Could Gil be responsible for them, too?"

"You're talking about an animal killer, Luanne. Never took kindly to kitten drowners or any other kind of killing. And a young kid like that…." He sat upright on the stool and shook his head.

We took all the ice from the refrigerator ice maker and dumped it over the bag with the dog, after placing it in a styrofoam cooler we found in the kitchen. Hoping it would stay cold until the sheriff could pick it up, we left it just inside the kitchen door where it would benefit from air conditioning. The smell was gone, at least in reality, but the lingering thought of it would stay with me the entire night.

I slept fitfully, rising often to gaze out the window at the Bono house. Close to dawn, a delivery truck pulled up the road and did its loading and unloading thing again. Mr. Bono, fully dressed, pointed orders to the men, while Mrs. Bono stood on the front steps in a bathrobe and viewed the operation. Gil was nowhere in sight.

CHAPTER NINETEEN

"You sure are a dare devil!" Chandler grinned at me after hearing the story of the dog in the bag and the cat off Ferguson's dock. "Tony said you'd do things no other woman would want to do."

"I didn't particularly want to do it," I said. "Just couldn't help myself."

"Went underwater at night," he chuckled. "You got nerve."

"Any sheriff's diver could have done it," I added, becoming a bit irritated with the emphasis on me.

"But you're a woman, and you did it." He laughed again. "Okay. Show me."

My inclination was to let Chandler get a big whiff of dead dog without warning, but Pasquin shot me a glance and spoke.

"You better cover your nose."

Chandler used the same snake stick to view Ferguson's dog. He held a paper towel to his face as he read the dog tag.

"We're going to have to question the kid, and I'll have to mention you," he said to me after shutting the styrofoam lid. "You ready for that?"

I stared at him and smiled a bit. He had just acted in male amazement that I'd swim underwater at night to fetch a dead dog and now he wondered if I could handle the wrath of a neighbor kid. I didn't answer him.

"Let's get this in the car," he said, avoiding my gaze now. Maybe he had caught on. Many men never did.

When Chandler slammed the trunk lid, he turned and stared down the lane. It appeared that someone thin and gray was walking toward the house. As the figure came closer, we both recognized Betty Stubbs. She wore dirty sweats, and her hair hung in strands over a haggard face.

"I seen the sheriff's car over here," she said, not venturing more than two feet toward the car. "I been out looking for my cat and her kittens. Ain't been born more than a few days."

I closed my eyes and saw the dead cat in the boat near Ferguson's dock. Its throat was slit, but the swollen teats were those of a female cat with young kittens.

"When did you notice it was gone?" Chandler placated the woman. He clearly saw her as a bruised child.

"Day before yesterday. I got home and they was gone. Kept them in a box on the back porch. I figured the mama cat got scared and hauled them off somewhere."

"Does your brother like cats?" I asked.

She gazed at me, the thought processes behind the eyes moving slowly. "He don't care one way or the other. Says they's my responsibility."

"We'll keep our eyes peeled, Betty," said Chandler. "You got a way to get home?"

"I'm walking all over today. Got to find my cat. She's yellow, kind of like Miz Keen's sign." She pointed toward the end of the lane, then turned and walked away.

We were still standing next to Chandler's car when a van pulled in the drive behind him.

"Vernon!" I said and silently cautioned myself not to dash forward and grab his sweet body.

"Early birds?" He grinned but his eyes were tired.

"Have you driven for hours?" I asked.

He nodded. "But I got stuff. And I'm glad you're here," he said to Chandler. "Won't have to drive to your office."

We sat at the cleared kitchen table. Pasquin made coffee and rested on his wicker stool near the counter. He wouldn't nose in to see the papers Vernon had, but he'd hear everything. No one asked him to leave. By now Vernon and Chandler knew the value of the man's wisdom.

"Bono owns the warehouse in Gainesville. He's got some others around the country, like Houston and Sacramento. He really does sell and ship furniture. Most of the orders are done online, but he sells out of the warehouses, too. Would be easy to sell other stuff—like drugs—in an operation like that, but I can't find anything that points to it." He turned to Chandler. "You need to get your computer techs on this to see if anything he's doing in the way of sales is illegal. Just on my surface scratching, I don't see any crime."

"The storage here at his house is a little strange," said Chandler.

"Yeah," added Vernon, "but things get a little stranger." He pulled out another set of papers, all of them with a fax address at the top. "These came into Tallahassee and they refaxed them to me." He read from the top one. "Paulette Henderson, age 88, disappeared two years ago. Her estate is still in limbo but has been placed in the hands of her only niece. The niece may be her heir, but we can't locate a will at this time. The estate, however, is worth about nothing as far as we can see. Miss Henderson, who never married, seems to have sold her home and spent most of the money on a retirement facility long before she vanished. She wasn't living in the facility at the time of her disappearance, but was still in the home she'd sold."

"Okay," I said when Vernon stopped to sip some strong coffee. "Who bought the place?"

He went to the second page. "Sheriff says a corporation. And, not only can't they find who owns the corporation, they can't find the retirement facility she bought into. Said they interviewed the niece once who appeared to know nothing about the sale or the facility. Said she seemed pretty agitated that nothing was left for her in the estate." Vernon sighed and poured more milk into his coffee. "Sheriff says the woman is gone, but he can't see that the niece had a motive to do away with her, so it's an open and cold case right now."

"Does he think the teeth we found belong to that particular Paulette Henderson?"

"Oh, yes. They tracked them to her dentist. They figure if the teeth were found, the body is buried somewhere. But the big deal comes next."

"Get on with it!" Pasquin's gravely voice sounded angry. "Old people abuse don't set too well with me."

Vernon gave him a deep nod. "The niece's name is Cara Henderson Bono."

The four of us sat in silence. The milk ran out, and Pasquin pulled out another carton from the refrigerator. Chandler stirred more sugar into his cup.

"So," I said, "the woman's teeth end up in her niece's neighbor's linen closet." I looked around the table. Pasquin stood behind Vernon now. "Anybody got any ideas how this happened?"

"State Police in New Jersey want to know that, too," said Vernon. He pulled out a full-page photo of Paulette Henderson, the white false teeth safely in place as she grinned for the camera. The gray hair had been permed and the makeup been applied a little too thick, but the resemblance to Cara Bono was there.

Chandler scraped his dining chair backward and frowned. "It's time, I think, to call in the entire Bono family for a chat." He leaned forward again and pulled out a small pad and pen. "Father has a questionable business; mother has a missing aunt with questionable financial dealings; and son has a penchant for tossing dead animals into the lake, weighted down like a mafia hit." He stood. "Don't anyone say anything to those characters next door. I'm going back to the department to arrange the interviews. In the meantime, let me know ASAP if anything happens next door."

He headed for the front door. I followed.

"Shouldn't we notify Tony?" I asked.

"I'll do that," he said, a sharpness in his voice. He hesitated before turning the handle and turned back to me. "You did a good job out there, Luanne. Lived up to your reputation." He smiled.

Back at the table, Vernon gripped my hand and squeezed it. "Tony knows it already. He read this stuff when it came off the fax in Tallahassee."

"Yeah, I figured that. But he won't know they're going to interview the Bono family." I sighed and sat down. Pasquin had taken Chandler's chair. "Wish I could be there." We all laughed.

By the time we finished the strong coffee diluted with milk, I had filled Vernon in on my night dive and the cat at the Ferguson dock as well as the morning visit from Betty Stubbs. He nodded and commented until his eyes began to close.

"You must have been staking out that warehouse," I said and squeezed his arm. Pasquin saw the gesture and his lips twitched.

"Whatever gave you that idea?" Vernon said. "I need a nap. Anyone mind?"

I pointed to the Keen bedroom. "Before you go, any word from the lab on that notebook I found in the water?"

"They have it by now. Remind me, and we'll call Marshall when I wake up. Too groggy right now."

"I can't sit here," I said to Pasquin. "You game to pay Burl Ferguson a visit?"

"Man ought to be at the hospital with his daddy," said Pasquin as he put his straw hat on his white head and waited for me at the door.

I left Vernon a note before we got into the Honda and headed down the lake road. A morning breeze had kicked up and the cattails were swaying and singing. Among their soft brown tops, hidden below the stalks, all sorts of danger swam, crawled, and sat perfectly still. The beautiful white egret, its long legs stretching like a ballerina's through the reeds, searched for frogs and snakes. The alligator, with only its eyes and bumpy back hide showing above water, lay in wait for the egret. However beautiful the scene, here was direct proof of Darwin's survival of the fittest.

Maybe Burl should have been at the hospital with his daddy, and for all we knew, he was. He certainly wasn't at his house—or better said, his daddy's house.

"The door is open," said Pasquin. He pushed it with his toe. "Wasn't even latched." Pasquin leaned into the living room and looked around, waving his straw hat as though clearing the air. "Stuffy in here." He stepped inside. I followed him.

"You know," he said, nodding to himself, "I bet he came out this door that day we found him on the road, without shutting the door, and nobody's been around to check it since."

"If that's true, then where is Burl?" My voice seemed to carry in the big living room in spite of the heavy furniture that sat in silence.

"You got your phone? Maybe you ought to call Chandler and have him look around. Man could be hurt somewhere." Pasquin moved slowly to the hall and kitchen doors. He looked around both and came back shaking his head. "Old Ferguson was cursing some boy. Think it could be his son?"

"We've heard him do it before. He resented his son going off for those years. Seems he thinks the boy should take care of him." I hesitated. "But I remember that moment at the hospital when Gil stood in the doorway. I don't know why, but it sure looked like Ferguson was scared of him." I took out my phone and pulled Pasquin after me to the porch.

Chandler sent two deputies to the house in less than ten minutes. Both put on gloves and kept their guns handy. I told them Pasquin and I had found the door open and no one was answering.

We waited outside, sitting in the dilapidated chairs on the porch while the deputies went in search of robbers, dead bodies, or nothing.

"Guess somebody just left the house and didn't close the door," one said as he joined us on the porch. He pulled off the gloves. "Didn't find a thing."

"Has anyone located Burl Ferguson? His father's in the hospital," I said.

The deputy nodded and pulled out his phone. After a call to headquarters, he shrugged and said, "He's still in Tampa. Says he's been in contact with the doctors and it's not so urgent he has to drop what he's doing there."

"What is he doing there?" asked Pasquin. He batted at gnats that threatened to get into his white hair.

The deputy shrugged again, but said nothing. He closed the door and left a note to tell the Fergusons they had been there.

"Let's go into town," I said. "We could do with some supplies."

Pasquin just looked at me and smiled. "Maybe visit the hospital?"

We rode past Old Hill's. Large delivery trucks were pulling into its back entrance, most likely unloading some modern soul's inherited furniture. It would sell, either at auction or on the floor, for enough to outfit an apartment in steel and glass.

Passing a mini-mall, we came to a light that stopped us right in front of a separate structure, a cottage-like building that called itself "Quinne's Jewelers."

"Quinne," I said. "Isn't that the name of the woman who visits Burl's bar?"

"Rosie Quinne," Pasquin said. "Think she owns this?"

"Or comes from the family who does."

We drove through town, its shopfronts looking either dilapidated or quaint. It had all given over to fancy malls on the outskirts or to mini-malls that dotted the intersections. By the time we had left the city limits again, we had seen two more Quinne's Jewelers.

"Selling diamonds must be lucrative right now," said Pasquin. "Lucrative anytime, I suppose. Never understood what people wanted with them. Look just like shiny glass."

"Yeah," I said, "cost about the same, too." I forgot my sarcasm for a moment when it hit me that Rosie Quinne could be quite wealthy, and maybe that made her attractive to someone like Burl.

"Mind if we go back and visit one of these stores?" I watched Pasquin grin and nod like he knew I was going to ask that.

We reached the closest mini-mall with a Quinne's at a time that didn't seem too busy. The outside wasn't the usual boxy utilitarian structure, but an update of the Mediterranean look complete with an arched door and picture window. Inside was all thick carpet and glass cases, some with lights that made the jewels shine even brighter. A man, looking very much like Hobbs from Old Hill's, greeted us. He wore a shiny diamond and gold ring that threatened to break his pinkie.

"We just came to look," I said and at once spied a photograph of a younger Rosie on the wall behind the register. "Oh, is that Rosie Quinne?"

"Sure is," he said, his face beaming. "She owns the stores. Inherited them from her husband's family."

"Yeah, I met her at a restaurant once." I swallowed hard to make Burl's place a restaurant.

"Lovely lady. She drops in now and then but pretty much leaves the running of the place to us." The man looked up nervously as two young men dressed in low-cut pants walked in.

I pretended to walk with Pasquin and look at a few watches until I saw the teens weren't going to pull guns. They were actually looking at wedding bands. One of them planned on getting married in a month.

"Think that kid will have to pay on time?" said Pasquin as we walked back to the car.

"Probably got more money than you or me," I said.

"Kind of like that Burl, huh?"

I thought about what Pasquin had said on the ride to the hospital. Burl knew how to dress, or at least he made some attempt to do it with local class. The colorful shirts and cowboy boots gave him that macho status, but the clean, pressed jeans would appeal to women, especially women of a certain age. I shook my head and scolded myself for falling back on stereotypes.

At the hospital, things had improved. Mr. Ferguson lay back on his pillow without oxygen and dipped ice cream from a cup. Color had reappeared in his face.

"Well!" he said as we approached, his toothless mouth grinning widely.

"We worried about you," I said in my most feminine care voice. "Looks like the nurses got you straightened out."

"Yeah. And I ain't had no stroke." He smiled even wider, the vanilla cream dripping from his top gum. "Just some kind of reaction to the sun and not eating properly."

"Why were you not eating?" Pasquin asked.

"Damn kid wouldn't feed me, and we ran out of groceries. I don't know where he'd got off to, but I had to get something. Decided to walk."

"Walk? That's a far way," I said.

"Couldn't sit there and starve, could I?" He swiped the last of the ice cream and handed the cup to Pasquin who tossed it in the trash.

"What kid are you talking about?"

"My son, who else?"

"He's in Tampa, I understand. Surely he would have left you food if he knew he was going to be away."

"Missy, that kid ain't been responsible for years now. Stayed away most of the past twenty years. He said he left money with that Bono kid to get some groceries for me, but the kid most likely didn't use it for that." A storm cloud hit his face, and the paleness returned.

"You got to take it easy," said Pasquin. "Too much anger and you will get a stroke."

"Damn kid—Bono kid—thinks he can march right in my house when he pleases. You know what he did one night? Just came inside and caught me in the bathroom buck naked. I was getting out of the shower. Nearly had a heart attack."

"He came in the house," I asked, "and went to the bathroom?"

"Yeah, said he needed to use it. I got so mad I told him to go find a bush outside. Wouldn't let him unzip his britches in my house."

"Funny," I added, "I thought most men would find a bush if they were outside like that."

Ferguson looked at me, his eyes flashing inside an ancient face. He nodded slowly. "Made me wonder what he really wanted."

"You got something a kid would want to steal?" Pasquin asked.

"Not me, but Burl's always had a collection of expensive stuff he says he got on his travels."

"Is it there now?" The open door set off an alarm in my head.

"No. Burl moved all that stuff a while back. Said he sold some, put the other on display at the bar." He let his head drop back on the pillow, clearly tired from all the talk. He hadn't had a major stroke but the experience left him exhausted.

We said goodbye and headed for a local grocery store. Outside, the sky was black and clear.

"You know, ma'am, I don't recall seeing any nice stuff in that bar," said Pasquin as he eased inside the car.

"It sure isn't displayed there. Maybe it's in the storage area."

The grocery store was a big all-night affair. We stocked enough for several people for at least a week. I phoned the house but got the answering machine Tony had hooked up. When I dialed Vernon's cell, I got the recorded voice there, too. Leaving a message for him to call me, I drove to the Keen house.

Vernon's car was in the driveway. My skin prickled with anxiety. I told Pasquin to wait in the car while I went inside. The house was dark except for the two night lights that came on with dusk. I made a quick glance of the kitchen and living room, and with a deep breath of dread eased toward the bedroom. I leaned against the door jamb and looked at the bed. Tousled, but empty.

I walked around the other side and saw nothing on the floor. My eyes riveted to the bathroom where the door was half closed. Stepping quietly, I held on until I was sure the place was empty. Breathing easier, I searched Pasquin's room and the rest of the house, closets and all.

"Vernon must be outside somewhere," I said. I shined a penlight into his car and saw no one.

"The garage?" Pasquin asked as he eased out of the car.

"I checked that. Nobody there…" And then I remembered something missing. "The canoe! He's got my canoe out on the lake, I'll bet."

I left Pasquin with the grocery sorting and headed to the Keen landing. It was too dark to see a boat unless it had a light or was close by. The dark water lapped against the marsh grasses. I listened for heavier laps to signal the approach of a boat but none came. In the distance, the whiteness of Mildred's house was barely discernible. The Bono house wasn't any better. All windows were dark, and no cars or delivery trucks sat in the drive. It was like the world had deserted Lizard Lake—at least the human world.

I sat on the hard boards of the landing, using a post to support my back. Taking out my phone, I called Vernon's number again and got the same leave-a-message voice. For at least ten minutes, I sat with my stomach churning. Something was happening, and I hated being ignorant of what it could be. Silence surrounded me, an alarm in any swampy place. I looked up but saw nothing. Could the frogs have sensed my presence and kept quiet? I doubted that. Frogs pretty much croaked again after the first alarm of someone in their midst. Something had to be disturbing them.

I nearly fell into the lake when my cell phone rang.

"It's Vernon," he whispered. "Just listen. I'm at the Culley dock.

Rowed over here in your canoe. That Bono kid has been walking around the lake. I saw him peek into the Keen patio like he was looking for something then move close to the water. He's got a bag of some sort."

"You want me to call Chandler?" I whispered back.

"If you do, tell him to come quietly. If the kid is stealing stuff, we need to catch him in the act."

I returned to the house, called and explained the situation to Chandler. Pasquin stood in the kitchen doorway and watched me pull my pistol from my bag and head outdoors.

"Will you be all right here?" I asked.

His old hands clutched a butcher knife and held it up in front of his face.

"You gonna be all right outside?" he said.

I tapped his knife with my gun, nodded and headed to the lake side.

I carried a large flashlight in one hand but didn't turn it on in case it gave me away. It wasn't going to be easy, and maybe not safe, making the journey in the dark. But reptiles weren't my worry. The frogs still weren't singing, and I heard no splashes of alligators grabbing ducks. Instead, something like a fullback tackled my legs and sent me sprawling into the wet reeds.

CHAPTER TWENTY

Lifting my face from the slimy, knotty roots of marsh plants, I heard a gravely voice shout, "Hey, you! Get away from her."

Through the water that dripped across my eyes, I watched Pasquin's old legs carry him with haste down to the water's edge. His butcher knife swung in the air. Half-raised on my forearms, something slapped me in the back and knocked the air from my lungs. I hit the water again but managed to roll over. Legs went splashing away, making sucking sounds in the mud. In a flash, I thought it couldn't be Gil, not clunky enough. And the smell. It wasn't just murky water and rotting swamp material. The face had been close enough for me to smell breath.

"Lordy, ma'am! Are you all right?" Pasquin stood in grass and mud above me. His face kept moving, looking about for the attacker.

"What happened?" I found myself sitting in the marsh mess and hoping I didn't have any critter seatmates.

"I was watching from the porch and saw you move off the landing and go into the shadows. Then this figure, kind of tall and slim follows you. Knew he weren't up to no good so I took the knife and came down here. Just in time, too. Knocked you right in the back."

"Yeah," I pushed myself to my knees and felt my head spin for a moment. When the dizziness passed, I stood. "Which way did he go?"

"Kept running that way," he said, pointing to the same direction I had been moving.

"He'll reach the Ferguson landing if he keeps in that pattern." My phone rang, remarkably saved from a soaking by the denim pocket of my jeans.

"I heard a yell," whispered Vernon. "What's going on over there?"

I explained quickly.

"It's not the kid. He's sneaking around the Culley house. Just go back inside for now and call Chandler's office again. Something's not right out here tonight."

After groping about in the mud for my gun and flashlight, I did as he said, feeling vulnerable and perplexed. I made the call and cleaned up while Pasquin poured coffee.

"What was he after?" I asked. "Did he know I was going to walk to the Culley house?"

"Could have been something more basic," said Pasquin. He had found a way to make one of the upright wicker chairs rock on its legs. The click clack sounds weren't reminders of nights on my front porch back at Fogarty Spring, more like expressions of an agitated anger.

"A rapist?" It wasn't a thought I'd harbored, not in an atmosphere of old lady murders. I put it aside. The man wanted something else. He hadn't been particularly vicious, only powerful, and as far as I knew he had no weapon. He ran fast when an octogenarian took after him with a butcher knife.

We sipped coffee and waited in the dark living room. When I could sit still no longer I moved to the kitchen and peered into more darkness outside. I thought I saw a movement in the distance, something large like a car, and knew a deputy had arrived to help Vernon. About the same time, I heard the soft click of a car door closing in front of the Keen house.

A tap on the door was followed by a male voice identifying himself as a deputy.

"Chandler and another deputy went to the Culley house. They sent me here. I got my dog Gertie in the car."

Gertie turned out to be a top-notch K-9 whose specialty was looking for "goons in swamp water" as the deputy put it. I showed him where the man knocked me down, and he ordered me back inside. We watched as he and big black Gertie took off around the lake.

There's something about waiting that is nearly unbearable. Humans are meant to act, not glue themselves to old wicker and stare at each other through shadows. The adrenaline alert is still there, causing every creak in old boards, every gush of a slight breeze, to pull up visions of monsters in the night. Thus, when the house phone rang, both Pasquin and I were on our feet.

"Tony, here. I'm about twenty miles away. Got a leave at the last minute." He sounded upbeat, not at all expecting what was happening at the moment.

I explained the situation and asked him to go sit in Ferguson's bar until I called him back. We didn't need car lights coming down the road right now. He agreed, but doing what I said must have hit a sore spot. He grunted as he turned off his phone.

Gertie and the deputy didn't take long. We heard the "stay" command on the patio and met the deputy at the door.

"Tracked somebody to the road. Probably got into a waiting car. Gertie couldn't pick up any other scents." The deputy leaned over and rubbed the dog's head. The dog wagged her tail once or twice. Anyone seeing her reaction would never know she would take up the bird stance for a human being lying in wait.

"I'll need some information from you," said the deputy and came inside to the dining table. Gertie lowered herself to the floor and kept an eye on her master.

"I smelled something when he got close," I said, trying to call up a description of the strong odor. "It wasn't unpleasant exactly. Kind of mintie or a heavy mouthwash smell. Medicine perhaps."

"Any reason for someone to attack you like that?"

"I suppose there are several at this point. If you're aware of the investigation going on here, you'll know I'm in the thick of it."

The deputy looked up from his note pad. "Not your garden variety rapist, then."

The blood flowed straight to my face and had he not looked back at his pad, he would have seen my anger. Instead, he heard it in the iciest voice I could muster.

"I suppose a rape victim isn't hurt as bad by the garden variety?"

He looked away sheepishly. "Sorry, ma'am. Habits, you know."

I let the room rest in silence. Pasquin didn't move. He still held the butcher knife across his lap.

When my cell phone rang again, Vernon talked in a full voice. "I'm heading back in the canoe. They caught the kid upstairs in the old lady's bed. He was eating potato chips and drinking beer, listening to rock music on a headset. He'll be charged with breaking and entering, but as far as they can tell, he didn't steal anything."

"What was in the bag he carried?" I asked.

"He says the chips and beer. He's under age so he'll probably get some charge on that, too."

As soon as I finished with Vernon, I called Tony's cell phone.

"This is a dark, dreary bar, you know. Lost souls sitting around

crying in their liquor. How does the man make a living here?"
Tony had found a nearly deserted bar when he pulled in to wait
out the commotion at his aunt's lake. "I even went to the fireplace
to see if the rattlesnake was still there—it is."

"Are there any cars parked around back?" I asked.

"Haven't looked." He hesitated, curious but unsure of following more orders from a female. "I'll look before I leave."

I told him to come to the house and we'd all get filled in on the
night's events.

The little living room was crowded with Vernon, Tony, Pasquin,
the K-9 deputy and Gertie. I sat on top of a wicker end table.

"The kid may be just nosy and have nothing much else to do,"
said Vernon. "But he's someone to watch, someone who can be
used by adults."

"He's not responsible for anything, including any jobs he takes.
Near 'bout let old man Ferguson starve to death. And goes about
walking right into houses, big as you please." Pasquin shook his
head in disapproval. "Kid needs a whopping with a tree branch
and lots of work to tire him out." He fell back on the expressions
of old ancestors, generations of child disciplinarians.

"And Burl, has anyone heard from him?" asked Vernon.

We all just looked at each other. I started to relate the story of
his being in Tampa when lights flashed from a car in the driveway.

Chandler stood at the front door; a tall, thin man stood behind him.

"We came to get some stuff straightened out," he said and
moved into the crowded room. He stood aside and let the man
follow him inside. "This is Mr. Oscar Valentine, or shall I say
Sergeant Valentine of the New Jersey State Police. He's down
here on undercover work—which he blew tonight when he decided to knock Miss Luanne into the mud."

I stood and moved close to the man, holding out my hand so he had to grasp it in a handshake. He half-bowed in embarrassment and said, "ma'am."

"That's him all right," I said. "What kind of mint do you use?" I still held his hand.

He blushed and pulled out a small mouthwash squirt bottle.

"If you plan to work undercover, you'd better leave off that stuff," said Pasquin.

Valentine began to stutter then apologize. "I had to stop you from going around the lake and didn't want to identify myself."

I glanced toward the K-9 deputy. "At least you weren't a garden variety rapist."

The deputy gave me a brief guilty glance. Gertie was fidgeting and trying to take a stance, the odor of her prey keeping her in an agitated state. The deputy finally gave her a command, and she followed him to his car. Valentine moved aside to give her wide berth as she headed outside.

"We're all here, so let's do a briefing," said Chandler. He brought two chairs from the dining room. When he and Oscar sat down, he turned to the man and nodded.

"I'm part of a team doing an investigation on elderly fraud, and maybe even worse, in Jersey." Valentine spoke stiffly, like an overgrown student who had been caught in the teacher's grade book and had to explain why. "Paulette Henderson lived in our area. She went missing, and her bank account was empty. We questioned her relatives, the only ones being those living next door to you." He pointed toward the Bono house. "Couldn't find a thing. Whatever the Bono woman inherited, she can't do anything with it until the old lady is declared dead." He cleared his voice. "When Chandler put out the info on finding her teeth, we thought it might be the break we needed. I've been down here about a week now, undercover."

"So why did you see the need to attack Luanne?" Pasquin's old voice commanded an answer.

"It wasn't an attack so much as a way to keep her quiet for a moment. I was going to hold her down and explain who I was, but when I saw the knife waving at me, I took off." He nodded in Pasquin's direction.

"Why did I need to be kept quiet?" I asked.

"I saw the man get into the canoe and head across the lake." He nodded toward Vernon. "I had seen the kid, too, and planned to follow him, when the father came out of the house and pushed off in a small boat. He rowed, never started the motor. He was skirting the shoreline with a flashlight, like he was looking for something in the reeds or just below the surface. He must have heard something because he turned out the light and let the boat drift. That's when I saw you come to the dock and take off through the marshy area. You were just a few feet away from him."

"I never saw anyone," I said, feeling the hair rise on my neck.

"I know that. I'm sure he saw you, but I'm not sure what he may have done if he realized you saw him. That's when I decided to step in. May have been a mistake." He shrugged.

Everyone sat in silence, each thinking what could have happened. Would Bono pull a gun or be scared off?

"What is it you think happened to Miss Henderson?" I asked.

Valentine shook his head. "We have to go on the assumption that the Bono family murdered her. Maybe they didn't. We've checked all the homes from assisted living to nursing centers down here. I've sniffed around their house enough to know she's not living with them. And the bank account money is really strange."

"Did she have any money prior to disappearing?" asked Vernon.

"Plenty, but she took it out in cashier's checks. Said she was going into a nice home for the elderly. Both she and the money are gone now. The Bonos say they don't know where she is."

"Funny both the Bono family and her teeth should show up here," said Pasquin. Underneath the gentle appearance, his eyes raged.

"That's what we thought, and I'm sure there is a connection," said Valentine. He sighed. "Just don't know what it is yet."

"There is a similar case here," I said, looking toward Chandler to get the okay. He nodded. "A lady sold her place, took out her money to invest in a retirement home, then took a fall in her shower."

Valentine nodded. "I know about Nell Culley. Heard it from a bank clerk yesterday."

"Well, ladies and gentlemen," said Chandler, "I think it's time we all cooperated here. We got the kid locked up in Juvenile Hall, waiting to pull in his parents, but we need to do some questioning, big time." He stood. "We'll call when this is set up and wait for you all to get there." He said goodnight and motioned for Valentine to follow him. Their car lights moved about in the dark like two swamp monster eyes until they faded into the distant reeds.

"I wonder," said Tony who had remained silent during most of the conversation until now, "where Bono, the father, is right now."

"Let's go," said Vernon who stood and nodded for Tony to follow him. "We need to go right up to the door and see if he's home."

"Wouldn't they have been notified when their son was arrested?" I asked, following the two men up the incline to the Bono house. Pasquin stayed behind, watching the events from the side of the house.

"Chandler tried to call them, left a message on a machine here at the house, " said Vernon. He touched the gun at his waist but didn't draw it. He nodded for Tony to head for the back door. "Luanne, you hide somewhere near the door to the storage area on the other side of the house. If anyone comes out, yell but don't approach them."

"Not even Lady Bono?"

Vernon didn't answer. He approached the front door as I skirted around the side. I planted myself behind some reeds, hoping the water moccasins had better plans for the evening. The door to the makeshift cellar was shut tight, or so it seemed from the distance. A sensor light came on when I moved around the corner of the house and lit up the area like a small football field.

The critters of the night grew silent when Vernon rapped on the front door. When no one came, he rapped harder. Tony stood at the bottom of the steps leading down from the back porch, his hand on his gun. A sensor light had come on there, too. It gave both of us a view of the entire back yard and the area leading to the lake.

Nothing happened and all remained dark for a long time, or at least what seemed like an eon. I edged out of mud, sucking sounds filling the night, twice before I met Tony in the yard. Vernon came around the side and we stood in the glare of the light.

"Something is way over there," said Vernon, pointing toward the Ferguson landing. "I saw car lights from the top of the incline."

The three of us waited, frozen until there was movement or sound. We couldn't see car lights, but suddenly a light came on the front of a small boat. Whoever drove, turned on the motor and headed straight for the Bono landing. Our cover was blown by the sensor lights. Vernon said we should simply wait on the dock and give Bono—if indeed it was Bono—the news about his son.

It was Cara Bono and a lot of boxes. She stared up at us from where she tied up, her chubby body dressed in black sweats. She had barely enough room to steer the boat.

"Is something wrong?" she said without trying to move out of her cramped seat.

"What is all this?" Tony asked.

"Oh, some supplies for our business," she said. "Why are you here?"

Vernon explained about her son.

Instead of a parent's panic, Cara Bono breathed deeply and shook her head. "It's just so tempting sometimes to say keep him and do what you will with him." She looked up from the boat again. "It's just too hard being a parent." Her eyes saddened on cue from a wrinkled brow.

"Where is your husband?" asked Pasquin who had walked over from the Keen house.

"He's back there with a broken-down truck," she said, a bit of anger seeping through the pathos. "I've told him so many times to get that thing replaced but he won't. We had tied up at the Ferguson dock and figured I could bring over these boxes while he waited for the auto club." She looked at the two men again, then sighed. "I'll wait until he gets here to get these into storage."

"Oh, no, don't do that," said Vernon. "The dampness will seep through the cardboard if you leave them out here too long. We'll help you." He moved immediately to hold one end of the boat steady and offered her a hand to the ladder.

"Really, I can wait for him." She hesitated, confused and rattled.

"Mrs. Bono, your husband may wait for hours for the auto club and your son isn't here. Now, give me your hand."

The woman moved but kept an eye on Vernon.

"Some of the stuff is breakable," she said. "My husband knows which and would better be able to move them."

"We're used to breakables," said Tony as he got into the boat and shoved it closer to shore with an oar. Vernon pulled it so they could unload the boxes from dry ground. "Just tell us where to take them."

"They have to be sorted. Better just stack them on the back porch." Mrs. Bono headed up the bank. She put out her hands in some invisible effort to keep the boxes from falling.

"Not a good idea," said Vernon. "It's damp there, too. Any room inside?" He winked at me as I watched from the bank. Pasquin had taken a seat on the dock.

"But, oh, no, there isn't any room. Ordinarily we'd stow them in the area under the porch but it's pretty full now." She looked around quickly as though trying to conjure up an empty room. "I think they'll be okay on the porch. I've got a tarp I can put over them." She had found her solution and smiled at her thought. Darting around the side of the house, she met Vernon and Tony at the back porch steps with a large blue tarp. "Just stack them against the wall."

Cara Bono trotted up and down the bank with the men for the first three boxes. On the fourth, Vernon stood behind me and quickly whispered in my ear, "Keep her down here."

"Mrs. Bono," I said, looking about for an excuse. "It looks as though one of the boxes is stuck up against the motor. Maybe you better go on board and move it. If the motor is hot, it could burn the box." I had no idea if this could happen, but it sounded like a legitimate worry. She took the bait and moved back into the boat.

"It's not against anything," she said. It had taken her several minutes to get her balance and move to the motor end. It would take her the same amount of time to come back. "I don't know what you're talking about."

"Must have been an optical illusion," I said. "This light doesn't make things too clear." I held the boat while she wobbled back to the shore end. "Sure is a lot of trouble to go through for a business venture. Hope you're making a profit."

"What do you mean *venture*?" she asked as she stepped on dry ground. "It's a legitimate business. Lots of people sell on the internet."

"What's the word, then?"

"Venture sounds so flighty." She trudged up the incline only to meet Vernon coming back for the next box.

"You got a few dents in some boxes already," he said. "Probably happened in the move from truck to boat."

Cara Bono looked worried but didn't reply. Again, she followed them up and back without saying anything but watching closely.

Pasquin seemed amused at the goings on until it bored him into fanning with his straw hat. He stood and walked to the end of the dock, gazing off into the direction of the Ferguson landing. At one point, when the other three were on the porch, he turned to me and said, "Ain't no lights coming from there. Not from a broke down truck or a tow truck. Don't see a thing. Nothing." He fanned until his thin white hair blew up at each stroke.

CHAPTER TWENTY-ONE

"Ma'am," said Vernon when he and Tony had finished carrying the boxes to the porch. "Don't you think you'd better call the sheriff and check in about your son?"

Cara Bono sighed again at the mention of her child. "I suppose so. Do you have the number?"

"I'll come with you if you like."

"No! Please, you've done enough. Just help me place the tarp over these boxes and I'll make the call." Vernon and Tony moved the tarp alone. She nodded and thanked them again but did not go inside until all four of us had crossed the property boundary.

"She's not telling the truth, you know," said Pasquin as he resumed his position in a wicker chair. He slammed his hat on the end table. "Bet that husband ain't nowhere around the Ferguson dock by now."

"She is nervous," said Tony. He smiled at Vernon.

"Those boxes have some sort of machine inside," said Vernon. "I made all that up about dents. Gave me the excuse to shove back a corner of one. I couldn't make it out but it sort of looked like a kid's pinball machine, or maybe a Vegas slot. I guess they sell those things on the internet."

"Funny way to get them to storage," I said. "Why not just rent a small warehouse and have delivery trucks take them there?"

Tony and Vernon stared at me for a moment. Neither had the

answer, but we all suspected illegal gambling.

The sound of tires on dirt road and car lights briefly came our way. I went to the window in time to see Cara Bono driving down the hill in her small car.

"Must be going to bail out her kid?"

"Could be," said Vernon, joining me at the window. "Care to take a ride?"

Tony and Pasquin stayed in the house. Too many things had happened in one night for everyone to leave the premises. Vernon and I piled into his van and followed Mrs. Bono at a distance. She headed straight for the Ferguson place.

"No broken down truck on this road," said Vernon as he made the turn into the drive. He had switched off his headlights. "We'll have to try and go beyond the yard and park near a big oak." He edged the van down the road and found a place to stop the engine. Breathing relief, we sat in the humidity and watched lights come on inside the old house.

"There's a truck around the side of the house," said Vernon. It was hidden in the shadows but if you stared long enough you could see the outline. "It's right at the edge of the porch, or at least the bed is. Great place to unload stuff."

"Or load it," I said.

Inside, the living room light clicked off and only the kitchen glowed. If Bono was there, his wife would be telling him about the boxes—and about their son, one would hope. I suggested one of us sneak around the side and see what was happening, but before I could move, the front door opened.

"We'll pick him up tomorrow. Take your car and go home. I'll be at the club." Bono went down the stairs first and looked back at his wife. "And lock that door."

Cara got into her car and backed around until she could head out. Her husband revved his truck as he waited his turn to move away.

"Lovely parents," I said as I stood. "Wonder what Chandler thinks of leaving the kid all night in Juvie?"

"From the looks of things, it's the best place for him." Vernon started the car and we headed back to the Keen house. "And I'll bet those boxes were stowed right here in the Ferguson house."

At the road around the lake, Mrs. Bono turned left towards her house, but her husband turned the other way, towards the Culley house. Vernon followed him. Instead of staying on the lake road, Bono turned onto the lane to the main highway. He drove for several miles along the deserted and dark road until he came to the outskirts of Ocala, the place where shoddy stores and gas stations began to dot the swampy landscape.

"He's heading right for Ferguson's bar," I said. "Want to take bets he'll pull in there?"

Vernon didn't answer but concentrated on keeping a distance. When the Fireside Bar sign came into view, sure enough, Bono slowed and turned into the drive. He didn't stop at the front entrance but drove to the grove of trees behind the storage area. Vernon continued on the road until he found an old drive that pulled into a closed field gate. The farmer who owned the land had long since given up using it to get to his house.

"Did you see how many cars were parked in that grove?" asked Vernon.

"Lots. And it's not the first time." I looked at him and we both knew something had to be happening there.

"I'm letting Chandler in on this," Vernon said. "We can sit in the bar if it's still open but I'm not barging into the back room."

I sighed. "Glad to hear that, my sweet. I have no desire to confront rattlesnakes—real or human."

Chandler agreed to meet us on the small road and, within twenty minutes, an unmarked car pulled up behind us. Valentine was with him.

"I see what you mean," said Chandler. He leaned over the window and gave me a nod. "Too many cars behind the bar. But we've got no reports of anything illegal back there. If Bono is keeping stuff in storage there, so what? Nothing says Ferguson can't do a favor for a friend, or rent the space to him for that matter."

"Why does he guard it with a live rattlesnake?" I asked.

"He does?" Valentine's face paled. "You mean it crawls about?"

"It's in a fireplace," I said. "You go near that back area, and the thing starts rattling like a flamenco dancer. It's a big diamond back with a slew of rattles."

Valentine looked at Chandler like a deer in headlights.

"Don't worry, man. We'll shoot it if it gets out." Chandler grinned at this Yankee fear of snakes.

"No, no, I'm not worried about killing the thing. It's the snake part." He hesitated before relating the rest of the Paulette Henderson story. "When we searched her house, we found a cage out back. Had a big rattlesnake in it. Now you don't see that in Jersey very often. And her neighbors were sure she never kept pets like that."

"Some pet!" said Chandler.

"It had to belong to someone else," Valentine continued. "We called animal control to pick it up, but when they got there, it was gone. Long gone. So was her little puppy. We figured she took them with her, if she left on her own."

"Oh, come on!" I said. "A little old lady with a puppy and a rattlesnake in a cage. What kind of scene is that?"

"Most likely the snake bit the pup, and somebody killed the

snake. May have bit the woman, too," said Vernon.

"Yeah," I said, "and the snake crawled all the way down here with her false teeth."

"Doesn't make sense," said Chandler. "Look, I can go in there and say I spotted Bono's truck and I needed to tell him about his son."

We agreed to wait on the hidden drive while he parked in back of the bar. Valentine pulled out his fancy field glasses from the valise he kept with him and aimed them at the grove.

"You can see things in this dark?" I asked.

"Night vision. I can just make out Chandler at the door. Someone has come to the door and is talking to him."

"Any lights shining behind the person?" asked Vernon.

"Nope. Total darkness. Chandler has tipped his hat and is leaving. Man is closing the door." Valentine dropped the glasses to his side and returned to lean against the car. "We need to get inside that place."

"Snake or no snake?" I tried to lighten the moment but the man's sense of humor had disappeared if he'd ever had one. He just nodded.

Chandler pulled his car back into the small opening behind Vernon's van. "Bono says his wife called him. They'll get the kid in the morning. Do him good, they say, to stay overnight. I asked him who owned all those cars. He says they're friends who park there. Ferguson takes care of them while people go on vacation." He leaned over and rubbed his thighs as though walking hurt. When he stood up again, he said, "Not a very good lie, if you ask me. I got as many license plates as I could in the dark."

"And what was going on behind him?" I asked. "Could you see anything in the doorway?"

"Nothing. There's a wall with a solid door behind him. He

answered from a kind of hallway that ran widthwise of the building." He wrinkled his brow. "Electric lines run into that place. Let's see what the power company says about that."

We all headed back to our places for the night. Tony would take up his position on the couch again. Pasquin kept us supplied with coffee.

"Too bad Edwin isn't here," he chuckled. "He'd love to see that big snake."

I snuggled next to Vernon. The thought of Edwin with his odor of leather and snake skin and swamp water made me uncomfortable, and I was glad this time we'd solve something without him.

Morning brought a squall of rain. We sat at the dining table, groggy from the confusing night, and ate eggs scrambled with bits of ham and pepper and drank strong coffee. It was time to listen to Chandler talk to Gil. Only Pasquin would stay behind at the house.

The hall where Chandler would sit with Gil and his parents was a bit friendlier than the standard one-way mirror interrogation room. Instead of gray walls, it was a light blue with matching plastic chairs. Tony, Vernon, and I crammed into an observation area and listened.

"This is only an interview," said Chandler. "I want to know first how you got into the Culley house, Gil?"

The boy's parents glanced quickly at their son and then away. They offered no help.

"The door was open. I just walked in," he said, his eyes big but not quite frightened.

"What did you do inside?"

"Looked around. I wanted a place to watch television but it

wouldn't turn on. Guess the power is off."

"You don't have a set at your own house?"

"Yeah, but I was bored in there. Just wanted to look around."

"And was this the first time you looked around Miss Culley's house?"

"Well, since she died, yeah." He sat up straight and glanced at his parents. They both had their eyes lowered.

"You were there before she died?"

"Few times. I sometimes went by to ask if she needed any work done. She didn't appreciate that and always told me to get away from her. She was like a lot of old people I know. Afraid of young men."

I groaned. "He sees himself as a young man."

"You ever give her any reason to fear you?" Chandler kept a steady gaze into the boy's eyes.

He shrugged. "Don't think so."

"Now what about the beer, Gil?"

He shrugged again like he didn't know what the question was.

"You're under age, son."

"I'm not your son," he said and his eyes darted to his parents. A slight grin appeared and disappeared in a second. I could swear his father looked up and made the same gesture with his mouth.

"Where did you get the beer?"

"From the refrigerator in our house," he said and broke into an obvious grin this time.

Chandler leaned back but never took his eyes from the boy's. "You've had trouble with beer before, haven't you?"

"Oh, that," he smiled. "Those guys at school couldn't handle it."

I stood up, wanting to throttle the kid. "He's joking about the whole thing, and his parents don't seem to mind. For heaven's sake! They're not even threatening to get a lawyer much less disciplining their own child."

"Chandler won't find anything to charge him with, Luanne. The kid didn't actually purchase the beer. Better sit down." Tony was chewing his jaw, meaning he was as angry as I was. "He'll let him off on a warning not to go into anybody's house without permission."

"Gil, you went into the Ferguson house and surprised the old man more than once, right?" Chandler changed the subject but neither the boy nor his parents appeared shocked.

"Yeah," he laughed, "that old croak never could remember when I was to come and do things around there."

"Like what things?"

"Shopping, cleaning the yard, moving stuff around." Gil's eyes make a quick movement toward his parents. This time, they held their heads up and stared at him.

"Moving what stuff?" Chandler had noticed the movement, too.

He shrugged. "Furniture, dishes and stuff he wanted sold or stored. I don't know. Never really asked. He paid me."

"Did you ever move any of this stuff to Mr. Ferguson's bar?"

"Yeah. He's got storage there, and then I got a job for a while."

"Do you still work there?"

"Sometimes, but I don't get along with that barbecue man. What a jerk!"

"And where is Mr. Ferguson now?"

"Which one?" It was either a stall or a dig, the kind of teenage smart remark that made you want to slap a face.

"Burl."

"He went on a buying trip, I think. I don't keep up with him and he doesn't tell me things like that."

"I'll bet," I said. "Is Chandler going to ask about the dead dog?"

In the next breath, he did.

"Well, it was like this. Ferguson's old dog kept getting locked inside our storage area and I had to get him out all the time. One day, I chased him out and hit him with a broom handle." He smiled and shrugged. "Guess I hit him too hard. He staggered off and died. Made a big stink. Pops made me get rid of the body." He smiled again.

Chandler looked at the father who shrugged just like his son. "Can't have a smelly dead animal lying about the place."

The Bono parents left with their offspring. Gil's unbalanced body stumbled over his own feet as he walked ahead of his mother to the car. Mr. Bono signed the papers, promising to give his son a curfew and watch his movements, and shook hands with the clerk.

"Somehow," I said, "I don't think there's going to be any guilty screaming fits from anyone inside that house tonight. It was almost like their son was doing just what they expected him to do."

"We need to see behind those walls at the bar," said Chandler, his hands resting on his hips. "It's not just storage."

"Search warrant?" I asked.

"Not reasonable cause yet," he answered. "But," he turned to face us, "we can look up some of those license plates, even get a report from the power company."

The three of us followed Chandler back to the sheriff's department. He led us to the computer room and, with one finger motion, had an operator dealing with the license plates. We waited in swivel chairs while he went to his office to make a phone call to find out how much electricity was pouring into the bar.

"Wonder if anyone has heard from Ferguson today," I said to

Vernon.

The computer clerk overheard, and without changing her attention to the monitor, said, "We got an alert on him. Seems he's still in Tampa."

"Are you monitoring his movements, too? I mean do you know which companies he's visiting?"

"I don't, but the deputy in Tampa probably does. He's been told to keep a record of places the man goes. It's not a tail. Tampa can't spare that much time. He's doing what he can."

"Is he traveling with anyone?" asked Vernon.

"I know that," said Tony. "The bartender said he was down in Tampa with his girlfriend. Said 'girlfriend' like she was Godzilla or something."

The clerk glanced back at us. "I'll check in a minute. Deputy should be sending the info back by computer."

I looked at Tony. "Girlfriend? The only girl I saw him with was one old enough to be his mother—Rosie Quinne."

We looked at each other and our thoughts clicked into sync. "Where's Valentine today?" I asked.

Vernon moved outside and pulled his cell phone. He tapped a number and talked for nearly ten minutes.

"Valentine is on his way over here with some of his files. He's got some new stuff on the Henderson woman in Jersey."

"Okay," said the clerk. "Here's a printout on who owns those cars. Some locals, some in neighboring counties. Shouldn't be hard to locate." She handed the paper to Vernon. "Now let me see what the latest is from Tampa."

"Visited one liquor warehouse. Stopped at some bars. One bank. Two retirement centers. City Hall and a beauty salon." She continued to scroll down. "No mention of anyone with him. I'll type in the question."

We waited, hoping whatever deputy in the Tampa area had been assigned the task of following Burl around would be in the car and get the message right away.

"Here it comes," said the clerk. "Dropped off an elderly woman at the beauty salon. I watched that because he didn't just drop her off; he went inside with her. Haven't seen her again. Ferguson is using her car, however, or someone named Rosie Quinne's car. At least that's who carries the registration. Expensive Cadillac." The clerk shook her head. "That's all I've got."

Chandler returned, his face red with anger. "Dealing with the power company is like communicating with the local idiot. Had to tell the kid who answered I'd be over with my badge and embarrass the hell out of him if he didn't give me the info over the phone. Lots of power going into that bar. New wiring was put in not too many weeks ago. He said the old wiring wouldn't be able to handle the use the place gets now."

"And there's no way to get inside?" I asked.

"Can't think of one right now, but let's see what we've got on the cars." He took the paper Vernon handed him. "I know a couple of these people." He chuckled. "This one spends all his energy trying to con the world. It usually cons him back."

"I'll wait in the lobby for Valentine," I said to Vernon, "if you want to go with Chandler."

"Valentine?" asked Chandler.

"Yeah," I said. "He's opening up the Henderson file for us."

CHAPTER TWENTY-TWO

"And these are pictures of whom?" I asked as Valentine spread photos in front of us on the dining table. The sheriff's office was having trouble finding spaces to meet as it tried to disband all the outside hurricane task forces. I suggested Valentine meet us at the Keen house.

"People, mostly men, she was seen around from time to time. We think we know who some of them are, but two can't be identified. When we heard about the teeth showing up down here, we started looking at these again." He touched two blurred photographs on the end of a row of six. "These are the two we don't know about."

I stared at the first photo on my left. Valentine named him and went on to another, named him and his occupation in lawn service. The third and fourth were probably construction workers who drifted to odd jobs between the big projects. The last two had beards. I stared at the first one, a bushy haired man whose growth of hair enveloped his face like a captured Saddam. It stood away slightly as though a breeze had caught him just as the camera snapped. He looked to the left and his expression was not of someone who knew he was being photographed. He looked familiar, but then any man with so much hair is noticed wherever he goes, and I thought I might be falling into type rather than knowledge. The last photo was even more blurred. This man had thinner hair and a beard that came to a little point. It was dark, like the first one, but spattered with gray. His eyes looked at the camera, and again he looked familiar. I stared for a several minutes, then took my hands and framed the eyes away from the rest of the face. I did the same with the other photo, going back and forth, until it hit me.

"How did you get these photos?" I asked.

"Mrs. Henderson belonged to a ladies group that met to play mah jong every Friday. The hall where they met has a security camera in the parking lot. Our agent has just now been able to see her car in the background, and a man getting out to open the door for her. They don't have parking attendants there. We are assuming that all these men at some time, dropped her off for her weekly game and picked her up later." Valentine poked his finger at the same background sign that appeared in all the photos.

"They're the same person!"

"What?" Valentine leaned over and stared so close I wondered if he didn't need glasses.

"Check the eyes. These two are the same or closely related. I'll bet if you get an expert to check the facial structure, you'll find even more proof."

Valentine turned over the four other photographs and used them to block off the faces, exposing only the eyes. He looked back and forth, comparing the shapes and corners.

"Do the Bonos deny knowing these men?"

"Haven't had a chance to show them yet."

Before we could go any further, my cell phone rang. It was Marshall Long.

"FDLE did the lab work on that diary you pulled out of the lake," he said. "Vernon said to call as soon as we knew anything."

"Well, you'll have to tell me. Vernon's out searching for cars with Chandler."

"Seems the tablet wasn't used much. Might have been just bought. Only the first three pages have writing on them. I can send you the exact transcript with each word as the tech found it, but the gist is Mildred found her sister's jade in F's house. She doesn't explain who F is. She says Mildred planned to take it out and hide it. It goes on about how 'Mildred and I' went inside the F house while the old man sat on the porch. And get this, she says, 'we found teeth in some jade.' The final part is about her cats disappearing after she caught the kid next door throwing rocks at them. She planned to check that out while the family slept."

"Spunky old lady, that Miss Keen," I said. "By the way, how do we know Miss Keen actually wrote in this tablet?"

"Techs can identify the handwriting if you want. But inside the front cover, it's got Marta Keen's name and address."

"Dates?"

"Only on the one entry she made. It's most likely just before she died."

I sat for a moment, picturing old Miz Keen sneaking out in darkness toward the Bono house. She'd have a flashlight, maybe wear dark clothing and running shoes. How quiet could an elderly woman be? And when she got to the door, could she open it? If someone was inside or maybe watched from a boat and came after her, what would she do? I saw her taking off in a fast walk toward the lake, heading toward her landing, and then trying to hurry to her own back patio. Anyone younger who was after her could overpower her and knock her down face first in the dirt, hold her there until she quit breathing.

"Luanne?" Valentine was staring at me.

I nodded to him, thanked Marshall and said Vernon would call him back when he could.

"And how did they get her tablet," I said to myself. "Or maybe she tossed it in the lake herself?"

"What tablet?" Valentine's brow wrinkled now, as though worried about me.

"I'm sorry, but there have been developments." I explained the FDLE report.

"The Bonos are in on this. I know it," he said. He sat lost in his thoughts for a moment, then collected the photographs and tucked them into his file. "I got some checking to do. You've got my cell?"

Pasquin had sat without a word during my discussion with Valentine. His eyes were closed, his head tilted back. But, the gnarled hand that held the straw hat fanned continuously. He heard it all.

"Think the Bono kid killed Miz Keen?" he asked without opening his eyes.

"Or the Bono father or the Bono mother," I said. "You fancy a ride to the Fireside Bar?"

His eyes came open and he slapped the hat on his head. "Can't let an old man rest, can you?"

Two cars sat in the lot of the main side of the bar. Both looked like they had been rebuilt on cement blocks in someone's front yard. Inside, what must have been their owners sat together at the end of the bar and poured down beer. From the looks of the empty bottles, they had been at it for a while. The bartender's eyes darted their way when we sat at the other end.

"Any word from Burl?" I asked after ordering our own light brews.

"None," he said and moved away, wiping the top of the bar.

Pasquin turned up his beer bottle and drank from it rather

than use the glass sitting in front of him. When he put the bottle down, he said, "You see that picture up there?" He pointed to a wall where Burl had put various photos of himself and some of the customers. "Man fancies himself with celebrities."

"Mind if I come back there for a closer look?" I called to the bartender.

He nodded at the wall. "Suit yourself."

I scanned the jumble of photographs. Most showed Burl with men in business suits. He was wearing cowboy boots and a hat that partially shaded his face. A few city council people had captions beneath their pictures. There was a shiny new one of Burl and Rosie Quinne outside the bar. To one side, the liquor license for this place had been framed along with a small facial photo of Burl. It resembled a driver's license picture. His name, followed by "proprietor," had been typed beneath it. I stared at it, and my skin froze.

"I'll be right back," I said and left my beer to get warm on the counter. Outside, I pulled out the cell phone and dialed Chandler. I asked him to try to get Burl's driver's license photo and to enlarge it if possible.

"We're just pulling up to the second car, Luanne. You got something?"

"I don't know, but I need to see an up-close version of this man's face. There's a familiar pair of eyes on the wall of this bar."

Chandler promised to phone in the order. I could pick it up in maybe thirty minutes.

"Any luck with those cars?" I asked before hanging up.

"First one wasn't home. So far, nothing."

Chandler wasn't going to tell me anything else. Like some other deputies, even Tony at times, he was overly cautious about giving out facts to a temporary.

I returned to the bar. The two men, their clothes stinking from old car oil had moved closer to Pasquin. The bartender kept his distance but stood looking at the three.

"You want to buy us a beer, old man," one said. The other one slipped off the stool and moved to Pasquin's back. He eyed his pocket and the outline of his wallet.

I moved quickly just as the second man slipped Pasquin's wallet and turned to run. With as much force as I could muster, I got beside him and kicked his shins with my foot. He got tangled up in his own momentum and sprawled into a table, finally landing on the floor with his arms spread out like he was crucified. He still held on to the wallet. I stomped hard on his wrist. He yelled and let go. I swept up the wallet and handed it over to Pasquin. The other man was off his stool and making some kind of move toward me, his eyes wide and fearful. I gave him even more to be scared of when I pulled my gun. He stopped cold.

The bartender didn't want to call the cops. He figured I had defeated the men, so let it be. I screamed at him, "If you don't call the cops, I will. And, I plan to tell them you refused to report this. Perhaps it's aiding and abetting?" He picked up the bar phone and made the call.

Lownde arrived before the sheriff got there. He headed toward the bar when he realized two men were sitting on the floor with their hands in the air, and I was holding a gun on them. Pasquin had moved to a chair, directly in front of the pair and stared at them. He chuckled every now and then and once said, "If there's anything a petty thief can't stand, it's being stared at."

Lownde, who had started around the bar to the kitchen for the day's ribs, stopped in his tracks. He then moved slowly back to the front of the bar. His size took up lots of eye space, and his slow steps were like a giant's coming after a couple of bad boys.

The dimness of the bar made him an outline almost, until his loud burst of laughter roared through the room.

"You white boys having a good time?" He laughed again. "Playing cowboys and Indians?" He pulled up a chair near Pasquin and sat down, staring at them. "What you tried to steal this time?"

Outside, lights from a sheriff's car flashed into the dim room. When two deputies burst into the door, the two men looked down. One thief squirmed and seemed on the verge of tears. Lownde laughed again. "Gon' haul your white asses right off to jail." He stood and headed for the kitchen.

"Mr. Ferguson," said the bartender, "won't file charges, I'm sure. He'll just tell them to stay away from here." He tried to talk calmly to the deputies.

"Well, maybe he won't, but we will," I said. "They didn't steal from the bar. They stole from an old man." I winked at Pasquin.

"And I'm filing charges," he said, his gravel voice shaking in anger. "What's to say they won't try to steal from me somewhere else. Mr. Ferguson ought to be ashamed of himself not to file charges on thieves." He slammed his hat onto the table.

Lownde had come out of the kitchen with a big tray of raw ribs in his hands.

"Put your asses in jail, right now," he said and laughed all the way to the barbecue pit. From behind the closed door, he shouted, "Takes one to know two!"

The bartender glared at the door, his face pale and stiff.

The deputies seemed to enjoy the pat down and cuffing of the two men. One said under his breath after reading them their rights, "neighborhood nuisances."

When it was all over, Pasquin and I sat at the table. The bartender continued to wipe the bar, glancing up at us as he made his way from end to end.

"Why wouldn't Mr. Ferguson press charges?" I asked.

The bartender shrugged. "The less we see of deputies, the better."

"Your words or Burl's?"

"Burl's," he said without hesitation.

"He doesn't care for cops around here?"

He didn't answer.

"I guess it doesn't sell alcohol to have a marked car out front. People might think something illegal is happening inside." I watched the bartender. He didn't look up.

"Is that right, son?" said Pasquin.

The bartender shrugged. "I got a job, okay. I plan to keep it if I can. Boss don't like cops around here, but that's the nature of all bars, I think."

I looked behind the counter at the wall of photos. "Is that license still good or has it expired?"

"Of course, it's good. Come around here and take another look if you must." He sounded disgusted but scared, and the last thing he needed while the boss was away was someone calling about an expired liquor license.

I stood and walked behind the bar. I moved my hand down the row of photographs until I came to Burl's photo. I placed two fingers above and below his eyes. I needed to see if the familiarity was really there, but I couldn't be sure. I'd have to wait for the blow-up.

I was still measuring the eye space when Vernon and Chandler crashed through the door.

"We heard the call," said Vernon. "You're all right?"

Lownde came back inside and laughed to the point of drowning out everyone else. "She put those boys' asses in jail, I'm tellin' you!"

"Pleased about that, Lownde?" said Chandler, who chuckled a bit himself.

Lownde just let out another loud roar. He walked into the kitchen, murmuring to himself, "asses in jail, asses in jail."

When his big body burst out of the door again, another tray of raw ribs in his hands, he said to anyone who would listen, "Pricks stole my spare tires and hub caps. Boss man didn't want to hear about it. Wouldn't even pay for the stuff." He made a high pitched giggle. "Little white asses in jail now."

We left the bartender nervous but recuperating. He had told Chandler that Ferguson almost never pressed charges when a fight broke out. "Takes care of his own place," he said. Chandler tipped his hat without saying a word and left.

"Follow us to the department," said Chandler. "We'll get that enlargement for you and show you what we got."

Chandler commandeered a conference room by pushing hurricane supplies to one end of the table. The computer tech brought in the enlarged photo. It took just seconds for me to realize why I'd been so mesmerized by the photographs I'd seen in the bar. I held both hands up to section off the eyes.

"They're the same eyes Valentine showed me just hours ago." I pulled out my phone and made the call. Valentine was sitting on the lake road in a position to watch the Bono house. He started the car and headed to Chandler's office.

"So you think Burl Ferguson is this man who was hanging around the Henderson woman in Jersey," said Vernon. "She disappears. Her teeth—and maybe her body—end up here."

"Along with her niece's family," said Chandler.

No one wanted to speculate what all that meant, at least not until we had a chance to locate Ferguson. Chandler took a deep breath.

"We got something else to do now. Hit the jackpot, we think, with one of the car licenses." He smiled the pleased look of a boy who had done a good deed. "We had a talk with one Mrs. Jeri Powers. Scared woman with an eating problem." Chandler spoke as he looked at the table top.

"Fat?" asked Tony.

"Skinny. Bone thin. Says she's anorexic and has been in and out of hospitals. Her husband wasn't home, but the car was. She got skittish when we asked why it was parked at the Fireside Bar. Said she didn't know unless he was there drinking. She got too nervous and began to hyperventilate right there in her own living room. We were just getting ready to call the medics when her husband came flying out of a back room."

"You've been involved with paramedics all the time we were talking to Valentine?" I asked.

"Nope. He gave his wife a paper bag and she calmed down. Says she does that a lot these days." Chandler looked up and breathed deeply again. "That's not all he said. Seems he gambles at the bar. That's when he clammed up and we brought him in for questioning."

"And you plan to do that now?" I asked.

"Gave the man a while to call his lawyer. Soon as he gets here, we start." Chandler smiled.

It didn't take long. Powers drummed up an old man who had defended him before in petty crimes. Sitting next to each other in the interrogation room, it was difficult to tell which was the suspect. Chandler sat across from the men with a uniform deputy next to him. The tape recorder light came on when Chandler began.

"You've gambled at the Fireside Bar, Mr. Powers?"

The man nodded. When there was no response, he leaned over and said "yes" into the machine.

"Tell us about that."

Powers rattled on about how there were lots of empty dining tables and he and his pals would just get up a friendly game once in a while. Chandler wasn't buying it.

"Mr. Powers, we're not talking about friendly, spontaneous gambling here. Not some dice tossing in a parking lot or even a game of Go Fish over the rib plate special." He stopped and smiled. I got the impression of a snake about to strike. "Tell me about the games in the back room, Mr. Powers."

Powers began to shake and look at the lawyer beside him. The other man leaned over, put his arm around his client and whispered for quite some time. Finally, Powers nodded.

"Maybe it's better," he nodded toward the lawyer and with watery eyes looked back at Chandler.

"Just remember he's the one telling you everything," said the lawyer.

Chandler nodded first to the lawyer then to Powers.

Powers' hands shook as he revealed what had been happening under the noses of a too busy law enforcement agency.

"Ferguson rented out that back space to Mr. Bono," he said. "I think they knew each other from somewhere else. Ferguson said they were in school together."

I looked at Vernon. "Most likely in crime school together."

"Bono outfitted it with poker tables and a few slot machines. Then he and Ferguson got people together who liked a card game now and then and sold memberships. The fee was for beer and stuff, and for the privilege of playing there."

"And how big a percentage did the house take of your winnings?" asked Chandler.

Powers shrugged. "They took their due. I never found out how much. Never won."

"No wonder his wife was anorexic," I said. "All the money was going out the door to feed a gambling habit."

When the interrogation ended, and Chandler joined us in the viewing room, I stared at both men until Vernon smiled and said, "It's illegal. And that fact gives us a reason to raid the place."

"When?" I asked.

The plans and the court order would have to be discussed among local officials. We left them and returned to the Keen house.

Valentine walked in as we were discussing the logistics of a raid. He huffed and puffed after he sat in a dining chair. Pulling out the file, he placed it in front of me. "The photos are in here. Tell me what you found."

I pointed out the photos of the hairy man and compared them to the blown up picture of a clean shaven Burl Ferguson. Unless a person was looking for comparison, he wouldn't see the similarity. In the eyes, however, the shape of the upper lids and the expression itself left no doubt.

"Damn man is an old woman scam artist," Pasquin said. "They get jollies from all the attention. He gets the money."

"And," said Vernon, "in this case, their lives."

"And he's in Tampa with Rosie Quinne, a rich jeweler's widow from here?" I shuddered. Where would we find her, if we did find her?

Vernon rose. "I'll ask Chandler to put out the APB now and have the man picked up. I'll get the lab to blow up and compare all three photos. FDLE might be able to do a facial bone match." He walked outside to use the cell phone.

Valentine's eyes twitched and he started to speak twice.

"What's the matter, man?" said Pasquin.

"I've got to do something. The Bono family isn't innocent of this elderly rip off. I'm positive of it."

"Then go spy on them." Pasquin had no patience with agitation that sat still.

Valentine looked at him for a moment, rose and headed out the door. He came back to gather his file and photos, telling us to keep him informed of everything. He left, closing the door softly and, we assumed, went to his car and then to the Bono stakeout.

"He may have a long night," Pasquin said.

"This may be a good time to visit old man Ferguson again," I said.

Vernon nodded and agreed to meet Pasquin and me at the hospital in an hour. He planned to get some kind of statement from the old man if he could do it without endangering his health.

"And the raid on the bar? When do you think that will happen?" I asked.

"I'm sure Chandler wants it done at night, when games are in full swing and all the members are present. Ferguson may not be there, but that's probably best. His clientele will talk more without him in the room."

"And Bono?"

"Now he probably will be there. It's his operation, remember."

"I want to be there, Vernon." I knew I wasn't a sworn deputy, even though both sheriff departments, with their adjunct use of my diving services, considered me an agent of the law.

"Tony will want to be there, too," he said. He looked back toward the department. "He's calling north right now to put his own department on alert."

"And will Chandler allow it, seeing as how Miz Keen was his

aunt?"

Vernon shrugged. "He'll give him a job, but it may not be inside the bar." He looked down at me. "He can keep you company outside." He broke into a wide grin and I wasn't sure if he was kidding or not. "Better yet, we'll put you on snake duty. You're a good shot. You can kill it before it bites somebody."

"Thanks a lot," I said, and waved Pasquin to my car. Vernon crawled into the back, complaining of having to fold himself like a letter to make it.

"Wonder if Burl has visited his papa yet," said Pasquin. "It's not nice, you know, for a kid to let his old man lie in a hospital bed with nobody but nurses around." He fanned for a moment, then stopped. "Of course if there's some rich old nurse around, you'll likely find Burl, too."

Ferguson had healed, at least physically. He was angry now like he had never been before. He sat in the visitor's chair in his own room, a hospital gown thrown over pajamas someone had given him.

"Damn kid! I'm cutting him out of my will. You can count on that." He hit the arm of the chair. "What kind of kid leaves his old father in a hospital and never shows up?"

I shrugged and patted his shoulder.

"Tell us about this kid," said Pasquin, who sat in the only other chair. Vernon and I sat on opposite sides of the bed. "How long was he gone from home?"

"Years! Hell, I don't know. He'd call or write once in a while. Never knew where he was most of the time. He'd say he was running a business that made him travel. Even had me mail him emergency money once or twice. But you think he'd come home rich or even care for his old man? No!" He put his head down and whispered, "No good, no damn good."

"What was his relationship with the neighbors?" asked Vernon.

Ferguson looked up, his eyes watery and wide with fear that showed through the anger. "Liked some, hated others."

"Any women friends?" asked Vernon, keeping his voice even and low.

"No woman was going to take up with him. Except old ladies who thought he was a young stud."

"And did he take up with old ladies?"

Ferguson breathed heavily and looked up at Vernon. "All I know is, we got a couple of old snoops showing up in our house. I run one out with a broom, just like I did that Bono kid. Don't know what it is but all Burl's friends think they can just march into my house, look around my kitchen, and take out what they please."

I wanted to ask what they took, but Ferguson had spent all his anger and the downright agony he felt took over. He broke into an old man stream of tears, his mouth wide and blubbery. Pasquin got up and patted him on the shoulder.

"I think maybe those days are over. We need to find your son. He's with a lady by the name of Rosie Quinne. You got any idea where they could be?"

Ferguson used the edge of his hospital gown to wipe his eyes and then his entire face. "He spends time over at her farm, I think. She's got a house in town, too, but the farm is where they visit." He looked startled for a moment. "You don't think…?"

"I don't think what?" Pasquin kept his hand on the man's shoulder.

"You don't think he's going to move in with her?"

"Might be good for you if he does. You could get yourself a nice woman to come in and clean and fix meals. Wouldn't have to bother with a son who won't do that."

Ferguson looked down at his hands and nodded. His face held the sadness of many years, mirroring other old men, alone and lonely, yet unwilling to move into the assisted living places where conventional wisdom said they'd be a lot happier. Clinging to one's roots, no matter how rotten, was the one last fight they had in them.

"Where is this Quinne farm?" asked Vernon who had stood up.

Ferguson gave us the directions. It was in the country, far from neighbors and encompassed nearly thirty acres.

"We'll look for him tomorrow morning, Mr. Ferguson. You get some rest. If you need a ride back to your house, call me." Vernon handed the man his card.

On the way back to the parking lot, Vernon added, "If he does call and we take him home, we'll have to do what those other nosy neighbors did—take a look at his house."

CHAPTER TWENTY-THREE

The Bono family couldn't be found, and it wasn't because Valentine didn't look. He stayed on night vigil, skirting the lake in his car and by foot through reeds, cattails, and pure mud. He had mosquito repellents lined up on the back seat of his car. At five in the morning, he gave up and knocked on the Keen house door. Vernon jerked on his pants and grabbed his gun. Tony had flown off the sofa and stood dazed in starched pajamas.

"Sorry," said a disheveled and itching Valentine. "I got pretty miserable out there." He moved inside when Vernon gave him the pass sign. Hitting a wicker chair, he pulled off his shirt and sat there in a sweaty undershirt. He rubbed his forehead as though it ached. "I'm not cut out for this anymore."

"Lordie, this place gets up too early," said Pasquin as he emerged from his bedroom in a tied robe over his pajamas. He shook his head but wandered into the kitchen to make coffee.

"They didn't come home all night," said Valentine, now leaning his head back, trying to crack his neck. "Where the hell are they?"

"Are you sure they weren't there all along?" I asked.

"If they've got some underground tunnel, maybe, but I checked out the windows, listened, did all kinds of tricky things I don't want to talk about. They aren't home."

I looked at Vernon. He nodded and gave Tony a glance.

"Go take a shower, man, and get some rest," said Tony, who shoved his linens from the sofa. "We'll check this out."

The three of us sat around in night clothes while Valentine used the master shower. Tony brought a suitcase in from the man's car. When he finally emerged, he sat on the sofa and took the coffee mug Pasquin handed to him.

"Sorry," he said and sipped the strong stuff. It didn't seem to bother him. "I got the worst headache."

"Need some food and maybe an aspirin," said Pasquin.

Valentine nodded. Later, he took both from the old man and swallowed them down in quick gulps. He face reddened somewhat for a time but went pale again as he rubbed his forehead.

"Just let me lie here," he said and leaned on a pillow.

I nodded toward the kitchen and all of us headed there to discuss how we'd go to the Quinne farm. Valentine began to snore almost immediately. The sound reverberated throughout the house.

Tony pulled out a map of the county and routed us to the farm. Pasquin would stay with Valentine and man the phone at the house, while the three of us would meet Chandler at the turn-off to the farmhouse.

"No one is going to be a hero if this gets ugly, okay?" He was looking directly at me.

"I'll stay with the car if you don't want me inside," I said.

Tony shot me a nervous grin. "I know better than that, Luanne."

Chandler positioned other deputies on the roads at the far reaches of the acreage just in case Ferguson had found another way to leave. We didn't really know if he was there, but as soon as we spied the big house with its antebellum pillars, we saw the Cadillac.

Chandler and one of his deputies climbed the steps to the massive front porch. He pushed the door bell and waited. Vernon,

Tony, and I stood near some thick camellia bushes, while two other deputies found a grove of heavy oaks.

A door opened, and a disheveled Rosie Quinne answered. Her hair was half in curlers, and she had on none of the makeup she normally wore. Instead of looking like a worn-out clown, she just looked worn-out, gray and blotched.

"Oh, sheriff, you gave me such a scare. I'm not in any shape to receive you."

"She knows how to put on Southern airs," I whispered.

"Had plenty of years to practice, not to mention the money," Vernon whispered back.

"I wonder if she knows how close she is to losing all that money," said Tony, his anger showing in the deep olive color of his face.

When Chandler asked about Burl, the old lady giggled. "I think he went in to his bar. He's been away, you see, and he needed to see to it." She giggled again.

"Is something funny, ma'am?" asked Chandler, smiling with her.

"Oh!" she said and slapped one wrinkled hand over her own mouth. "I'm just so thrilled. I got married on the trip." She giggled some more.

"To Burl?" asked Chandler, his voice taking on an alarm that made Rosie stop her girlish laugh.

"Why not?" she said and poked her arms stiffly at her side. "I can marry whom I wish to marry."

Chandler turned to face the yard and rolled his eyes. When he turned back, he said, "You say he's at the bar? You do know his father is ill?"

"Oh, yes, but the doctor has that under control. And poor Burl was looking all over the Tampa area for a suitable place for his father." She lowered her voice. "Feeble old man like that shouldn't be living in a rickety farm house by himself."

Chandler must have been outraged and couldn't resist. He said, after looking over the front porch, "Well, maybe you could bring him here. You've got enough room for a father-in-law."

Rosie's mouth drew into a thin line when she realized the irony of two ancients living under the same roof, one of them being the daughter-in-law. Her face grew stern.

"He'd never be happy here. He's going to a home in Tampa."

"Yeah, well we need to speak to his son." Chandler turned away from the woman. Shaking his head, he joined us near the camellias.

"Being married changes everything." He called to a deputy and told him to get back to the office and confirm that it really happened. "I'm going to see a judge about a search warrant on the bar."

"Look," I said, tapping Chandler's arm, "she said old Mr. Ferguson is going to a home in Tampa. Nell Culley took her money out to pay for an assisted living place but nobody ever said where that was. And Paulette Henderson had the same idea. Burl must have been taking these women for a ride, offering to help them pay for a home but taking their money instead."

"And doing them in while he's at it?" Chandler stared off in the distance. "Excuse me." He took out his phone and called someone in the department, ordering a thorough financial search of Ferguson's assets. "Happens all the time," he said after he closed his phone. "Old lady gets hooked by flattery and taken by a crook."

"But not Rosie Quinne," I said. "She married him. Maybe she changed her will?"

"Something is strange about this. I need to get back to the office."

Vernon went with Chandler to the Sheriff's Department. Tony had to return with me to his aunt's house. He had remained quiet during most of the visit to the Quinne house, but his jaw worked and his face reddened a couple of times. He was still in the middle of this because he was a victim's heir. The frustration at not being the one in charge worked at him, but he would never say it out loud. We rode in silence until my phone rang.

"You need to get back here," said Pasquin in a hurried gruff tone. "I had to send that lawman to the hospital in an ambulance. He doubled over right here with chest pains."

"Did the paramedics say it was a heart attack?"

"Yeah, and they got here just in time. Same hospital where Ferguson is."

"We'll go straight there," I said.

When I explained the situation to Tony, he got on the phone to Chandler.

"Hurricanes seem tame right now," he said as he closed the phone.

"Well, this end of the hurricane anyway."

Valentine was in stable condition by the time we reached the hospital. His office in New Jersey was sending down help and would take over whatever job he was doing.

"I'll watch the Bono house tonight," said Tony. "Let's check on Ferguson while we're here."

Mr. Ferguson was dressed and sitting in a chair when we entered his room.

"They're sending me home," he said. "Told me some lady would drop by to cook meals if I wanted her." He shrugged and took on the hound dog sadness again. "Have to. Ain't no son going to cook for me."

"Mr. Ferguson," said Tony, "how well do you know Rosie

Quinne?"

"Rich old lady. Her husband owned jewelry stores around here for years."

"She's friendly with your son?"

Ferguson looked up as though surprised. "My son ain't friendly with old people. Mostly he hates them. Says we're—or at least I am a nuisance."

"You don't know of a close relationship between Burl and Rosie?"

"What? You think my son is nuzzling up to that old broad? Not hardly. Nuzzling up to her money maybe, but not to her."

I moved to a position where I could sit close to the old man. "Mr. Ferguson," I said, "have you ever considered going to assisted living instead of staying in that big old house?"

"Not ever!" He glared at me. "I ain't leaving the house my father built and I lived in most of my life."

"Has Burl ever suggested it?"

"No! And he better not."

A nurse came with a wheelchair. She said that they'd found a woman who would take the man home and cook his meals. He would have someone check on him, but he would be alone at night. "At least for now," said the nurse. "He may have to hire live-in help soon." She smiled at us, patted the man on his shoulder, and wheeled him out the door.

"Poor guy," I said. "He has no idea that Rosie and Burl are planning on putting him in a home."

"They aren't," said Tony. "They'll go through the motions of finding a nice expensive place. Then the old man will die of this or that, and the money is Burl's. Rosie will go pretty soon after that. And he'll get her money, too." He sighed. "We've seen this kind of thing before. Why can't we stop it?"

"Of course, if the old man doesn't die soon enough, Burl will help him along."

"That's what I meant," said Tony. "You got a son who won't show up when his dad's in the hospital, who gets married to a rich woman on the sly, you got a suspect."

"Shouldn't somebody watch Rosie," I said. "I mean she's in danger, right?"

Tony stood silent, clenching his teeth. He nodded and walked away. It was a gesture I was used to from years of having him treat me with silence. It was no wonder to me that, handsome though he was, he could not sustain a relationship. He shut out people too often.

Pasquin brewed a fresh, full pot of Cajun coffee for Tony who positioned himself for nightwatching in alternating spots: the patio, the living room, and the hall bathroom. He provided himself comfort with pillows. "I'd do it outside except the mosquitoes would eat me up just like they did Valentine." He grabbed a flashlight and headed toward the Bono house. There was no car out front, but Tony had to satisfy himself that no one was home.

I watched from my bedroom window as he strolled first to the landing, then along the shoreline edging his way toward the house. He moved to the wall beneath the kitchen window and listened, his ear against the boards. He rounded the house, most likely doing the same thing under other windows. Eventually, he headed back to the Keen house and sat on the patio.

"Nobody is home, unless they're sound asleep or dead."

Darkness came with a cloud cover. If Tony were to see something, it would have to have a light on it. I waited with him until my eyes drooped. Pasquin had long since retired. Tony sat like stone, still sipping the strong brew.

Sometime after midnight, I awakened to a roar coming from

the road. From my window, I saw Tony's light move from the back of the house to the roadside just in time to flash against the side of a paneled delivery truck. It made a precarious move onto the soggy shoulder and turned around in order to back into the Bono drive.

Three men huddled to talk about whatever task was at hand. One dug into his pocket and pulled out a key chain. He went to the other side of the house, and I imagined, unlocked the door to the storage area. The others followed him. Soon, dollies came out of the truck, went to the other side and came back with large boxes. They appeared heavy because it took two to lift them into the truck.

The movement of boxes went on for half an hour. I couldn't see Tony but knew he surely must be watching all this. I stood in the darkness of my room, trying to make out the men who only had the light of their own truck. One looked familiar.

"Stubbs!" I whispered. "You'll work for anyone." He had been the one with the key, the local boy who probably knew where everybody's secrets were kept.

A low voice suddenly came from the doorway to my room.

"Luanne," said Tony. "I've notified the sheriff. Cars are on their way here."

"Can they get them on anything?"

"Maybe not, but they can get some information. Where is Bono and where are they taking this stuff?" He joined me at the window.

"That's Stubbs with the other two. You don't think he might be stealing stuff, do you?"

Tony shrugged. "If he is, Chandler will catch him in the act. Most likely he's not stealing. He wouldn't risk the noise and the lights."

The deputy patrol cars showed up without sirens, three of them lined up on the road and blocking anyone from driving to the main highway. When they stopped, they left the bubble lights flashing, and the night resembled the silent landing of three space saucers. Six deputies got out, their guns drawn. The first car used his speaker and told the men to put everything down and raise their hands.

The expressions on the men's faces were bewildered as they did what they were told. I knew then that this was no robbery, but a paid for transport job. Bono must have hired them. After speaking with the men, searching them for weapons and checking the contents of the truck, the deputies holstered their guns. Two cars drove away; the third moved to the side of the road to allow the truck to pass.

"Damn!" said Tony as he went outside to meet the deputies. I followed him.

"They got a letter from Bono telling them what to get and how much he would pay them to do it. Gave Stubbs a key. We can't arrest them for that—unless you see it as disturbing the peace this time of night."

"Any word about where they're taking the boxes?"

"Fireside Bar, they said."

"You think you could follow them?" Tony asked.

"Get in," he nodded to Tony.

I stood back as I watched the car drive to the main highway. I held up my own phone to signal Tony to call me when he knew something. I wouldn't hold my breath, not unless he needed me for something, and there were no swimming holes in the Fireside lot.

I sat on my bed and looked at the Bono house for a long time. It had no lights anywhere. The stillness was eerie, not even a breeze blew the clouds away. Leaning against the window sill and about to fall asleep again, I caught something—a sound, maybe a sight, but it seemed to come from the Bono's back porch.

Grabbing my phone, gun, and a light, I moved to the backyard. A light had been switched on inside the Bono kitchen. I could make out Gil standing there with a glass of water in his hand. I phoned Tony.

"Watch him," he said. "I'm still sitting in this patrol car. As soon as the last box is moved inside, Chandler is coming with his warrant. Talk about a midnight raid."

I eased toward the Bono house. Another light, the glow of a television, came from the living room. The sound was some kind of chase scene. Gil wouldn't hear me on his porch. And when I found the door unlocked, I eased it open. The noise of the television chase drifted outdoors, shutting off the frog chorus.

From a position in the kitchen, I could stand out of sight but see through the crack left in the partially open door. Gil sat, teenage style with his shoulders and back hunched onto the seat of the couch. He feet rested on the table. He had a bag of chips across his stomach, and every few seconds he rustled the bag to feed himself. An opened beer sat on the coffee table. He checked his watch a couple of times, and when it seemed he wanted to get up, I slipped out the back and hid beside the house.

The television sound and light went off. Gil came through the kitchen, rummaged in a drawer and slammed it hard when he had what he wanted. He came outside, his beer bottle in one hand, a knife in the other. He took a long swig from the bottle, turned it over, poured out the rest, and tossed the bottle into a clump of cattails. He shoved the knife in his belt and grabbed a flashlight from the porch.

I followed him in the darkness until he came to a group of

reeds. He reached into the cluster and pulled out a black garbage bag that moved. When the mews of kittens emanated from the bag, I had a good idea what he planned to do.

He propped his flashlight by anchoring it in the soft mud. Its light shined upward like a beacon. From the bag, he removed one kitten, its body tiny and shaking. He twisted the opening so the others couldn't escape. Removing the knife, he held the yellow cat by the scruff of its neck over the light. The tiny animal squirmed and closed its eyes against the bright light. Gil took his knife and held it close to the animal's neck.

"Stop! You little creep," I said and pulled my gun.

Gil's plump head moved slowly toward me. He acted like someone high on drugs, his eyes glazed with the joy of the kill.

"You touch that knife to that kitten and I'll shoot you dead!" I meant it.

He looked back at the cat, still in the air, and the knife in his other hand. His body jerked slightly, and he let the animal down.

"Toss the knife out here near me," I said.

Gil never said anything. He did as I told him, including sitting down on the damp grass where I could see him. I called the sheriff, something that seemed commonplace out here now.

CHAPTER TWENTY-FOUR

"What the hell?" said the deputy as he stood over Gil.

The kid looked up at him, his big eyes full of nothing. He appeared dazed, as though he had no idea what he was doing. Two uniform deputies pulled him up by the arms and cuffed him. They charged him with cruelty to animals.

When they took him away, he stumbled over his own big shoes. I followed him to the car. Looking at me, he said in a soft voice, "They made me do it."

"Made you kill animals?" I said. "Who?"

He shook his head. "It, they made me do it."

I followed the deputies to the jail where they booked Gil and put him in a juvenile holding cell. Again, it was a task to locate his parents. I had a feeling I knew where they were.

"We're going to recommend this kid see a psychiatrist," said the deputy. We stood outside the cell with its big window. The bluish cast in the lighting that shined on Gil and the blue steel bench and walls made his emotionless face seem like something out of a surreal computer game. "Too many serial killers liked doing in animals as kids. If we can catch one in the making, maybe somebody's life will be saved later."

I shuddered. The chubby kid next door who gave beer to his classmates and roamed about the lake with a bag of chips—this could be the makings of a killer? I nodded to myself. It had happened too many times before.

I gave my formal statement to the deputy and left him my cell phone number. Leaving the station, I headed for the Keen house, knowing the direction would take me by the Fireside Bar.

The darkness made my trip seem even more unreal. Mine was the only car on the road for miles, and the headlights cleared a mere patch in front of me. On some curves, the lights would suddenly hit high reeds on the roadside, sending a shock through me. I've often had the fear of a deer darting in front of the car— and I've seen plenty of dead deer on the sides of roads to know it does happen—or a slow alligator making its way across the pavement right in front of me. I forgot my fears of animal roadkill when I saw the flashing patrol lights surrounding the bar. The raid was in progress, or perhaps over by now.

I drove slowly past the building until I saw deputies standing under a tree and chatting without urgency. A sheriff's truck had pulled into the back lot and deputies were loading boxes and tables inside it. I parked up the road in a solid looking place where someone had dumped gravel to make a turn-around, and walked back to the bar and phoned Vernon to let him know I was nearby.

"We arrested one entire party of gamblers, both Bono's, and the bartender," said Vernon who had cleared me to join them at the bar. "Ferguson wasn't around unfortunately."

"And all this?" I motioned to the truck loading efforts.

"Evidence of gambling," Chandler said. "We'll do a search when we get all this out of the way."

"Gil is locked up again," I said and explained the near kitten massacre. "He mentioned something about 'they made me do it' and intimated 'it' wasn't killing animals."

Tony joined us in time to hear about the kid. "Killing, perhaps? If he likes to kill animals, are humans far behind?"

The loading stopped and Chandler gave the go-ahead to lock up the truck and haul everything down to the station. Two patrol cars remained behind with Chandler to help carry out the search warrant.

"Okay, let's do it," he said. I followed him inside as did Vernon and Tony. He went straight to the fireplace.

"First thing is to get rid of this big rattler." He talked over the frantic dry rhythm of the snake's tail. "He's been doing that during this entire raid."

"You don't propose to just open up the fireplace and shoot it?" I asked.

Chandler looked at the bolted glass cover. Whoever unscrewed that and pulled it away would have a hard time dodging the angry fangs.

"Isn't there a door behind this wall?" asked Vernon.

We moved back into the gambling area. It was actually a large area with cubical walls that made private rooms. The lighting was low except right over the table areas. Pocket ceiling lights had been installed there to shine directly on the cards below. The place smelled of stale cigarettes.

"This door," Vernon said and rapped it with his knuckles. The snake's rattle sounded faintly through the walls. "It's got to be a back up to that fireplace. Maybe this is where Ferguson tossed in the mice. At least it will give us more leeway to shoot and dodge."

Chandler nodded. He tried the knob and found it locked. A deputy came forward with a sledge hammer and knocked off the handle and lock.

"The rattling is louder," said Tony. "Be careful." He reached inside and found a light switch.

In the wall directly in front of the door, there was a wooden flap with only a hook to keep it closed. From the sound, the snake and fireplace were on the other side. It looked high enough to be out of range of a strike and an easy place to slip in some poor animal for the snake's meal. But after the shock of that natural danger, we focused on the rest of the room. It had been painted a dark green and fitted with matching shelves. A small Indian rug lay on the floor and a single overstuffed chair sat at one end. Pocket lighting had been installed here, too. Civilized quarters just off the snake pit, I thought.

The shelves were filled with knick-knacks. On two shelves, an entire collection of jade sat dusted and spotlighted. The water bird pattern appeared on all of them.

"Nell's jade," I said. "This is where he brought it."

"Think he had that box with the Henderson woman's teeth in it, too?" asked Vernon. "Maybe Mildred found it in the Ferguson house. That's why he made space here.

"And maybe she just didn't have time to find these," said Chandler. His gloved hand pointed to a similar jade box he had opened with one finger. A set of false teeth rested inside.

"An expensive-looking necklace over here," said Tony. He held his hands behind him to keep from touching anything. "A hymnal, a box of talcum powder, and a long metal object."

"It's a tatting shuttle," I said. "It's used to make lace. My grandmother had one."

"Dear God!" Chandler said. "This looks like a human thumb." He pointed to a petrified looking piece of someone's anatomy encased in a round jade pot. He backed up and said, "Let's kill this snake and turn the room over to the scene techs. I got a feeling I know what this room is about."

There was no question of animal rights in this case. The snake was an evil agent of an evil man, and good ol' boy justice was about to be done. Everyone stepped outside the room except

Vernon and Chandler, but we all had our hands on our guns. Vernon held his gun in both hands and stood away from the wall. Chandler twisted the bolt and jerked the wooden flap toward him so hard it came loose from its screws. The snake went wild, its big head darting upward but not quite far enough to strike into the room. Chandler stood back and let the snake's sense of heat follow him. Vernon moved in quickly, aimed his gun into the opening and fired. It was a direct hit. The rattling stopped, and we all felt our bodies relax.

"Good," said Chandler, patting Vernon on his arm. "That thing becomes evidence. Scene techs are going to have to box him up, too."

A group of techs in white coats had come into the large room before the gunfire. Now they huddled away from the small room door.

"Include the reptile in your report." Chandler removed his gloves and headed outdoors. "And be careful of those fangs. They're full of poison."

"You know what all that was, don't you?" He said as we stood in a circle.

"Trophies," I said. "They are trophies from people he has murdered, namely old ladies."

Chandler nodded. He looked at Tony. "You might find something of your aunt's in there, too."

"I don't think so," I said. "Ferguson didn't kill her. I have a feeling I know who did."

The next day, I left Pasquin to his own devices but told him to call if there was any sighting of a Ferguson near the house. He had pulled up a wicker lounger and was reading the paper when Vernon,

Tony, and I left for the jail.

Gil had just finished a large bacon and egg breakfast with hot cakes when we saw him inside an interview room. A young public defender had been assigned to him, primarily so he could be handled away from his parents. They were jailed in the adult areas, charged with all sorts of racketeering and gambling crimes.

A juvenile counselor joined the lawyer, placing Gil between them on one side of the table. Tony had to stay on the other side of the mirror. He didn't like it, but he said he would have done the same thing in Chandler's shoes. Vernon and I joined Chandler at the table.

We went through the events of the evening. Gil appeared confused and sad that he had almost killed some kittens.

"I don't really want to do that," he said. "It's just sometimes, I get this feeling all over me." He stared ahead as his eyes went glassy. "I want to hear them meow, and then watch the blood run down the fur. It's," he sighed, "it's almost like the meow is sliding down their bellies and out into space."

The room went silent. The counselor's face paled, and she turned slightly to look over Gil's head at the lawyer. The lawyer avoided her eyes but said nothing.

"When it's done, I bury them or throw them in the lake.." He put his head down.

"Gil," I said when no one else could speak, "you said last night, they made you do it. What exactly did you mean by that?"

The counselor nodded slightly as though she knew he would say something about voices, that maybe this was a schizophrenic who couldn't help himself. She was wrong.

Gil stared at me for a moment, then blinked. "We caught that woman who lived next door trying to see in our windows. She ran down to her landing but my parents headed her off. She tried to

run to her house, and my mother kept yelling 'Get her! Get her!'
I was off to the side of the landing. My dad told me to get her, so
I ran after her. She was old. I got up behind her and pushed her
down. She hollered some and tried to get up, but I got her back
of the neck and held her there. She stopped hollering." He looked
up, his eyes afraid now. "I didn't know it right then but she died.
That's why she stopped hollering. She puked a little and made a
little sound, but she stopped that, too, and then she was quiet."

I thought of Tony in the next room. He would be gripping
something to contain his anger.

"And the writing tablet?" I asked.

Gil looked a little surprised. A slight grin moved across his
face, turning him from scared child to killer. "We went inside her
house that night. My father found a notebook that talked about
us. He told me to get rid of it. I tossed it in the lake."

The lawyer turned to his young client. "Did your parents tell
you to do anything else?"

"Like what?"

"Something you thought might be wrong?" We all saw where
the man was headed.

Gil shrugged. "Don't know. They told me to do things but I
never asked much. Told me to get jobs with that Ferguson man."

"And how did you like working for him?" I asked.

"He wasn't around most of the time. Just told me to do this or
that and he left."

Vernon leaned forward on the table so that his face was level
with Gil's. "Did you ever see the rattlesnake in the Fireside Bar?"

Gil broke into a big grin. "Yeah. He's neat!"

"Did you see him from the fireplace side or the back room
side?"

"Both. Burl let me feed him once. I took a live mouse inside the room, and got to drop him inside the flap. Then I ran around to the fire side and watched him swallow it whole."

"Did you see anything in that room besides the snake door?" Vernon still sat at eye level.

"Stuff," Gil shrugged. "He got me to put something in there once, on a shelf."

"What?"

"It was a little painting of a cat. It belonged to Miz Keen. I think it was one of her favorites."

"Did it have a caption—you know, something printed on it?"

"Of course, Miss Priss, like all her cats. He said he would put it over the bar one day."

"Did Ferguson spend much time in that room?"

"Lots," he said and a darkness crept over his face along with a smile.

We left Gil with his lawyer and counselor. As far as we could tell, he didn't yet know his parents were in jail.

"Valentine wants out of that hospital so bad he can taste it," said Chandler. "Unfortunately, this other guy coming from Jersey will sit in on the questioning. That's going to be a story and a half."

"Do you think the Bonos know their son is, well, like he is?" I asked.

"They know, and they used those talents," said Tony.

We left Chandler to his catches of the day and headed to the Keen house. As soon as we hit the chairs in the cool living room, we all felt the emotional exhaustion. And we smelled the gumbo. Pasquin had made a huge pot of the stuff. It was his way of connecting us to the tranquility of life.

"The kid may get off, you know," said Tony as he spooned the Louisianne soup from his bowl. "His parents will get the book thrown at them. Seeing a penchant for killing animals in their own child and using him. Now that's pretty disgusting."

"And if he gets off," I asked, "will he kill again?"

"Let's hope he gets some help, big time, while he's in a cell or juvenile hall." Vernon dipped a store-bought roll into his gumbo. "I don't want to retire by putting a grown up Gil Bono on death row."

"When are you going after Ferguson?" asked Pasquin. "He's likely to murder his old man and his new wife now that his casino has been ruined." He tipped over a bottle of hot sauce and cursed under his breath when he realized it was empty.

"Chandler's got rotating deputies watching the farm, and Rosie's place, too."

"Wonder what she thinks of her prince charming now?" I asked.

"If she's like most of the women I've seen taken by a con artist like him, she'll defend him for a long time," said Tony. "It's like this is the last hurrah, and fate isn't going to interfere with happiness."

"She'll have a ton of money to defend him," said Vernon.

"When New Jersey and Florida, and who knows where else, get through with him, it won't matter how much money she's got." Tony smiled, and I had to believe it was in honor of his aunt.

I stirred my gumbo. "I guess those kittens were taken to an animal shelter. Any way we can rescue them?"

The men shrugged. They had no answer to something they would have considered a womanly thing.

We settled in front of the television after filling our bellies with gumbo and ice cream. The newscaster made a point of show-ing how the last hurricane's effects hadn't been repaired and already there was a new tropical storm in the east Caribbean. It was headed for Miami and would probably strengthen if it continued into the Gulf.

"We need to get this cleared up before the rains begin," I said.

No one commented. We had just captured a criminal family. Now it was Mother Nature that would come back to haunt us at least one more time.

CHAPTER TWENTY-FIVE

Sitting still while deputies searched the Bono house had taken its toll on my nature. I had to get out, to do something. I tried sitting on the Keen landing. When a light rain began, I moved back to the patio and watched the techs remove computers and boxes from the house. Pasquin napped and made small conversation, but I could sense his restlessness, too.

"You want to go home, don't you?"

"Yes ma'am, I do," he said. "I been down here just one day too long. Got a garden that needs tending to, and," he turned and grinned at me, "I just need to ride my boat down that river."

I knew what he meant. My own house less than a mile from his sat in the humid swamp, gathering bugs and mildew. I needed to be home, to once again eat at Mama's Table, the best seafood cafe in the state, and walk to the river's edge with Plato, the dog who had more or less claimed me as his number one owner. There were others but he chose them by the turn of the tides.

"I'm going to make a call to the animal shelter," I said and went to look up the number in the phone book.

"You planning on hauling those cats back to your house?" Pasquin yelled. "Plato might not like the company."

"No, I've got other plans. I'm going for a ride," I said.

Pasquin waved me out. He wasn't interested in chasing the locals anymore.

I took the road past the Ferguson farm. A deputy sat at the entrance to the drive. I stopped and rolled down my window.

"Is old man Ferguson okay?" I asked.

The deputy shrugged. "Seems so. He's got a nurse coming in daily to see him."

"No sign of Burl?"

The man shook his head.

The animal shelter sat at one end of a mini-mall. No one questioned why I'd want all four kittens that had been rescued from Gil that night. They were just happy someone could take them. The clerk gave me a high-sided box with a drop cloth in the bottom to transport them. I stuck them on the back seat where little mews and scratches told me they were safe and sound.

Continuing far into the countryside, I came to the Quinne drive. A lone deputy stood next to a marked car.

"She just left in her Cadillac," he said.

"And Burl?"

He shrugged. "Haven't seen him."

I turned the car and headed back toward the Keen place. I went the way of the Culley houses, wanting to be sure deputies were watching them, too. At one point, I met two trucks speeding around the lake road. Betty Stubbs sat in the back of one, laughing. It was the first time I'd ever seen her do that and wondered what had made her happy. I had traveled to the highway when I spotted a Cadillac just like Rosie's headed down a side road. It traveled fast, kicking up dust on the unpaved surface. I turned and followed it. When it slowed at an intersection, I noticed the white haired driver making a quick check for cross traffic, then slam on the gas and take off toward high reeds. I suspected she knew I was following her. We were the only two on the country road. She made the curves on the ruts and her car swayed dangerously close to the watery ditches on the side.

"You can't outrun me on this road," I said. I had slowed but following her dust was easy.

We moved liked this until I saw a familiar rooftop. Rosie Quinne was headed to the backside of the Ferguson house.

I pulled out the cell phone and reported this to the Sheriff's Office. The deputies on the front end promised to make their way through the property and encounter her near the holding pond.

I raced the Honda across bumps that sent the top of my head into the ceiling upholstery. In the distance to my right, I could see another patch of mud flying. I caught a glimpse of the two muddy pickup trucks racing down a road, their cabs swerving like a giant gila monster in the mud. "Kids muddin'," I said and focused on the Cadillac.

The dust ahead of me turned to sand slings and finally mud. The Cadillac came to a sudden halt and the passenger door opened into tall reeds which caused it to slam back into Rosie's knee as she tried to get out of the driver's seat. But the knee didn't look much like anything on a petite elderly lady. It was covered in trousers and the foot wore a steel tipped cowboy boot.

I parked the car around the curve, got out and hid in some reeds. The driver had white hair, coiffured in Rosie's style, but it sat atop the head of Burl Ferguson who was trying his best to move from the car to the muddy shore of the pond. He pushed himself hard and fell into the reeds. When he stood, he opened the back door and grabbed a rifle. I stayed put. I had left my own gun in the car. "Dumb!" I said to myself.

Ferguson's face had been smeared with red lipstick. The deputy who let him pass must have been half-blind to think he looked like Rosie. From a distance, maybe he did, but not up close. His eyes darted around and he headed to the front of the car where he paced up and down the narrow bank of the pond. He spied something and darted into the reeds. I moved closer, using the Cadillac to hide my movements.

Ferguson jerked a rowboat onto the shore and began pulling some rope from inside it. He turned back to the car and came at a trot toward the back. I shoved into the reeds as far as I could.

Burl glanced around him and opened the trunk. He leaned into the opening and seemed to be moving around. I could barely see his legs, but they kept moving. The entire car shook. When he stood again, his face was red and the lipstick had spread to appear as though his mouth was bleeding. The white wig still sat atop his head. I noticed for the first time that he wore a frilly top, something feminine, over his jeans. He slammed the trunk shut again and ran down the road a ways. I supposed he was looking to see if someone was still following him. When he returned to the car, he took a deep breath and opened the trunk again. Dragging something out, he staggered in the mud and half dropped his bundle. The bundle had feet—tiny, old lady feet.

I saw that Burl had dropped the rifle in the trunk while he worked. It was still there. I walked toward him and, before he saw me, I slammed it shut. He stood up, startled, a tied-up Rosie Quinne at his feet. She was bound almost entirely in rope, like a mummy in hemp. Her mouth was wrapped in duct tape, but her eyes stared out like a frightened cat. In a flash, I saw Gil as an older man and what the kitten had become.

"Let her go," I said. "The sheriff is on his way. Do you want another murder on your charges?"

Burl froze and stared. He seemed to be dazed under his wig and lipstick.

"What a creep," I said. "You should see yourself. No more

charm for the rich old broads in that getup."

He said nothing but made a dart for the trunk. I held up my cell phone in both hands and took the stance of a cop in action.

"Just stay right there, sir," I said, hoping he took the phone for a gun.

He didn't move. His face began to contort as though he might cry. He began to back up until he stumbled into the reeds. Using their cover, he headed for the boat. I ran after him, both of us trampling through the tough reeds and cattails.

Burl pulled on the boat as he waded into the dirty water. It wasn't deep, but I guessed he would head for the other side and make a run for the house. He didn't look like a swimmer, and I figured this was it. I had to make an effort to keep him here until the cops came.

He stood waist deep in the water at the end of the boat. I approached the end that still sat on shore and shoved it at him. He staggered in the mud and water but held on until he was able to fall over head first into the boat. I took both hands and rocked it back and forth. He had grabbed an oar and was attempting to smack me with it, but his back was to me and it took too much effort to turn around. He got lucky when he pushed the oar into the mud and shoved off. I slipped and went almost completely under until I rebalanced myself and grabbed hold of the moving boat. Shaking it was too hard now. I jumped on it, using my weight to pull it to one side. It tipped at last, and Burl with his white wig fell into the pond.

It was too shallow to to be really dangerous, but the water was dirty and the bottom was pure mud. Burl's cowboy boots didn't move well. He splashed around, trying to stand and at the same time trying to slam me with the oar. I used the overturned boat to slam him in his gut. That's when he let go of the oar and fell backward into the water. I grabbed the oar and moved around to the back of his head. He tried to come up, all the while spitting muddy water, but I placed the oar handle under his chin and held it tight.

"Be still or I'll choke you right here!"

He went limp, his big arms floating beside him. The white wig slid off and got stuck between his neck and the oar handle.

"Okay, okay," he said and the tears began. His face twisted and his throat choked with sobs and pond water and the pressure of the oar.

I dragged him to shore like an old boat. He lay there, half in the water, half in the mud.

"You make one move and I'll crush your skull," I said as I stood over him with the oar.

That's when he stopped blubbering and stared at the sky. I let my guard drop for only a second. He turned and grabbed my ankle. I let the oar come down on his side. He yelled but wouldn't let go of my leg. I poked at him frantically until I lost my balance and fell beside him in the mud. He grabbed hold of my throat. That's when I heard the voice in the reeds.

"Let go her!" Two hands came down and took hold of the frilly shirt. Someone rolled Burl over and sat on his chest, his legs straddling the man. "You don't do things like that to a lady!"

I coughed and squinted in the sun. A skinny fellow with rotting teeth held Burl's throat with one hand and the other was raised above him in a threatening fist.

"Stubbs," I said, "thank God."

Burl attempted to roll from under his captor, but Stubbs let go with a sock that echoed throughout the lake area. Blood spurted from the face on the ground.

Burl closed his eyes, and whispered, "No more, no more."

The two deputies came running after they found the muddy road. Their first encounter was the tied-up Rosie, lying in the marsh grass behind her fancy car. She was in and out of consciousness but she was alive.

"Bring your handcuffs!" I yelled when I heard them approach.

One came to the shore of the pond and looked down at Burl Ferguson, a white wig hanging off his shoulder, a mixture of blood and lipstick across his mouth, and tears running down his cheeks. They helped Stubbs to a standing position.

"How did you both get wet?" the deputy asked, looking from me to Burl.

I breathed heavily and nodded toward the pond. The rowboat floated upside down near the shore.

"Dang!" he said and stared until I yelled for him to arrest the guy. My throat hurt from the effor..

When they finally had Ferguson in the car, I looked up to see Betty Stubbs poking at the rope across Rosie Quinne's chest. She cried silently as though doing it out loud would have hurt the woman even more. I walked toward her and pulled her from her kneeling position.

"The deputies will take care of her, Betty. Come with me."

I led her to my car where I pulled out the box of kittens and handed them to her. "I'm sorry. I wasn't able to rescue their mother, but I wanted to make sure you got the babies back."

The woman, her face and hands covered with dried mud from the fun ride she was having in the back of the truck, took the box in a gentle fashion. She sat down on the wild grass and with one finger began stroking the tiny kittens. A smile turned into a wide grin.

Vernon, Tony, and Chandler arrived about the same time as the ambulance. Rosie was placed on the stretcher, all the while mumbling about her sweet Burl and how he took away her jewelry stores.

"He planned to dump her in the pond," I said. "He would have drowned her."

We watched as the deputies placed the man into the back of a patrol car. Chandler had picked up the white wig and held it for a scene tech to bag it when they arrived. "Dressed like an old lady. I wonder what the psychiatrist will say about this."

"I wonder what his own father will say about it," I added, brushing dirt from my shirt and jeans. The skin on my neck was tightening from the trauma.

Stubbs stood aside, his eyes wide in bewilderment. I walked toward him and shook his hand. All I could do was nod. The lump in my throat had nothing to do with choking.

CHAPTER TWENTY-SIX

We stayed in the Keen house long enough to hear how the Bono family had met Burl Ferguson in New Jersey when he became friendly with Cara's Aunt Paulette Henderson. Somehow, their warped attitudes drew them together and all the parties came together to do in the old lady and share the profits. Burl knew how to handle the cashier's checks and property titles by then. He had ripped off several old ladies and was about to do the same to another in Florida.

"He came home and took up with Nell Culley." said Chandler. "Convinced her to sell out and use the money to move into assisted living. Thing is, he let her live only long enough to take her money and her property."

"Mildred and Marta found out and went after him, right?" I asked.

Chandler nodded. "We can't get anything out of Ferguson, but we pieced together what the Bonos have said. Both the ladies were bold enough to walk right into the Ferguson house and look for things. That's why Burl began to sell some of the stuff and move his trophies to the bar." He hesitated. "And that's why Burl broke into Mildred's house the night of the storm. He must have realized she'd found the jade box with the teeth or her sister's watch. He went after her. She did her best to run." He shook his head. "But he shot her in the back."

"When did the gambling thing come along?" asked Vernon.

"It must have been Bono's idea. He handled the operation. Burl knew the people who would join and keep quiet about it, but JoJo knew how to manage. And since they had murdered the old lady, they were bound to each other."

"Where is the Henderson body?" I asked.

"In Jersey. Bono and his son buried it in the woods. Their state police should be looking for it about now." He looked up at us and gave a sarcastic laugh. "Gil, the kid, told us how Burl took the old lady's teeth at the last minute. Just shoved them into his pocket."

Pasquin cringed. "Ought to draw and quarter that man."

"Well, we plan to do something like that," he said. "And Jersey has the same thing in mind for him." He turned to me. "You know, I've been after those kids who go muddin' for a long time. Now, I have to look the other way. Stubbs was driving one of those trucks when he saw you chasing the Cadillac."

Chandler didn't wait for a reply, just saluted me and turned to all of us. His last advice was to head out soon. The latest storm was turning into a hurricane and threatened to cross the southern end of the state.

Pasquin squirmed in the Honda as we sped up I-75. He had been angry ever since he'd heard about Rosie nearly dying.

"And what's going to happen to old man Ferguson?" he asked.

"He'll be fine, Pasquin. He's got enough insurance and income to take care of himself. And his property is worth something. It's still in his name, thank goodness."

We didn't speak for a time, just listened to the storm news on the radio. The weather man kept going on about the tropical wave becoming a tropical storm, then a hurricane with force one, and finally, when it hit the warm waters of the Gulf, it could become a deadly force five.

"That kid is like that," said Pasquin.

"Gil?"

"Yep. He starts out giving beer to kids and tossing rocks at cats. Then he kills them. Then he helps his dad bury an old lady. What's the next step in his storm pattern? Killing old ladies and taking trophies," he answered himself.

I thought about what he said for a moment. "Could we have stopped his storm surge by catching him early?"

"Just about like we could stop the hurricane by catching it early," he said.

Recommended Memento Mori Mysteries

Viv Powers Mysteries by Letha Albright
DAREDEVIL'S APPRENTICE
BAD-LUCK WOMAN

A Katlin LaMar Mystery by Sherri L. Board
BLIND BELIEF

Matty Madrid Mysteries by P.J. Grady
MAXIMUM INSECURITY
DEADLY SIN

A Dr. Rebecca Temple Mystery
by Sylvia Maultash Warsh
TO DIE IN SPRING

AN UNCERTAIN CURRENCY
Clyde Lynwood Sawyer, Jr.
Frances Witlin

A Suzanne LaFleshe Mystery by Hollis Seamon
FLESH

THE COLOR OF EMPTINESS
a crime novel by Cynthia Webb

Other books by Glynn Marsh Alam:

RIVER WHISPERS

Luanne Fogarty Mysteries
DIVE DEEP and DEADLY
DEEP WATER DEATH
COLD WATER CORPSE
BILGE WATER BONES

Glynn Marsh Alam is a native Floridian. Born in Tallahassee, she is familiar with the live oak forests and cypress swamps of the area. She also knows the sinkholes and reptilia that abound there. She often swims in the cold, clear springs above the openings to fathomless caves. These are the settings for her Luanne Fogarty mystery series (*Deep Water Death, Dive Deep and Deadly, Cold Water Corpse, Bilge Water Bones*) and for her literary novel, *River Whispers*.

After graduating from Florida State University, Glynn worked as a decoder/translator for the National Security Agency in D.C., then moved to Los Angeles where she taught writing and literature and earned an MA in linguistics. After many years of traveling back to Florida twice a year, she has now moved there and writes full time.

Visit Glynn Marsh Alam at www.glynnmarshalam.com.